DEFINED

ASSASSIN SERIES BOOK 1

MARY ELLEN QUIRE

ENIGMA HOUSE PRESS

ISBN: 978-1-948374-01-9

Enigma House Press
Goshen, Kentucky 40026
www.enigmahousepress.com

DEDICATION

To my family who gave me roots in which to grow and provided loving acceptance. And then to show me the world is not a perfect place, introduced me to a lesson in conflict. It was from this, I was able to move forward, leaving the past where it lay and define normal for myself.

"Bad things happened, it was how we navigated the fallout afterward that really defined what our new normal would be."
— Jay Crownover, Leveled

ACKNOWLEDGMENTS

There are many people to thank for making this book come to be, and honestly I cannot even begin to thank them all, but I shall make the attempt. Thanks to Tony Acree at Hydra Publications who saw enough promise in this book to give it the chance it needed, my eternal gratitude to you. Thanks to my editor, Ryan McDaniel, whose suggestions made the writing stronger, more believable, and breathed life into the characters I created.

Thanks to all of the wonderful people I've had the pleasure to work with at Crestwood Animal Hospital, for you all more than just friends, you are family. Last but certainly never least, I want to thank all of my readers, for I write because it pleases me and I share it in hopes it pleases you.

PREFACE

I developed the idea for Defined during a very difficult time in my life (which if you live long enough and are within spitting distance of other Homo sapiens, difficulties are sure to come at some point or other). Frustrated with the lack of aid from any figure of authority, I began wondering about vigilantism and what it would take to even the score, so to speak. Too financially strapped in reality to hire my own mercenary, I allowed my mind to wander and began to put all of those frustrations on paper (uh, well, computer screen), thus an assassin was born.

First and foremost, Price MacCann had to be female, no way around it. Call it woman power, call it penis envy, or call it whatever you like but I needed her to appear the underdog, yet be damn good at what she did (a success rate rivaled only by the legendary grim reaper). I also needed to make her human otherwise she was just another Bond character going through yet another mission. As a writer, that is my cue to screw things up royally for her. I kill off someone who wasn't meant to die and I make her watch. I fill her with such grief and guilt that only Job himself could have withstood what I dealt out. And then as cream cheese icing upon the carrot cake of her life, I give her the ultimate challenge. Mwwaahaahaahaa! I give her family.

A normal familial group might have made for a normal Price MacCann, but there's no story there because people live "normal" lives all of the time. No, what she needed was a family just as abnormal as she was, and then to add a bit more flavor, she needed the burning desire to just be a regular Joe.

I wrote and rewrote, my final product morphing into the book which you now hold in your hands. Defined can and will be pigeon-holed into a lot of categories; action, adventure, comedy, maybe even romance, but I will always look at it as a story about self-discovery and self-acceptance. Regardless of how it's classified, my hope is that you enjoy reading it as much as I have enjoyed writing it.

--Mary Ellen Quire, 2018

PROLOGUE

"DON'T LET GO!"

"Price, it's useless. Just go!"

"I'm not leaving you!"

An explosion smothered the sound of my proclamation. It blew out in all directions, billowing up choking black and gray smoke nearly obscuring the man hanging from a beam near the ceiling of the cathedral. He'd caught it on his way down and his body swung gently like a pendulum just above the inferno lying in wait, the flames eating away at everything beneath him.

I shoved my gun back in the shoulder holster, grabbed the beam I'd been squatting on and kicked out to hang from it. The smoke was thick but I could still make out the beam below where the man hung for dear life. I let go of my grip and dropped down, balancing effortlessly as I'd learned to do when I was a child. I knelt on one knee, keeping as good a hold on the beam as I could.

"Grab my hand!"

A gunshot blared to the right and I felt more than heard the bullet whiz past my head. I glanced over and saw the shadowy form moving fast along the beam, heading to the balcony.

"There's no time!" the hanging man yelled. "You save me and you'll lose him!"

To me, it would always be the one brief moment in my life which seemed to last forever, a sick and twisted slow motion film of thought. There was another gunshot, the bullet going wide, missing both of us by several feet. The shooter was on the run, hard to aim when you're moving. I grabbed the hanging man's arm tight, the flesh was slick with either blood or sweat or both, and my hand slid upward. There was no way I'd ever have enough traction with just my hands to be able to pull him to safety. It was a fact I guess we both knew.

"Get him, Price."

He let go.

ONE

THANKSGIVING IS an American tradition and most people know how it started. They learned it in elementary school along with how to make a paper turkey by drawing an outline of your hand and adding those few essential characteristics to make it look like a turkey. One eye, because all kids know you only need one to make it look proper, two stick legs with three stick toes, one wing, and a wattle shaped like a tear drop. When it was finished it became the masterpiece on the refrigerator for the next several weeks until the Christmas art took over. Countless debates on whether or not the history books provided an accurate account of the first Thanksgiving have surfaced over the years and I'm sure the battle will rage on long after I'm gone. But one thing is for sure, Thanksgiving is the time where families and friends get together, overeat, and either plot out their tactical plans for Black Friday shopping or participate in the glories of dysfunctional family drama. Personally, I was just hoping they wouldn't overcook the turkey this year.

My name is Price MacCann and I was born the second child in a line of four, the oldest daughter out of three, and since my younger two sisters are identical twins they count as the package deal of one, which in turn puts me as the proverbial middle child. My parents married young and have bragging rights on happily staying that way after many years. I don't really know much about my Dad's side of the family because he never talks about them. In fact, I'm not even certain there is a "them", but that's beside the point. When he married my mom, he just blended in with her very large and quite peculiar family.

Our family is spread all over, and during Thanksgiving we all travel home to my grandmother's house and make it a long weekend. Some stay in nearby hotels, some bunk in with my grandparents. For the past twenty-five years, I have been among the bunkers, along with my parents, sisters, and my brother of course. It's been going on long before I was ever thought of and it was a tradition I planned to break this year. Don't get me wrong. I love my family but I'd had enough nightmares about people running around with their hair on fire, looking like a flaming matchstick on Road Runner legs, to last a lifetime.

My flight was the only red-eye scheduled to arrive at three in the morning on Thanksgiving Day. My plan was to take a cab out to my grandparent's house, climb into one of the guest beds and sleep until close to dinner time. No one could possibly think badly of me for it, after all, I'd spent my sleeping hours just trying to get there, right? When dinner was over, I could scoot back out to catch the only flight leaving on the holiday and resume my life as I'd left it.

I would be using the old "I'm-working-Thanksgiving-night" excuse and topping it with "there's no way I can get out of it" lie. They would believe it whole-heartedly since what I do for a living isn't your typical job with nine to five hours. In my line of work, things don't shut down just because there's a holiday on the horizon. I don't get a day off until the job is done. To be done, someone has to die and to get paid, I'm the one who has to make it happen. You see, I am an assassin. Occasionally, I'll take on a freelance job, but most of the time I work for my family. Crazy, right? But trust me when I say that working for them isn't nearly as crazy socializing with them.

Now, no family is perfect. Some have skeletons rattling around in the darkest recesses of their closets. Some have black sheep grazing out in the family land's back forty. And some just can't get along when they are within spitting distance of one another. That's just life, so what's the problem?

Well, the problem is that I discovered just how different my family was from everyone else pretty early in life; probably too early to deal with it properly. And this realization became apparent when my third grade teacher, Mrs. Schultz assigned the class an essay on what we did during our summer vacation. We were to write the stupid paper and then stand in front of the class and read it. I was last on the list of presenters by seating position, not the old alphabetic standby.

So I sat back with all the rest of the students and listened. No one ahead of me had written anything about a member of their family going to jail or committing any sort of act which could possibly land them there. There were no stories about learning to pick locks or pockets, lessons on handling weapons or self-defense of any kind, or recitations of federal, state, or international laws. Instead, my fellow students stood at the head of the class and read about vacations, swimming, playing games, and generally every other normal activity leading to a blissful summer break. It was the turning point for me and for the first time I saw my family for the Batman-wanna-bees they really were. Class time ran out before I was supposed to read mine, and I immediately went home, trashed the essay I'd written and composed a brand new one filled with complete and utter falsehoods. I guess you could say I wimped out, but every kid wants to be accepted by their peers and that's all I wanted.

Regardless, family is family. And although ours is filled with enough eccentricities to fuel the National Enquirer for a good decade should they ever get a whiff of us, I still love them; which is why, on

Thanksgiving Day at a little after three in the morning, my plane landed at the airport. The flight had been on schedule and uneventful; the cab ride even more so, with the traffic so sparse so early in the morning. I arrived expecting my family to be in a peaceful holiday slumber but every light in the house was burning bright. The door was thrown open as soon as I topped the porch steps and they were all up and anxiously awaiting my arrival. My parents were first in line for the hug-fest followed by my grandparents, aunts and uncles, brother and sisters, and finally my cousins. Everyone gets a hug.

Ushered inside the warm and cramped house, I couldn't help but notice every window was thrown wide open, regardless of the fact it was thirty-five degrees outside. I detected the smell of things already cooking in the huge oven. Turkey and pumpkin pie were the scents most prominent.

My grandmother gave my hand a good-hearted squeeze and led me through the house to the kitchen. "Bet you thought we'd all be asleep."

I didn't have the heart to tell her it was what I had hoped for, so I just went with a benign smile and a nod. She seated me at the small kitchen table and my mother placed a cup of hot, black coffee into my hands.

"Thought you could use a cup or two," Mom said sweetly. "We wouldn't want you falling asleep and missing out on everything."

"No," I replied, "we sure wouldn't want that."

One of my uncles pulled up a chair beside me and set his own cup of Joe down on the table in front of him. He's my mother's older brother and my favorite uncle.

"Uncle Sandor, how are you?"

He gave me a genuine smile and slung an arm around my shoulders. "Oh, I can't complain. Not really. But you, my dear, have every reason to gripe. Working on a national holiday such as Thanksgiving, it's almost sacrilege. Who are you doing the hit for? You say the word and I can have him begging for you to take the whole weekend off."

I needed a diversion, something to change the course of this conversation which would surely lead to the whopper of a lie I'd told my mother when I'd phoned her about my visiting plans. It took less than a second to come up with it.

"Oh, I'm sure you've never heard of him," I replied, just as my elbow made contact with my coffee cup, tipping it over and taking Uncle Sandor's cup right along with it. We both jumped out of the way of the hot coffee tidal wave.

My mother rushed to the mess with a couple of towels to sop it all up and a stern look for my uncle. "No more shop talk, Sandor. It brings bad luck. Remember last Thanksgiving?"

Uncle Sandor nodded. "True. Sylvia's hair is just now coming back in."

I couldn't help but feel a little sick because Sandor's wife was indeed the running matchstick in my nightmares. She'd been unfortunate enough to be in close vicinity of one of my cousin's newly-lifted flame-throwers when he'd been demonstrating it in my grandparent's back yard in hopes to sell it to one of my sisters, both of whom happen to be arms dealers. Aunt Sylvia's hair lit up like a candle wick, probably from all the spray she used to keep it in immaculate condition, and it took all of us to catch her when she took off running. Two fire extinguishers and a bucket of iced tea later, we finally put out the flames. Luckily, she didn't suffer severe burns as there was enough fuel in her hair to buy us time to put it out, but I knew for a fact she'd been forced to wear a wig until the middle of this summer.

My mother gave him a pat on the back. "Let's just enjoy the time we have with her and be thankful. No shop talk. No bad luck."

My opinion was bad luck didn't have anything to do with it, but stupidity and physics did. I kept that particular opinion to myself.

Mom replaced our empty cups with steaming new ones filled with Joe, and we all small-talked our way past a half hour before I was thrust head first into the whirlwind of dinner preparation.

TWO

LIKE I SAID BEFORE, I have two younger sisters who are identical twins. We can tell them apart, but anyone outside the family usually experiences both difficulty and embarrassment in doing so. One twin, Remi, is very feminine and has fine-tuned the art of makeup application to a genuine science. She is also the queen of fashionable clothing with a marked specialty in accessorizing. Her identical counterpart, Demi, is the exact opposite. She has more tom-boy like qualities, preferring serviceable attire to the latest style and combat boots to stiletto heels. Cosmetics are reserved for situations requiring war paint to successfully accomplish her goal.

However, if their business calls for it, they can switch characteristics better than any con could hope to do, which is why I've always believed their chameleon ways were better suited for con-artistry, but whatever, I don't run the show I just dance in it.

"Price," Mom said, "I want you working on the cornbread dressing with your sisters."

My mother always followed the old family adage about food tasting better when everybody has a hand in the cooking. I personally didn't hold this view since a couple of my Aunts were notorious in the craft of poisoning. Somehow, that knowledge just isn't very appetizing to me even though I know they'd never taint family food. My mother passed out cutting boards and knives, then arranged the three of us around my grandmother's kitchen island to chop away at turkey innards and various vegetables. A few minutes into the task, Demi broke the blessed silence.

"Price, you should let Uncle Sandor help you in postponing the hit. He's helped us before. That way, you can stay the weekend. It'll be just like old times. We'll stay up and watch old movies, eat popcorn, maybe do each other's hair, and then we can all go out for Black Friday shopping."

I glanced over at my Mom who looked pleased as punch at my sister's plan, then back down at my cutting board. The onion I'd been cutting into nice and neat cubes was looking more and more minced. I moved the knife away from the cutting board in an attempt to stop the abuse.

"Can't," I replied, sticking to my big fat lie of a story, "I'm locked in the contract."

Demi gave me her famous sad puppy dog eyes, not realizing this particular ploy stopped working on me years ago when she'd located my diary, picked the lock and Xeroxed copies for her friends to read. I wasn't amused or moved by the expression then and I refused to be moved by her now. So I went back to chopping the onion, hoping they'd take the hint and let me be. That's when Remi nudged me in the side with her elbow. I glanced up to see her wink at me.

"There's no contract, is there?" she whispered, dicing a stalk of celery like a mad chef. "It's a guy, isn't it? That's why you're leaving early, right?"

I narrowed my eyes. "No."

"Girl then?" she asked, giving me her trademark deviant smile.

"No, no girl," I replied, careful to keep my voice down. I couldn't help but be thankful for the chatter in the kitchen which muffled this stupid conversation. "Can we just get on with chopping?"

"Come on, Price. You can trust us," Demi whispered back.

"She's right," Remi agreed. "If you tell us, then maybe we can help get you out of here faster to meet with him or her."

I lifted my cutting board and swept the minced bits of onion into the huge metal mixing bowl with my knife, grabbed the other half of the onion and repeated the process. The only thing going round in my head right now was the fate of the poor housefly. You know the one, buzzing around the spider's web as the spider whispers for it come into the parlor to see the many curious things there. I glanced up at my sisters. Yep. With four more appendages and several more eyes, they could be twin predators, just waiting for the chance to web me in, read my diary, and display it for the world to see. Me hold a grudge? No way. I looked over at one of my aunts and smiled my own deviant smile.

"Aunt Lula, can you tell us about the time you and Mom were trapped with that rich oil guy in Saudi Arabia? What was it you poisoned him with to escape?"

My aunt turned and simply beamed with joy. She reveled in the telling of past stories, especially when she was a participant in the events. Her tales were long and usually always common knowledge in our family, but she told them as if we'd never heard them before in our lives. It was a sacrifice I would have to make, but it was a better fate than the one the spider twins were trying to lock me into. Aunt Lula squeezed her short plump body between my two sisters and wrapped her arms around their waists in her own spidery clutch.

"It was hemlock, my dear," Aunt Lula began, "and it all started when..."

THREE

SMELLS of the pumpkin pies baking in the oven were now overpowered by the aroma of hot roasted turkey cooling on a side counter, awaiting carving. Most predominate were scents of sage from the dressing my sisters and I had put together, bacon and onions which had been simmering with green beans for several hours, and just a hint of cinnamon from the sweet potato casserole my Mom had recently tucked in the oven. Way ahead of the cooking schedule, we found a little time on our hands and the old adage about idle hands being the devil's workshop suddenly came to mind. My grandmother brewed up another pot of coffee (this time in her forty cup coffee urn) and announced what she hoped would be the start of a new tradition. I just hoped it didn't involve the fire department.

"This is just for us girls," my grandmother said, "and we can all thank Price for starting us early and giving us time to do it."

I winced as it appeared her thanks involved the largest bottle of Irish whiskey I'd ever laid my eyes on. She'd extricated it from the very back recesses of one of her bottom kitchen cabinets and plopped it on the table with a definitive thump.

"I've been saving this one for years," Grandmother said as she rustled around in another cabinet and pulled out a sleeve of large Styrofoam cups, "just waiting for the right moment and I do believe this is that moment. For as long as I can remember, the women in our family have cooked the Thanksgiving meal while the men sit out in the living room watching football and parades. It's tradition."

It was, in fact, tradition. The men in our family are grillers not cookers. They slave over the fire in the spring and summer months while the women took to the stove in the fall and winter months. Granted, our Fourth of July get-to-gathers always had store-bought potato salad and such, but at least the men were the ones responsible for it.

"Well," she continued, "this year we've got time to start a new tradition. Edith, pull out the whip cream."

I leaned against the wall and watched anxiously as my grand-mother started pouring coffee into the cups, passing them on to my Aunt Lula who added the whiskey, my Aunt Clara (also an artist in poison) who added the brown sugar, and then on to my mother, Edith, who squirted a pile of whip cream on top of the hot mix. The spider twins and a couple of my cousins passed them out to everyone in the kitchen. I took mine with a smile and a nod, wishing with all my heart I'd chosen to spend my time with the Neanderthals in the living room where the only threats were profanity, men farts, and possibly a spilt beer.

"To Thanksgiving," my grandmother announced, raising her Styrofoam cup high in the air, "the only holiday that's polite enough to come with its own menu." Then she gave a broad false teeth grin. "May you all get stuffed."

"PRICE, I have to hand it to you," Aunt Clara slurred as she threw her arm around my neck, "this is the first Thanksgiving where I haven't felt guilty about sticking my hand up inside a turkey's butt."

I grimaced, glancing down at her hand and hoping she'd washed it well. "Aunt Clara, how many coffees have you had?"

Her wired-rimmed glasses were askew but she didn't seem to notice. A smile slid across her plump cherub-like face and she swayed a little. "I don't rightly know, dear, all the cups looked the same."

I led her over to a nearby chair, releasing myself from her arm as I eased her down. "Sit here and rest a minute, okay?"

"Okay dear."

She caught my sleeve before I could get away. "Say, did I ever tell you about that summer in seventy-five when your mom and me got caught up in the Playboy mansion?"

I winced. Here it comes. Every eye in the kitchen whipped in our direction.

"I knew it!" my grandmother exclaimed.

My mom was at my side like a shot.

"Clara, hon, let me take that cup for you," she said as she pried my aunt's chubby fingers away from her cup and setting it on the kitchen table. "I think you need to lie down."

"You said you were both taking a sabbatical at that California convent in seventy-five," my grandmother said. "I had my doubts, but your father thought I was being paranoid."

"Now's not the time, Mom," my mother said.

"Nonsense, it's the perfect time," grandmother replied as she moved into position, maneuvering her twig-like body around us as if we were just trees rooted to the ground. "I knew I'd get the truth out of you sooner or later, but I honestly thought I'd have to hear it on my deathbed. Now, Edith, I want the true story, and don't you try and soften it with any Hail Marys either."

My grandmother, well known in the family for her evil eye, stood sentry at the kitchen doorway blocking my mother's exit. She crossed her skinny arms over fallen bosoms, which had succumbed to gravity probably around the time Jimmy Carter took office, and leered at my mom. My mother ignored her and hefted Aunt Clara to her feet. Poor

Clara swayed, smiled the broadest smile I've ever seen on a human face, and farted.

Mom rolled her eyes and frowned. "Come on, Clara. You need to go lie down."

"Sounds more like she needs a toilet," my grandmother said, waving her hand around to shoo away the smell. "Smells like it too. Clara never could hold her whiskey. Now, spill it Edith before I lose my cool."

Remi broke the shocked silence of our mass first. "Mom, is it true? You and Aunt Clara stayed at the Playboy Mansion? You're kidding me, right?"

Demi followed. "I can't believe you'd even step foot in that place without a crucifix."

Now, allow me to interject a fact about my family. We are not Catholic. Not now, and as far as I know, not ever. Our family does believe in God, the Bible (especially the eye for an eye bit in the Old Testament), and the hereafter. But Catholic we are not.

Mom let out an aggravated sigh.

"It's all right, Mother," Clara slurred in the general direction of my grandmother. "We had our crucifixes with us. Fat lot of good it did us though...we probably should have converted first...didn't ward off the Heff at all, he was already in the," she let out a loud, croaking hiccup, "habit."

My grandmother smirked and I could see everyone else straining to keep from laughing except for Mom who seemed too horrified to laugh, Aunt Clara who was too intoxicated to really laugh (without fear of losing bowel control, that is), and me, who now just wanted to eat turkey and go home.

"You posed as *nuns*?" my grandmother asked.

My Mom nodded slowly. "In our defense, we really were staying at the convent that summer."

"You *posed* as nuns in the Playboy Mansion?"

"Yes mother, we posed as nuns," Mom replied.

My grandmother's smirk turned into a deepening frown. "And you met the Heff, did you?"

"Yes. Yes, we met him alright."

My grandmother took the infamous lecture stance I'd heard so much about as a little kid. You know the one, with one hand on a hip and the other wagging her finger in reprimand.

"I cannot believe you two snuck off and met the Heff without me!"

And that's when the smoke alarm started screaming.

FOUR

HIGH NOON STRUCK and since my grandparent's house is really too small to hold a table big enough to seat our entire family, the meal is laid out buffet style. A line of sorts is formed and everyone serves themselves. Once you have your plate filled, you find a place to sit or crouch wherever you can and chow down.

This year's turkey took on a slightly overly brown hue. The stuffing was somewhat dehydrated, requiring more lumpy gravy to make it less crunchy, but the biggest casualty of too many cooks drinking Irish coffee in the kitchen seemed to be the pumpkin pies which suffered third-degree burns when the smoke detector went off during the Heffner fiasco. They were simply inedible. My brother, Michael, was kind enough to scoot out and hook us up with some freshly made ones from my grandparent's neighbor who always makes extras. They weren't my Mom's, but at least they weren't charred. In the buffet line, I'm right behind my Dad who was some-what befuddled at how something could possibly overcook with nearly twenty women in the kitchen and since the line is at a stand-still, he decided to turn around and question me about it.

"Gran just thought it would be the start of a new tradition," I replied, stabbing a piece of turkey breast with the meat fork. It was so dry it took me two tries to get the fork into it. "She made a toast and everything."

Dad moved on to the bowl of dressing and shoveled a spoonful onto his plate. The dry bits scattered around on the thick paper surface, sounding more like potato chips than Thanksgiving stuffing. He grimaced. "Nobody looks especially snockered except for Clara. Surely somebody should have noticed the smoke coming from the oven."

I passed on the stuffing and moved on to the green bean casserole. It looked safer. "Yeah, I know, but there were other distractions."

Dad liberated some gravy for the mashed potatoes and then took a second dip to try and moisten the stuffing. He replaced the ladle and turned back to me. "Such as?"

I didn't know if my father knew about the event involving my mother and Aunt Clara, so I wasn't about to open a can of worms right there at the buffet table. I was sure he'd hear about it shortly, but it wouldn't be from me. So, I just shrugged and said, "What can I say except there was whipped cream."

"Well, that's explains it all then." He took a step to the cold salads and spooned some from the bowl filled with Waldorf. Not my favorite. I skipped the salads altogether and moved on.

Behind me was Uncle Vinnie, my mother's youngest brother. He was a Navy Seal who specialized in covert operations. After twelve years, he retired and shook hands with the folks at the CIA where he stayed for another ten. He's a freelancer now, and a good one. Whenever I need information for a job, he either has it or can get it without a hitch.

I felt someone tap my shoulder. I didn't have to turn around to know it was Vinnie and I knew beyond a shadow of a doubt he was on a fishing expedition.

"Yes?" I asked, focusing on the prize at the end of the line, my grandmother's famous homemade yeast rolls.

"Word is, the whipped cream wasn't the cause of this fiasco," he whispered in my ear.

I sighed. "Check your source," I whispered back. "Whipped cream is a dangerous commodity."

"Your grandmother found out, didn't she?"

I moved my hand at him in a shooing motion, snatched a roll off the pyramid shaped pile and made my way out of the line before Vinnie could say another word. It was too late. He was a hound who'd caught a scent and he followed me to the counter where the beverages were nestled and iced down in their cups. I plucked one up without bothering to see what it was and moved quickly into the empty living room. Vinnie took a seat right next to me. I responded by shoveling the food from my plate into my mouth and not making eye contact.

"Come on, Price, I know you're stalling," he said in the low ominous voice, he usually reserved for interrogation purposes. "Is it the nun incident?"

I glanced up at him and pointed to my mouth which was full of the rather dry turkey, more like a bad kind of jerky really and nearly tasteless from being overcooked. I should have chosen the roll. If I kept the stuff in my mouth much longer I was going to choke. He put his napkin in my hand, one of those large paper ones with the cartoon drawing of a plump turkey with a pilgrim hat on top of its head.

"Spit it out," he said with a smile, "and answer the question."

I shook my head and looked longingly at my glass of iced liquid (could be tea or cola, I really couldn't tell in this light), but if I tried to take a drink, I'd probably spew dried turkey jerky bits all over the place.

"Okay then," Vinnie said, "Just nod you're head if I'm right."

I took a quick look at my uncle's plate. No turkey. He'd been wise. I spat the bite discretely inside the turkey napkin, wrapped it tightly around the unpleasant bits and set it on the table nearby to toss away with my plate.

"Well?" he asked, raising his brow.

This time, I took a bite of the homemade roll and savored its buttery goodness. He gave me his notorious stare and I knew he wouldn't stop until I answered his question. So, I gave him the universal answer to any question ever asked. I shrugged.

SOMEHOW, I'd managed to elude my Uncle Vinnie, mainly because he realized polite interrogation wouldn't work on me. It didn't stop his quest for answers though, he just moved on to weaker links, as in my sisters. When he saw they were going to sit down at the small card table in the corner of the living room, he excused himself from me and continued his hunt. The look of delight on their identical faces let me know they had no qualms with sharing what they knew, not surprising since family gossip was one of the things they enjoyed most. I continued eating and ignored the satisfied grin Uncle Vinnie sent my way when his question was answered by one of the twins.

The seats next to me on the couch were finally filled with two of my cousins, one specializing in false identification documents and the other in the art of computer genius aka hacker. They are the twin sons of my Uncle Sandor and there's nothing spectacular about them except for the fact they are quiet, for that I was thankful. It allowed me to eat in peace. When I'd finished, I tossed my trash and headed for the pumpkin pie. My brother, Michael, was in front of me, mounding Cool Whip onto the huge slice he'd served himself. I grabbed a paper dessert plate, cut a slice, and was just about to lift it onto my plate when he asked me to join him on the front porch. Michael is a man of few words, even as a kid he didn't say much. He used to specialize in con artistry, teaming up with Uncle Sandor's twin sons Jake and Jessup, but for the past couple of years he has partnered up with my Dad doing what we like to call people extractions (rescuing those who fall victim to either domestic or international kidnappings).

The house was so warm I didn't even need a coat when I walked outside and the snap of brisk wind felt merely cool on my skin. I sat in one of the rocking chairs on the porch and Michael took the other. We ate in silence. I pondered over grabbing another slice, tossing the idea when I stood up. My jeans were already cutting into my waist, another piece of pie and the button would pop. Michael lit a cigarette and sat silent for a few moments, smoking away. I gave him a moment before I broke the silence.

"You're not going to ask me about Mom and Aunt Clara, are you?"

"Nope."

"Good."

He didn't say anything for a minute and I started to get antsy. "So, what do you need to talk to me about?"

"You really working tonight or is it just an excuse to scoot out on the family fun?"

I let out a sigh; my breath billowing out much like my brother's exhaled cigarette smoke. I started to reinforce my lie with an affirmation but I canned the thought immediately. Michael was a liar by trade and he was good. If anybody could see through me, it would be him.

"Why do you want to know?"

"If you are working, then so be it, but if you're just trying to skip out, I need a favor."

I raised my brow.

"If you do this, it'll keep you honest and you'll be able to get out of here before the nun incident hits the fan."

"What's the favor?"

"I need you to take a Grinch out of circulation."

I stared ahead at the bare trees in the front yard, mulling over his reply. There are several assassins in his little black book of resources, most of them in our own family. If he needed a quick and quiet kill, we had more than a few poisoners who'd be willing to take on the task right here.

"Why me?" I asked.

"The target's paranoid," Michael replied. "He has food tasters on staff, body guards, and the whole nine yards. You're a genius with that kind of target. If anybody could get the job done, I know it would be you."

My gaze flicked over to my brother. "What's he done?"

"Mostly child trafficking, which should have sent the FBI banging on his door, but hasn't. Now he's not just bringing new ones into the country he's using the ones that are already here."

I felt a twinge in my stomach making the meal I'd just consumed twist around like a gut full of bricks, the result of overcooked turkey and human atrocity mixing it up in my belly.

Michael continued. "He stays off the internet and somehow out of the view of the fed's watchful eyes. Somebody in the belly of the law is keeping him off the radar. I just haven't figured out who it is yet, but there's no word he's even suspected of any wrong doing. And trust me when I say, if anything was said, I'd hear it."

"But how's that possible? America gets off on child protection. It's like a fetish."

I knew this to be true because I'd seen first-hand how a national concern for safety could turn into a sour witch hunt. In fact, I'd interceded in a couple of those cases where a few lies by a foe almost caused the complete destruction of innocent families accused of crimes they didn't commit. And since nobody wants to address that particular issue, nobody does anything to help, which unfortunately, is where I'd come in; execute the person, delete all records, and extinguish the problem.

Michael shrugged his shoulders. "Are you in?"

"You know I'll need to know more," I replied.

And he did. He knew I'd never take on a job without getting all of the information. There's a lot of money to be had working as an assassin, but there's also a lot of guilt to lug around. Michael took a few minutes to give me the particulars.

"It's your call," he told me at last. "No pressure at all. So say no if you want to. I won't hold it against you. However, if you do decide to do it, you could get there, do the job, and get back here in time for another cup of Irish Joe."

I narrowed my eyes playfully. "Uh-huh."

"Or," he gave a chuckle as he said this, "you could get the hell out of Dodge and just keep going before--"

Something crashed loudly from deep inside the house. Michael and I bolted back in the front door and fought through the crowd of relatives just in time to see Aunt Clara sprawled out on top of the buffet table which had collapsed under her weight. Food and broken dishes lay all round her. Her glasses were off and she was covered in lumpy mashed potatoes and gravy, cranberry sauce, cool whipped salads of varying and questionable ingredients; all of it highlighted with bits of dressing which stuck to the rest of the mess. Her shirt was off and twisted in her hand, leaving only her bright red Victoria's Secret bra to satisfy what modesty she might still have.

"What the heck is going on?" I exclaimed.

My mother and Aunt Lula looked horrified. My uncles, cousins, and sisters stood stock still, too frozen in shock to react. My grandmother, however, was cackling so hard I feared her Depends underpants wouldn't hold up to the strain. She was sitting in one of the folding chairs against the wall, pounding her fisted hand on her knee with one hand and holding her belly with the other.

Michael started laughing and I gave him a quick jab in the ribs with my elbow. "Don't you start it too, it's not funny."

"Price, you need to loosen up," he said, rubbing the place where I'd planted my elbow. "You're as uptight as Mom."

FIVE

AN HOUR LATER, Aunt Clara and the mess were cleaned up. There was a unanimous vote to toss every bit of leftover food, with the overall assumption it was now contaminated (whether it had been located on the collapsed table or not) with Aunt Clara cooties. My aunt was tucked into one of the guest beds and snoring the snore of the highly intoxicated. She'd been scrubbed clean of her covering of Thanksgiving staples, compliments of my mother and Aunt Lula, and dressed in her flannel pajamas completely unaware of her destructive show. Michael was on the phone in the living room, setting up the arrangements I needed made for the hit.

I leaned against the counter listening to Mom answer each of my grandmother's questions about the Heffner incident. Exasperated and slightly embarrassed, Mom let out a sigh.

"Nothing really happened at the mansion," she assured my grandmother. "I know you're disappointed, but we only went for work. Yes, it was during a party, but we went in, scouted the place for our target and kept tabs on him during the night. The rest is pretty much ho-hum. You didn't miss a thing."

"I just wished you'd have let me in on it," my grandmother said.

"It could have been a great memory to add to the bank, even better than Clara doing the shimmy with a half eaten turkey."

I could feel my cheeks redden, not from sympathetic embarrassment for my mom, but for the fact this was a perfect example of why I was spending less and less time with my relatives. Thanksgiving was supposed to be about tradition, normal tradition, not craziness. No one was supposed to do a striptease act during dinner. Nobody was supposed to set someone on fire with a stolen flamethrower. Nobody was supposed to shout out family secrets as an appetizer. And nobody was supposed to do all the other inappropriate things which had been happening every year for as long as I could remember. It was supposed to be normal; a norm, like Norman Rockwell. There were no flamethrowers in Rockwell's paintings of Thanksgiving. There were no half-naked dances of short plump aunts. There was peace, harmony, and food.

I felt tears fill my eyes and I quickly wiped away one which tried to escape. My grandmother sidled up next to me, her bony arm wrapping around my waist in a sidelong hug.

"I know what you're thinking," she said, keeping her voice low. "You think today should have been just a wonderful feast of thanks with family and friends, but let me tell you something. Run-of-the-mill memories are not memorable. They blend in too much and become a blur until they are forgotten. But events such as this will provide memories for a lifetime, and maybe even further into other lifetimes if the stories are told."

"Don't you ever just wish things were a little different?" I asked. "That we were just a normal family?"

My grandmother gave me quizzical look. "Define normal."

MICHAEL FOUND me on the couch next to Dad. We were watching the Thanksgiving episode of WKRP in Cincinnati, the one where the station manager decides to run a promotion by tossing live turkeys out of a helicopter while flying over a shopping mall parking lot. It always makes me laugh, not because I hold anything against turkeys but because the entire show is done without ever seeing one of these unlucky birds. It's a classic and like I said, it always makes for a good laugh.

"How many times have you seen this thing?" Michael asked as he plopped down next to me.

"I lost count years ago," I replied with a shrug.

The closing line of the episode played out showing the station manager, Arthur Carlson, saying with complete and utter disbelief, "As God is my witness, I thought turkeys could fly!!!"

He let the credits roll before he said anything. "Well, everything's in place. Are you ready?"

I nodded.

"Say your goodbyes and I'll drive you to the airstrip. All the details will be on the plane."

Doing just that, I made my rounds giving and receiving hugs and pecks on the cheek, watching as the living room slowly emptied out until it was just me and Dad.

He pulled me into a tight hug. "Vinnie told me what all of the hubbub was about."

I winced and leaned back, meeting his amused expression.

"The only person who didn't know about the nun escapade was your grandmother and those too young to understand at the time."

"Are you telling me Grandpa knew about it?"

"He's the one who sent them there. He didn't tell your grandmother because he knew she'd want to go. Too risky, she'd stand out like a sore thumb, so he played dumb and it became this big family secret."

I couldn't help but laugh. We finished our goodbyes just as the aroma of coffee started wafting into the room. I glanced towards the entryway of the kitchen as my brother sauntered our way, a knowing grin accentuating the dimple in his left cheek. I barely got the uh-oh out of my mouth before the sound of Grandmother's voice cracked like a whip in the silence of the living room.

"Edith, get out the whipped cream! We're gonna make that nun party of yours look like a stroll through a kindergarten class!"

Dad took two strides with his long legs straight to the front door. "Well, don't just stand there, go. She's about to get jiggy with it and trust me when I say you don't want to see *her* table dance."

The door opened, we ran, and hell followed Michael and I out of town.

SIX

"WHAT DO you mean you won't do it?"

I shrugged and then gave the fat balding man my most defiantly severe glare. "It means exactly what you think it does. I won't do it. Not today. Not ever. Not if you were the last chubby, middle-aged bald monkey on the face of this planet."

I emptied hot coffee over his inbox and slammed his empty cup down hard enough to upset the framed photo of his unsuspecting wife. It hit the hardwood floor, the glass front shattering as I whipped around, walked right out, and left him to in his own stew of impropriety.

The next morning, I stared at the nice pile of bills stacked neatly on the kitchen table awaiting payment. They began taunting me at the end of my second cup of Joe. Sure, I'd get my last paycheck and it would satisfy some of my debts, but not all. So, I did what a lot of other unemployed and ticked off woman would do, and stomped the short distance to a friend's house.

I'd met Kelly a few weeks after the hit Michael had asked me to do, in the local Kroger grocery store of all places. My cabinets and refrigerator were worthy of what would have been expected if a really good famine came riding into town. Condiments jiggled around when I opened the fridge door of course and there were the mystery bowls which held the beginnings of a crop of penicillin. I hadn't shopped in weeks because I refused to step one foot out of my apartment after the funeral. Hunger finally drove me out and while perusing the produce aisle for anything to toss in a salad. Kelly was doing the same, only with a very irate three-year-old boy in tow. We'd been friends ever since, meeting for lunch, grocery shopping and occasionally taking in a movie; but most of the time we'd just slurp on coffee in her kitchen, griping about things which didn't go our way or the trouble with the things which did. I'd confided in her many times, but never once had I ever told her about my life as an assassin. I needed a friend, not a judge, and she was right there for me.

"I don't know why you agreed to work for the horn dog anyway," Kelly said as she plucked a freshly dried towel from the white plastic laundry basket.

"Starvation and homelessness are great motivators," I replied as I watched her fold, "they also lower your standards. Beggars can't be choosers and all."

Kelly plopped another fluffy towel on the pile and grinned. "He really wanted to do it right in the office, right on the desk?"

"Yep, he's nothing if not cliché."

She laughed. "I thought crap like that died out decades ago."

"Nope, it's alive, well and kicking me as it goes. My price for morality is one job I hated anyway."

"Well, good riddance," Kelly replied, adding the last folded towel to her leaning tower. "So, what are you going to do now?"

I pulled the rolled up newspaper out of my winter coat pocket and laid it on the table.

"I was hoping you'd have time to help me search the Want Ads while your kiddo is still asleep. Are you in?"

Kelly plopped the towels back in the basket and set it on the floor. "Sure, I figure we've got an hour before Trent wakes up from his nap and at least two before my husband comes home for lunch, demanding to know what I did all morning."

I unrolled the paper and began smoothing it out on the table. "I don't know how you put up with him. What were you thinking?"

Kelly shrugged. "I was thinking I was unmarried, six weeks pregnant, and freshly kicked out of my parent's house."

I sighed. "Touché."

As I'd expected there were only entry level positions posted, which wasn't a problem, but they came with entry level pay, which was. I left Kelly's and went to the next logical level, the job counselor. Luckily he was an old family friend and was nice enough to get me into his office without an appointment. Unfortunately, he was an old family friend, meaning if I didn't tell him to be quiet about my state of unemployment, then he would probably tell someone in my family which was exactly what I wanted to avoid.

"Price, it's so good to see you again."

I gave the counselor a hug and a peck on the cheek. "Good to see you too, Jonas. How are you doing these days?"

We parted and he smiled. Jonas Vale was nearly six foot three and sported the figure of Santa Claus. His hair was down to his shoulders and as white as snow, a well-trimmed white beard covered his chubby chin and cheeks, and when he smiled his eyes sparkled behind half-moon wired rimmed glasses like the twinkle of Christmas lights. Because Jonas resembled jolly old Saint Nick, he's held the job as town Santa from the day after Thanksgiving until Christmas for as long as I can remember. He took the appointment seriously, maybe to make up for past transgressions or just because he wanted to bring a little magic to a world starving for it. Regardless of his motives, he stood before me now in red velvet pants with red suspenders, a white thermal undershirt, and shiny black leather boots. His red velvet coat and hat hung at the ready on a coat rack by the door.

"Better than I deserve," he said. "How are you?"

I shrugged. "At the moment, I'm unemployed. I was hoping you could help me out."

He patted the chair reserved for his visitors and took a seat behind his desk. "Care to tell me what happened?"

I gave him the rated G version of my parting with the law firm. He didn't need to know all of the details. I knew Jonas well enough to know he wouldn't tell my parents if I asked him not to, but I also knew him well enough to know he'd seek retaliation against my ex-boss for me, probably by tucking something very explosive into his Christmas stocking.

"I went through the classifieds, but there's nothing promising," I told him. "I was hoping you had some openings somewhere that paid more than minimum wage."

He chuckled, and yes, his belly shook like a bowl full of jelly. "Did you want to stay in the law field?"

I grimaced. "I think I'm over being a secretary."

"Administrative assistant," he said with a grin as he turned to the screen on his desktop computer. "That's what they call them now."

"Fancy title, but it really means gofer. Any chance you have something a little less subservient?"

He tapped a few keys and studied the screen. "Well, let's see, the hospital is looking for somebody to man the admissions desk." He glanced up at me overtop his wired-rims. "They don't fetch coffee for anyone and it looks like the starting pay is twelve dollars an hour."

Twelve bucks an hour was nothing to sneeze at, but there was a problem. I hated hospitals. They smelled funny and they were packed with sick people.

"Anything in there that won't expose me to a communicable disease?"

Jonas smiled as he moved his computer mouse, clicking the button a couple times. "Well, there's the job you're really good at."

"I don't want to do that anymore, Jonas," I replied. "I just want a normal job."

He peered over his glasses at me again. "Define normal."

I LEFT Jonas's office with a recommendation for a position on the other side of town in an antique shop. It wasn't secretary work and it paid more than minimum wage, but just barely. I went in person to inquire about it and the owner gave me an interview right on the spot, which I wasn't expecting. I left, not only with the position, but also with the knowledge that my new boss was indeed an old friend of the family. Good ol'Jonas.

SEVEN

ARNOLD ALVEREZ MET me with a smile and a handshake when I reported for the first day of my new job. He was a slight man, about my own height of five feet four inches, and probably weighing in about ten pounds lighter. Scant bits of grayish-brown hair in a comb over style did little to hide the fact he was balding. Black horned-rimmed glasses framed his gray-blue eyes and sat low on his hawk-like nose. If I hadn't been certain of my place in the present state of the universe during my first meeting with him, I would have sworn I'd been hurled all the way back to 1950, even his clothes sported that nifty-fifties look.

"Glad to see you came back," he said.

I smiled back at him. "Why wouldn't I have come back?"

"I find most new hires don't return once they have a good night's sleep and time to think it over." He ushered me to a broad wooden counter where a vintage register stood at one end. "Perhaps there's not enough excitement in the antique business to catch their attention or perhaps it is because we have no computerized gadgets lying about here. Who knows?"

"Well thank you for hiring me, Mister Alverez."

"I've been friends with your family for years. Call me Arnie. Mister Alverez was my father, my grandfather, my great-grandfather, and so on. That's enough misters for one family."

I laughed. "Okay, Arnie. So, what will I be doing?"

He lifted his hand and swept it in a flourish to indicate the tour was starting with the cash register. "This is off limits for now. It's not that I don't trust you, but mistakes can be easily made and there's no sense in starting an employment on the wrong foot."

I shrugged. "Fine by me, I'm not all that happy about being responsible for someone else's money anyway."

"I like that," he said with a lopsided grin. "Now, one of your jobs will be to keep house, you know, dusting and keeping the floor clean. I know it sounds monotonous, but it's needed."

"Did the monotony of dusting keep your new hires away?" I asked.

"I doubt it," he replied. "You're the first person that's gotten this far."

Arnie showed me around the shop, pointing out housekeeping duties, one of which included washing windows. If I hadn't been in dire need of this job I would have left on that note because I hate cleaning windows, but I swallowed my distain for the task and began my new position of shopkeeper's maid. I went home filthy, my nose filled with so much dust I needed an antihistamine before I went to bed. The next day, I repeated the process, this time on another part of the shop. By the fourth day, I had the dust and grimy windows under control and Benadryl was my new best friend. When Arnie took me into the basement storeroom I nearly passed out from dismay. The room was packed with crates, cardboard boxes, and antiques either too gaudy or too large to fit into the storefront.

"Arnie, please tell me I don't have to dust in here."

He raised his brows. "Dust? Why would I have you dust in here? It's a storeroom, there's no point. Sweep, maybe, but no dusting."

I gave a sigh of relief. It was short lived. He handed me a clipboard. It was one of those wooden backed ones holding about a half inch worth of paper under the metal clip. I glanced down at the first sheet. It was a list of items going from top to bottom, in a font like one would see from an actual typewriter. I lifted the page to see the same number of items, next page, it was the same thing. I glanced up at Arnie.

He smiled and clapped me on the back. "Congratulations. I've just promoted you to inventory."

My face paled. "Thanks."

He gave a lighthearted chuckle and walked off, leaving me alone with just the list, a crap load of junk to count and the burning desire to beat him heavily about the head and shoulders with the wooden clipboard. That night, I went home and scanned the classifieds and the internet for another job. There was nothing. So, I called Jonas on my lunch break the next day.

"Give it a little longer," Jonas said. "Arnie's a good guy."

"He's a slave driver."

"You wanted a normal job, remember? That's what you said. Arnie's place is as normal as you can get."

"What's that bell ringing?"

"I'm doing a gig for the Salvation Army," Jonas replied.

The bell clanged louder in my ear and I had to pull the phone away to keep it from bursting my eardrum.

"Can you stop with the bell for a second?"

"No can do. I've got to raise money for the kiddies. You wouldn't want to make a contribution over the phone, would you?"

"No. I'm calling to see if you've got another job opening somewhere else."

The clanging stopped. "Well, there is one opening I know of, but I'm afraid it's not a normal job."

I groaned. "Not with my family."

"Your choice, but the pay is better and you'd be doing much needed work."

"I don't do that anymore, Jonas."

The bell started again. "Well, that's a shame. HO! HO! HO! Merry Christmas!"

And then he hung up.

EIGHT

ON FRIDAY, I left the shop and deposited my paycheck in the bank. Arnie was more than generous, tacking a hundred dollar bonus on for enduring an entire week in his employ. I left feeling like I'd made the right decision by not quitting on him. I went home, wrote out payments for bills due and then called Kelly to see if she would like to have a late lunch and go to the store with me. I pulled the phone away from my ear when three-year-old Trent started screaming at the top of his lungs.

"You are an angel," Kelly said with an exasperated sigh. "Let me call the sitter and I'll meet you at the usual place in a half hour."

The usual place was McDonald's, a restaurant with a menu both of us could afford. If we were on lean funds, we ordered from the dollar menu. The value meals were reserved for when money wasn't so scarce. I ended the call, scribbled down a quick list of groceries and stuff I was in need of, and then headed on over to the land of the golden arches. The place was packed as usual on a Friday night, but I found an empty table near a window on the entrance side of the building and watched for Kelly to arrive. She slid through the door about ten minutes later with a huge pink leather purse slung over her shoulder. It was large enough to carry anything you might need if an apocalypse happened by and it bounced against her hip as she walked.

Since it wasn't sunny outside and Kelly wasn't necessarily a slave to looking cool, I knew immediately why she was sporting the Miami Vice look. I shook my head in dismay and took a deep breath, leaving my car keys on the table to save our spot as I met her at the counter. We ordered, grabbed our food and self-serve drinks and sat down.

"You're gonna do that one of these days and those keys are gonna be history," Kelly said as she opened the box containing her Big Mac.

I smiled. "Let's just say I like to live dangerously."

Opening up my quarter pounder box, I dove in like I hadn't had a meal in days, savoring every salty, fat-laden bit of goodness it had to offer and cramming in the best fries in the universe between burger bites. Kelly picked at her food for a while before she finally lifted her sunglasses up slightly so I could see what lay beneath. A freshly bruised ring of light purplish skin surrounded her left eye. It was accompanied by a slightly pinker than normal hue to her left cheekbone. She'd used a cover stick and foundation to hide some of bruising, but makeup can only do so much. She let the glasses drop back down into place.

"What was it this time?" I asked.

Kelly took a sip from the straw in her Diet Coke and studied the sandwich in front of her. She'd given up lying to me several months ago so I knew the moment of silence wasn't to work up a believable excuse. It was, however, the moment she needed to keep herself in check. No one wants to cry in their fries at McDonald's, it kind of goes against their whole motto of I'm Lovin' It. Besides, any crier over the age of six is sure to get some unwanted stares. I gave her all the time she needed until finally she looked up and gave a half-hearted shrug.

"He was having one of his headaches, you know? I just wasn't quick enough to quiet Trent during one of screaming tempers."

I grit my teeth, taking my own moment to reel in the temper I felt building up. Everything I could have said about her situation, I'd already said. My opinion of her son, however, I'd kept to myself. I'm not a parent and I don't have nieces or nephews in which to compare, so I honestly have no idea what's to be expected of someone that age. But from my naïve point of view, three-year-old Trent was an incorrigible asshat, announcing in great wails and ear-piercing screams he was indeed the spawned demon apple which had not fallen from far from the tree of Hell.

"You're gonna let him do that one day and your life is gonna be history," I said, revamping her warning about my keys to add a little punch which I hoped would get through her hard head.

Kelly gave me a slight smile. "Touché."

———

KELLY and I spent the rest of the afternoon not discussing her jacknut husband or little Trent. Instead, we finished lunch and then scooted out to the grocery store where we shopped (a chore I'd found somewhat more tolerable since Kelly and I had become friends) until we'd completed our lists. She dropped me at my car, still parked at McDonald's and helped me move all my bags to the back seat before we parted ways. The drive home was short and it was already starting to get dark when I pulled into the parking lot. The two measly security lights on the side of my building were all the illumination provided by the building managers, much to the complaints of many of my fellow tenants. But since this location offered me a pest-free apartment and neighbors who kept their noses in their own business, the lighting problem was low on my list of priorities. I got out of my car, grabbed all of my grocery bags, and trudged inside the building.

The building is a four story stone-sided monstrosity. There is no elevator. The first floor is open to the elderly or handicapped. The second, third and fourth are for anyone who does not mind hiking up and down steps. I live on the third floor which offers more exercise than the first and second, but doesn't go all crazy like the fourth floor.

Most of the tenants on the fourth floor are physical fitness junkies. They're marathoners, cross-fitters, and ex-military. I have nothing against exercise or the people who do it, I'd just prefer to treat it as it really is; a successful pathway in the execution of the fight or flight response. It's also a good way to fit in your jeans, but it should not be a lifestyle.

I lugged my grocery bags up the stairs, listening to the crinkling sounds the thin plastic made as I moved and praying they'd hold up long enough to make into my apartment. I don't know whose stupid idea it was to create bags thin enough to see through in order to carry stuff, but I've wanted to have a word or two with them since the time I was unfortunate to have a bag split on me while crossing the street, scattering my groceries all over the place (rest in peace little can of ravioli squished under the tire of an oncoming truck). I doubted I would ever get the opportunity.

I topped the third floor steps, gave the stairwell door bar a push and continued down the hall to my apartment where I stopped dead in my tracks about twenty feet from a man leaning against the wall right beside my door. He had on one of those brown corduroy caps with white faux wool trim and ear flaps. A dark brown parka covered his upper half; faded loose-fitting blue jeans and steel-toed work boots were on his lower half. He turned to me, his dark brown eyes smiling right along with his mouth, and I knew if he wasn't sporting the graying beard, I would have seen two dimples on either cheek.

"Hey Dad, how are you?"

He moved toward me and took the bundle of grocery bags, freeing up my hands to unlock the door.

"Better than I deserve, I'm sure."

That was the answer my father always gave to anyone who asked, just like Jonas. And like Jonas, his motto was 'No matter what may come your way in life, good or bad, it's always better than you deserve'. Dad isn't a church-going man, not in the organized sense, but he does believe in God, and he's never ceased to amaze me with his steadfastness.

I led him inside my one-bedroom abode. While he piled the bags onto the tiny kitchen table, I shed my coat and purse.

"You want some coffee?" I asked. "I can put a pot on."

"Sounds wonderful," he replied.

I put the coffee on to brew and started making us a ham sandwich a piece. Dad offered to help, but since there isn't much to do aside from slathering mayo on bread and topping it with meat and cheese, I told him to just sit down and take a load off. When the coffee was ready, I poured two cups and set them and the sandwiches on the table. I'm a real Betty Crocker, I am. We ate in silence while sipping coffee, both of us preferring it strong and black. I wasn't worried about the silence while we were munching. I knew he'd get around to why he was here eventually. We finished the makeshift meal and I topped off both of our half-empty cups.

"Bet you're wondering why I'm here?" he asked.

I put on my best daughter smile. "Is it because of my award winning personality and good company?"

He laughed lightly. "You and I both know you're not a company kind of person, but then again, neither am I. Jonas tells you me you've got a nice job with Arnie at his shop."

"It's employment," I replied. "Dusty employment, but it pays the bills."

"Get tired of the paralegal world?"

I paused. There was no way I was going to tell my father about the sexual harassment which had let to my quitting. Like most dads, he'd take it personally and go off to defend my good honor. It would not bode well for the greasy sleaze ball, not that I thought for one minute my ex-boss didn't deserve a good strangling, but if anybody was going to do it, it would be me. So, I took a less complicated path.

"Yeah, it was getting boring. So what brings you around?"

He took a sip of coffee and set the cup down in front of him. "Tell me the truth. Are you really happy doing the nine to five?"

I paused. This was a loaded question.

"It's not really a nine to five job, more like ten to three, but it's normal."

He reached across the table and took both my hands in his own, squeezing them gently. "I know and I know that you've wanted a normal life for a long time. I'm sorry for everything you had to go through to get that. You know I'd take away all the pain if I could."

I tilted my head in a slight nod.

He gave my hands another squeeze. "It's been over a year."

"I know."

"I think it might be time to get back on the horse that threw you."

"I shot that horse, Dad," I said with a sigh, "he's long gone and buried."

Dad managed a smile. "You know what they say about burying stuff? Somehow it always resurfaces."

"Not this horse. I dug a pretty deep hole and I'm still mounding dirt on top."

"Price, you couldn't have stopped what was set in motion. Nobody could. Some things just happen. There's no rhyme or reason to it. And nobody blames you."

I eased my hands out from under his and sat back in my chair, noting the immediate hurt look in his eyes. True, we'd had both lost someone we loved, but he wasn't the one who had to carry a burden of guilt around on his shoulders. A guilt so heavy it was an effort just to get up in the morning and try to make it through the day.

"I'm sorry. I can't come back now and I don't know if I'll ever be able to."

"I'm not asking you to come back permanently. I just need your help with one job."

I felt my blood pressure starting to rise, a sensation which was nothing like me. Keeping your cool was always rule number one in my family. It's what kept you alive and out of the electric chair.

"Pricey," he said, calling me by the pet name I'd been given since before I could remember, "I wouldn't ask for your help if I didn't need it. You know that. And I would never shortchange anyone's need to mourn, but this is important."

I glared at him with the look I'd perfected in my adolescence. "And there's no one else you can heap this on besides me?"

He sighed, leaned back in his chair and crossed his arms over his chest. "Nobody I can trust."

"Give me a break," I replied. "There are plenty of people you can trust to do this and most of them are related to you."

"Okay, so there's no one I can trust to succeed but you. I've exhausted all my resources just trying to get valid information on the target. You have a way of getting things done where no one else can. It's a talent."

"Talent, huh?" The word just tasted bitter in my mouth. I took a sip out of my cup, more bitterness. "My talent in life is death. Thanks Dad. You really know how to rev up a person's self esteem."

He studied me for a moment. "Not death, sweetheart, justice. And whether you like it or not, it's a part of you. I know you want to let go of everything and just be normal, but look around you. Normal people get hurt too. It's why we do what we do."

I closed my eyes and groaned, rubbing both my temples to decrease the throbbing pain beginning to make its presence known. "Who is it?"

"Artemis Van Oliver."

"The Gestinian Cult leader?"

"The only Artemis Van Oliver I know of walking this Earth."

"Please tell me you're joking."

"You know I never joke about a target."

I sat stunned for a moment. The Gestinian Cult was a New Age group which had surfaced nearly a decade ago. They were the standard apocalyptic following, much like the Branch Davidians or Heaven's Gate. They prey on the weak to increase their numbers and as most people are aware, these groups rarely have a happy ending. Artemis Van Oliver was not only the leader of the Gestinians but the freaking founder. So he might not be the guy mixing the Kool-Aid but you can guarantee he would be the one picking out the flavor and choosing the poison spike to go with it. Regardless of this idiot's place in the world, being a lead idiot of a bunch of naïve sheep really wasn't a way to get onto my Dad's radar, so in my mind it certainly wasn't a good enough excuse to drag me into the mess, and that's when he told what *had* caught his attention. I sat stunned for a moment.

"Van Oliver has people on the inside," Dad continued. "Sure, reports are taken but they disappear quicker than the time it takes to write them. What's more, the press won't even touch him, not even the tabloids. Somehow that son of a bitch has managed to stay buried."

"Give me a break. What about social media? Facebook and Twitter should be blasting the story out everywhere."

"Buried," Dad replied flatly. "All buried."

And buried is what always *did* find its way on my father's radar.

NINE

DAD LEFT with my promise to mull it over. It had been a year since I'd killed anyone (a confession you won't typically hear in a normal conversation) and I wasn't sure it was a road I wanted to go down anymore. I tossed the unopened envelope he'd left for me onto the kitchen table. It was heavy enough to make a smacking sound when it hit its mark, all of the information he'd collected on Van Oliver tucked inside just waiting for me to get curious enough to open it. I poured the leftover coffee from the cups into the sink, grabbed a clean glass out of the cabinet, and pulled a bottle of Wild Turkey out of my freezer. Then I settled onto my couch with a good helping of emergency bourbon. I'm not a big drinker. In fact, I hadn't bothered with the stuff until I'd decided to adopt this new way of living. The first week in my paralegal world prompted a visit to our friendly neighborhood liquor warehouse outlet where I could obtain a bit of liquid comfort for around twenty bucks. It wasn't the position which stressed me out as much as the inability to do anything about the legal situations which came knocking on the door to the firm. All actions were executed within the boundaries of the law and more often than not, it was the victims of the crimes committed who suffered. Coming from a life of vigilantism, the feeling of helplessness is extremely tough to take, hence the bourbon.

I took a gulp out of the glass and winced as it burned down my throat, making a trail down to my stomach. I sat there, thinking and sipping for a few minutes, then went into the bathroom and showered in the hottest water I could stand, not to help me think so much as to relax me enough to forget. I dried off, downed the remaining swig left in my glass, and crawled into bed naked. The sheets were freezing at first, but they warmed quickly and I fell asleep soon after. I didn't wake up until my alarm clock woke me.

The next day my job with Arnie was all the ho-hum I could hope to expect. I worked the morning away, counting crap, writing it down, and then counting more crap and writing that down. Lunch was a quick run to the deli across the street and it was the only break in the monotony. I returned to the antique shop for more of the same and left Arnie to lock up when the shop closed. I picked up some Chinese takeout on my way home, checked my mail box in the lobby which was completely packed, and made my way back up the flights of stairs to my apartment. A plain white business envelope taped on my door right overtop the peep hole caught my attention, so I pulled it off, unlocked the door and went inside. I settled onto the couch with my television and sweet and sour chicken, opening mail between bites and commercials.

Since my apartment building tacked the cost of utilities to my rent, I didn't have to worry about the water, electric, gas, and trash companies mailing me the bills. However, the cable company had no qualms with billing me for the cable, internet and cell phone in the little package deal I'd signed up for; nor did the credit card company or the nice people at the bank who provided the loan for my car.

I winced each time I peeked at the amount due on the invoice, and then made a brand new stack-o-bills to be paid. I took a bite of pineapple and chewed with vigor as I made my way through the rest of the mail which was mostly seasonal junk, setting it aside for the trash can. Who the hell buys cars and furniture for Christmas presents anyway?

I reached the bottom of the pile revealing the envelope I'd removed from my door. There was nothing written on the outside so I tore the seal on the flap and took out a single sheet of paper expecting it to be something like a notice from the building manager about maintenance or a rent increase. Instead what I got was a standard white sheet of copier paper cut down to fit the dimensions of the envelope with a name typed dead center. John Mathison. Nothing else; not a dear so-and-so, not a sincerely yours or with deepest regards, not even a screw you, lady or a have a nice day.

Puzzled, I stared at the name for a few seconds, then set it aside and finished my dinner. After I stored the uneaten portions of the cartons into my fridge, I retrieved my lap top, accessed the internet and Googled John Mathison.

Most people would probably have freaked out at the very idea of someone leaving something like this on their door, but then most people don't start trying to live a normal life in their mid-twenties either. My search engine provided so many results I could have spent the next week going through all of them and still not have made a good dent. Apparently, John Mathison is an extremely common name. I moved out of Google and logged in to Facebook where I do have an account, but don't make posts. Call me old fashioned, but I'm really not all that excited about sharing any information with people I'm not close to, much less publishing it on the net where anyone can see. I tapped the name in the search box and waited. The list was shorter than Google so I began going through page after page of John Mathisons. When nothing out of the ordinary could be found on any of them, I went back to Google and rooted through the first ten list-ings. The eleven o'clock news came on pulling my attention away from the screen so I shut the laptop down and called it a night.

The next day was Sunday and Arnie's store was closed, so I slept in. When I finally got out of bed, it was after eleven in the morning. My head felt a little too big for my shoulders, which always happens to me if I sleep for what my body considers too long. I stumbled into the kitchen, put on a pot of coffee and made myself a plate of pancakes with extra butter and syrup (a nutritionist's worst nightmare). I ate until my stomach couldn't handle another bite, then I spent the remainder of the day giving my apartment the good cleaning it needed with the added hope all of the scrubbing might count as good exercise and work off the mass amount of carbs and calories I'd consumed. When I finished, I showered and flopped onto the couch as a reward to myself for some quality TV time. National Lampoon's Christmas Vacation was playing and I settled in to watch Chevy Chase deal with family and his own overzealous expectations during the holidays. I kind of felt a little kinship with poor Clark Griswold as he just wanted to be a part of a normal American family making normal American family memories. Of course, the point of the movie was he always failed and the results turned out much like my family's gatherings; funny as hell when you aren't the one going through it.

The afghan I was huddled under was warm and cozy so I fell asleep an hour into the movie, dreaming about a house covered in Christmas lights and a very angry squirrel jumping out of a fully decorated Christmas tree onto my shoulder. The silly thing was stomping around, pressing its sharp nails into my skin and chattering away. What's more, it gave off a sweet spicy scent that was starting to make my eyes water.

The dream was annoying enough to rouse me awake and when I opened my eyes, Santa Claus was leaning his jolly bearded face overtop mine, poking me in the shoulder.

I blinked, recognizing the smell of the Old Spice aftershave he always wore. It tickled my nose and threatened to make my eyes water.

"If you brought Rudolph in here, you're cleaning up after him."

"Ho. Ho. Ho."

"Not funny," I growled, rubbing at my eyes and sitting up.

I didn't bother asking Jonas how he got in my apartment. What was the point? Like the real Santa, he didn't need a chimney to get into your house, though I doubt St. Nick picked many locks in his legends. I pushed the blanket I'd been snuggling under off of me and turned to glare at him.

"What so important you felt the need to break into my apartment?"

"You called me for another job, remember?"

My brow furrowed. "Why didn't you just use the phone?"

"I tried, you didn't pick up."

I swiped my phone off the end table and sure enough he'd called five times and left two messages. I must have really been out of it. Santa Jonas was making his holly-jolly behind comfy on the end of my couch when I look back at him. He was grinning. I didn't like it.

"If it's a job with my family, I'll have to turn you down. Dad's already put in his two-cent bid for me this week."

"Don't worry. It's not with your family."

"Is it legal?"

He shrugged. "Depends on your idea of legal."

I rolled my eyes.

"Price, it's for me."

I paused at the sincerity in his voice. I'd never known Jonas to really ask me for anything. "What is it?"

"Several homeless people in the area are missing. The police can't figure it out. No bodies. No witnesses. Just poof. Gone."

"Why don't they just put someone undercover?"

Jonas gave me a grim look. "They did. He's missing too. Not a word. Not a warning. Nothing."

"What do you want from me?" I asked.

"I need a partner."

I shook my head. "Nope. I'm not elf material."

"I'm not asking you to be an elf."

"I don't do the Mrs. Clause thing either." Then I added, "Or the reindeer."

He laughed. "No Mrs. Claus and no reindeer."

I felt my forehead wrinkle and my brows rise. "Then what's left?"

"Bag lady."

"Shit."

TEN

I PUSHED my beat up grocery cart down the sidewalk. One of the wheels kept pulling to the left, probably because there was a small chunk of wheel missing causing it to sound like the blown out hard plastic tire that it was. Ka-chunk. Ka-chunk. Ka-chunk. I corrected the path of the cart for the umpteenth time to keep it from barreling out into the street, although the thought of watching someone smash it to bits with their vehicle sounded very pleasing to my ears which were freezing by the way. I pulled the sock cap further down to cover them with one hand and steered the cart with the other. As I expected, it started to veer left again. Being a bag lady is not easy work.

I corrected the cart's path and made my turn into the alley just off First Street, it was like trying to fight the wheel of an old Cadillac with no power steering. The load of crap Jonas heaped up in this battered metal monster wasn't helping matters and I was forced to crane my neck around the mound of plastic trash bags to be able to see where I was going. I stopped the cart right in front of a huge dumpster midway down the alley for a moment. Correct that, I just stopped pushing. This cart wasn't moving anywhere without someone providing it with a little momentum, so no push no go. The alley was wide enough for a trash truck to back in, attach itself to the dumpster, and do its thing. There was less than three feet on either side for correction, so the trash man would have to be accurate with his backup skills. Three feet doesn't give you a lot of room for maneuvering a truck, but it does accommodate a person very well so I scanned the area on both sides of the dumpster for shadows waiting for their opportunity to move.

Lucky for me the city had seen fit to provide street lighting, unlucky for me, the building owners did not. So my view of anything beyond the dumpster was darkened by their uncaring negligence. I thought about taking a tour around the dumpster, but that would probably throw suspicion my way. Our local homeless population was aware of the disappearances, so I doubt they'd be likely to take cover in total darkness, regardless of the police hounding them as vagrants. If I wanted to keep my cover, I needed to make it look real, so this little old bag lady was going no farther. I kept my stance stooped, but at an angle where I could keep a better eye on my surroundings. This was the bad part of town so I was just as likely to be approached by your run-of-the-mill mugger, rapist, or murderer as the predator I was waiting for. Pulling my raggedy coat closed with my fingerless, gloved hands, I waited.

Out of the corner of my eye, I saw a tall, chubby derelict in a tattered army jacket and dark toboggan moving down the sidewalk. It was Jonas. He'd charcoaled his white facial hair to tone it to a dirty gray, ditched the glasses, and grimed himself up a bit. I hadn't seen his disguise before I'd left him to start my bag lady impersonation, but it didn't matter. I knew a homeless Santa when I saw him. He moved at a slow but steady pace carrying nothing but the grim expression of the downtrodden he was pretending to be. If I didn't know him personally, I would have believed he was just another vagrant. His disguise was good and his acting skills were impeccable. I shifted my gaze away from him and he passed on by without either of us expressing any acknowledgement of one another.

Like all well used streets in a populated town, there was still motor traffic even at this time of the night. It wasn't bumper to bumper, but the flow was pretty steady, mandating the need to keep in character. I rooted through the garbage bag on top of the heap in my cart and pulled out the small bottle of cheap whiskey included in my makeshift vagrant kit. I twisted the top open and took a swig of the foul smelling concoction. It was a prime example of what rot-gut whiskey would probably taste like if it got mixed in with a smidge of turpentine. I kept my eyes to the ground and swallowed, making sure I didn't start to cough or gasp. Cough after a drink and people tend to notice you, homeless or not, it's just an ingrained human reaction to someone in trouble. A car passed by slowly just as I'd swigged, the driver never bothering to look my way, which was a good indicator I was blending in to the background.

I screwed the cap back on, tucked the bottle into the bag from whence it came, and drew out a cigarette pack. I flipped the top on the box and glanced inside. Jonas had seen fit to provide a cheap Dollar General Store lighter and a few ciggies inside the pack to complete my loitering ensemble. I pulled one out, lit up, and inhaled deeply. My lungs fought back, trying to make me expel what I'd drawn in, but I won the argument with a gentle exhale of cloudy carcinogenic smoke. Don't mind me. I'm just a bag lady taking five from the gruel of cart pushing. I leaned against the handle bar of the beaten up cart and made the cigarette last as long as I could while I casually kept my watch on the area around me.

When I could no longer keep up appearances, I moved on. I'd seen vagrants huddling up in the shadows of the city park before, so I steered the infernal cart off the walk, through the still open gates, and onto the pathway leading to the grounds. Maybe I could pick up some information from one of homeless still awake and wanting to talk. I made my way to a remote section of the park where the security lights threw weird shadowy forms all around the grass, giving the picnic shelter up ahead a menacing appearance. It was the perfect hunting ground for all manner of boogers of the night and it made me wonder if Jonas might have thought the same thing and taken a position nearby. There hadn't been any information on where the victims disappeared from so the only real plan we had in place was to keep within a two block radius of each other. For safety, we were both equipped with a disposable cell phone. If it was lost or needed to be ditched for some reason, it would be no big loss either. I kept mine on silent and tucked down in the only pocket of my tattered coat that didn't have a hole in it.

I stopped the cart next to the picnic shelter for another cigarette break. I'm not a smoker by habit so I was really not looking forward to another lung full, but since my other two options were the whiskey (which I was more repulsed by than the cigarettes) or bedding down for the night (which would be suspicious to anyone with a brain as I was all by my lonesome), I chose the cancer stick. I propped up on one of the wooden picnic tables and lit up with the hope that somebody would see the cherry bit of fire at the end and get curious. Most importantly, I hoped they noticed quickly. If I had to be out here much longer, I might get more than just a tad cranky, I might end up with a lung infection.

I didn't have to wait long before I caught sight of a shadowy form coming my way. It was too thin for Jonas, so I took another puff off the cigarette and made myself ready.

"Cold night out, huh?"

The man's voice grated against my ears, deep and rough sounding. One of the security lights was at his back, so his features were shaded but I could still make out the general shape of his face and the long, stringy hair hanging just beneath his sock cap. He was tall with a thin build and a hawk-like nose no shadow could hide. He stopped just shy of a foot from me and I made sure to keep up a wary appearance.

"It's cold," I replied flatly.

"I don't think I've ever seen you around here before. Are you new in town?"

I nodded slowly and flicked ashes at his feet, keeping my gaze on his head and hands. In my experience, it's usually the hands which will provide the first strike if there is one, feet and legs used for kicking usually come second. There are always exceptions but since you can't use your lower extremities to shoot, stab, or bludgeon your opponent, they rarely come first. I've been fooled before but the fact is there just aren't a lot of Kung Fu ninjas disguised as homeless people traipsing around in general public areas. A professional can keep his facial expression neutral while he carries on whatever his hands desire without giving anything away, but the normal person cannot.

"I know a place where you can bunk down for the night," he said. "Nice hot meal and a warm bed."

"I'm not interested," I replied.

He took a couple steps toward me. "It's not a shelter if that's what you're worried about."

I took another drag off the cigarette. Keep relaxed. Keep focused. "Do I look worried?" I asked, letting trails of smoke ease out of my mouth as I spoke.

"Nah," he grunted, venturing another couple of steps closer, "just cold."

"You a cop?"

He laughed. "No, I'm just someone who could get you out of here. What's your name?"

I narrowed my eyes at him. It was all part of the game. "Don't have one. Do you?"

"Name's Hawk," he said, moving closer and extending his hand.

Bingo. No more shadows. I could see him completely now. His face was too thin to support the nose in the middle of it, making him look almost like somebody's version of a homeless caricature. He had a couple days growth on his slender cheeks and chin, supporting his vagrant appearance, but I wasn't fooled. A couple days growth meant he'd managed to shave a couple of days ago. In this cold weather, most all of the men walking the streets would welcome a beard just to keep warmer. I drew in a deep breath through my nose, taking in his smell. It sounds ridiculous, I know, but God gave us five senses, it'd be a shame not to use them when you should. The cigarette smoke was pungent but not overwhelming so I could still smell the scent of male deodorant (some version of the Degree brand from the sharpness of it), not the normal smell of a vagrant. He could just be a helpful citizen or a member of a church community trying to help the down and out, but I trashed the idea immediately. Why? It was his eyes that gave him away. I was familiar enough with the homeless to know destitute when I saw it and there was absolutely no despair in his eyes. Also, I spotted no compassion, contradictory to the words he spoke about helping me. This guy was definitely not concerned about my welfare.

I didn't shake his hand, too many things can happen when you take the hand of someone you don't know and most of them can get you killed. Instead, I tossed the cigarette into the darkness, never taking my eyes off him. "They call you Hawk because of your nose?"

He retracted his hand. "Yeah, that and because I've got eyes like one."

"You don't smell homeless, Hawk. You smell like a hunter. What I want to know is what or who are you hunting?"

His body tensed and I caught a faint whiff of perspiration breaking out on him. "Do you want to get out of the cold or not?"

"I don't want to spend the night in jail, Hawk."

"I told you, I'm not a cop. Look, follow me. If you don't like what you see, then leave."

I doubted I'd be leaving any place where Hawk took me. Jonas's last words as I'd pushed the dilapidated cart out into the frigid night air were, "Do whatever is necessary." It's a code phrase in our family which literally means do not leave a predator to chance with the law. Since this was more of a reconnaissance gig, I needed to get this guy to talk. Trust me when I say doing this is a lot harder than you would think. Having the upper hand doesn't necessarily give you answers to questions asked, but being defenseless will sometimes do the trick as human predators holding weak prey tend not to monitor what they say. It's like the proverbial villain monologue which spills the beans on the whole plan, once they have you in their clutches blah, blah, blah. This doesn't work every time and my success indeed depended upon Hawk's stupidity, so I got down off the table and waddled over to my cart to play innocent and defenseless bag lady Price who was now leaving. I wasn't a bit surprised when Hawk shadowed my movements. I didn't pull my hand away from the cart's handle when he made his grab, giving my wrist a hard squeeze which actually hurt.

"Leave the cart. It's too noisy."

I met his eyes with a hateful glare, laying it on as thick as I could. "Everything I own is in that cart."

His squeezed harder. "Nobody will bother it. Come on."

I held on to the handle bar, defiant, while Hawk's inner predator flooded his eyes and confirmed my suspicion. I didn't need to see the knife to know it was there. I just knew. Call it a sixth sense if you will, but I'd been in danger enough times to know when a weapon was pulled and ready to dish out damage.

"I said come on. I don't want to have to hurt you."

"That's a big knife you've got there, pardner."

He responded by jerking my hand, tearing it away from the handle and yanking me away from the cart, the knife in one hand, my hand held tightly in the other. It's not exactly the best way to keep someone under control, too much room to move in my opinion, but he had been intelligent enough to pull me out of the light and into the shadow.

"Where are we going, Hawk?"

"Just shut up and walk."

"Tell me or I'll start screaming my head off."

He whirled around at my threat, his face barely an inch from mine and veiled in the shadows. I felt the tip of the knife against my skin just below my left jaw, letting me know Hawk was a right-hander. He'd slice me from left to right since I was facing him.

"Try it and I'll cut your throat right here."

I shrugged. "I'm homeless, Hawk. You'd be doing me a favor. So either tell me where we're going or kill me now."

I felt the point of the knife dig in a little deeper, enough to cause a nick in my flesh. I feigned a look of surprised horror but in reality it was getting harder to cover up the true disappointment and boredom I was feeling at the moment. I'd been dealing with shit like this for years so it really took a lot to impress me. His gorilla chest-pounding just wasn't doing it, but I needed to make him feel like it did. I managed a shudder and pulled a whimper out of my bag-o-terrible acting skills. When Hawk's mouth stretched back in a satisfied smile, I knew I had him. My own mother wouldn't have fallen for that whimper even if it came with a whole batch of alligator tears.

"We're going to Bade and Nally."

"Why are we going there?"

Hawk's smile got bigger and it came with the sick sound of a chuckle not meant for anyone but him. I've heard light laughter like it before, usually right before the Thorazine drip starts taking effect.

"You're a lucky woman, you know that? Why, you've been chosen."

Another feigned shudder racked through me. "Chosen for what?"

Hawk let up on the pressure he had on the knife and I felt the tip ease out of my wound. He didn't pull it away from my neck; instead he slid it slowly across my skin slicing a shallow cut until it reached the center, holding it pointed against my trachea.

"You're going to be a part of the harvest."

"What harvest?"

Hawk brought his left hand up and ran one of his fingers down the side of my face. "They'll probably take your eyes first. They usually do. That's always my favorite part. Then they'll start to pull out the big money makers; heart, kidneys, the liver..."

I paused. The black market organ trade wasn't even on my list of potential causes for the missing homeless in this town. In fact, I'd ran through quite a few probabilities in my head when I agreed to help Jonas (serial killers, slavery which is usually always of the sexual nature, and possibly even somebody high up in government to take care of the increase in our homeless population with a good culling) but the organ black market wasn't one of those.

"Oh you'll feel everything they do to you, but you won't move. You can't even scream."

I clenched my jaw. There were quite a few chemicals which caused paralysis, ketamine or curare were the first two that came to mind.

Hawk stopped smiling. "Is that good enough for you, old woman? Are your questions all answered now?"

I contemplated the idea of disarming the fucker, knocking his ass out, and finding Jonas so he could deal with this sick piece of work, but it wasn't more than a passing thought. Something inside me just clicked to a stop and then began spinning wildly around, echoing past thoughts back to me. I didn't want to do this crap anymore. I didn't want more blood coating my hands and I didn't want to be there to see death staring back at me with its cold dark eyes. The cathedral job, the hit, the fire, all of it swirled in my head, whipping and whirling until all I could see was the last look in my brother's eyes. It was the sound of Hawk's voice which ripped me away from the subject of my nightmares these days.

"Will you shut the fuck up now and come on, or do I start making their job easier and begin a little cutting of my own?"

I stared at the shadowed angles in his face for a moment. Hawk was a prime example of why I'd become an assassin in the first place. Just like so many monsters, he'd be arrested and tried. And like many of those, they wouldn't have a damn thing to keep him away from society (or maybe they would find something and a technicality would rear its ugly head) either way, he'd skirt free from the long arm of the law and be out before next Christmas to hunt again. I couldn't let that happen, no matter what fresh hell of dreams I'd unearth with this death. A soothing sense of calm washed over me and I smiled. It was too dark for Hawk to appreciate it as much as I did.

"Don't worry," I told him, "I promise I won't say another word to you."

And I didn't. What I did do was jerk my knee straight up between his legs, shoving his balls up as far as they could go. The action caused him to double over with a grunt, taking his armed hand with him and the knife to boot. It skipped over my windpipe but cut against the skin on the other side of my neck, digging in a slightly deeper trek than the opposite side. It stung more than the shallow one of course, but wouldn't be enough to cause any real damage. I'd survive. I grabbed the hand which still gripped the knife at the wrist, turning it inward as I rotated its point toward him, all while pushing against his bowed torso, straightening him up just enough to give me the space needed. More concerned about the pain in his testicles, Hawk didn't block me and I rammed the blade straight up under his ribcage all the way to the hilt. The steel was long enough to meet its mark and wide enough to slice into a lung as well as the heart. He sank to his knees with barely a sound. I released his wrist and gave both of his shoulders a shove. He fell back onto the snow soundlessly, still holding the handle of his own knife in one hand and his balls in the other.

I turned away, grabbed my shopping cart and left. The park would soon be crawling with cops and bystanders. It was no place for a little old bag lady like me.

ELEVEN

"BADE AND NALLY," Jonas said, "the law firm? You sure you heard right?"

"Yeah," I replied, wincing as he dabbed the disinfectant on the cut on my neck. "I heard right."

"I'll make a call," he said, putting a couple butterfly bandages along the length of my wound. "Bade and Nally is a staple in this community. It won't be an easy sell."

I'd already stripped off the bag lady outer wear, laying it on top of the already heaped up shopping cart. The stupid sock hat was the first to go. I now had hat hair with just enough static electricity in it to cause several strands to stand up and out as if I'd put my finger in a light socket, very attractive. I pulled the thick, red wool sweater over my head which only added to the buildup of static, and stepped out of the worn-looking boots. The rest of the apparel I'd have to shed in the privacy of the bathroom.

I looked up at Jonas who'd stripped off his jacket and hat and looked pretty much the way he always did, except like a grungy Santa Claus after a night of sliding down filthy chimneys.

"Do what you have to do," I told him. "That Hawk guy was a

nasty creature. If they have more like him, then it's no wonder the police haven't a clue. But you better move fast, cause once who's ever in charge finds out Hawk's dead, it's going to get complicated."

"Point taken," Jonas replied. "You need a lift home?"

"Nah, I'll change my clothes and take the bus."

He gave me his best Santa Claus smile. "Welcome back."

I leered at him. "I'm not back."

He didn't say a word, just kept smiling. I left and less than an hour later, I was back at the door to my apartment. I was tired. I needed a shower and a nice, warm bed. I unlocked the door and stepped inside, flicking the light switch on as I went. The envelope on the floor caught my eye just as I stepped on it. Somebody had slipped it under the door. I lifted my foot, plucked it up and secured the door, doing a quick walk through to make sure the envelope was the only thing invading my apartment. Nothing appeared to be missing or touched but I made another sweep, this time looking for something smaller than a human; bugs, cameras, incendiary devices, anything that could possibly ruin my night. When I was satisfied nobody had broken in, I carefully lifted the lip of the envelope and pulled out the slip of paper inside. Two words, one name, in type, John Mathison. Again.

"Who *is* this guy?"

I tossed the envelope on the table with the first one and jumped into the shower. When I scrubbed as clean as I could possibly get, I pulled on a tee shirt and sweatpants and went to bed. Arnie was expecting me at the shop in the morning and if I was going to have to count crap and write it down all day or lug around a broom and dust-pan, I was going to need some rest. I fell right to sleep and I didn't dream a thing.

———

ARNIE PEERED at me overtop his glasses when I handed him the clipboard. I'd finished counting and told him so. He flipped through the papers, pausing ever-so-often to study what I'd written and then flipped on. Finally, he looked back up at me.

"Looks like you're finished."

"That's what I said. What do you want me to do next?"

Arnie glanced down at his watch and then back at me. "It's only an hour until close. Knock off early."

I sighed. "You sure you don't want to take the time to train me on something else, like maybe your steam punk looking cash register?"

He smiled. "Nope. See you in the morning."

I left and went home satisfied with a hard day's work. I ate dinner, a kind of throw together pasta dish from a box I'd liberated from the cabinet and washed it down with a glass of iced cold Coke. The Charlie Brown Christmas special was playing on one of the channels, so I settled in to watch as I searched through more of the John Mathisons on my computer. Nothing was popping out as out of the ordinary. Finally, I picked up my cell and phoned my Dad. He answered on the first ring.

"Have you made your decision yet?" he asked, not even bothering with a courtesy hello.

"About the Gestinians? No, but I do have a question for you."

Dad didn't sound surprised or disappointed. He knew me well enough to know I couldn't be pushed into making a decision. He'd given up on trying a long time ago.

"Shoot," was all he said.

"You ever hear of a guy named John Mathison?"

"Common name but nothing rings out."

"You're not kidding. There's quite a few to root through online and I'm not really sure what I'm looking for."

"What's going on?"

I told him what I knew, which wasn't much, about the envelopes and the persistence of whoever was leaving them at my door. He listened without interrupting, as only my Dad was known to do, and stayed silent for a few seconds after I'd finished.

"Dad?"

"I'm here," he replied. "Let me check around and see if I can dig anything up on the name. Sandor may know something."

Uncle Sandor used to be an assassin but took over the organization part of things when my grandfather retired. He's a stickler for information like my Uncle Vinnie, so if anything was known on John Mathison, he'd either already heard it or he'd find out about it. I thanked Dad for the favor and hung up. Then, out of guilt more than anything, I moseyed into the kitchen and fetched the file he'd given me off the table. I figured I owed him to at least look through the thing.

Charlie Brown was over and the television station was now playing a sappy Christmas movie I had no intention of watching. I don't do sappy. It's annoying. I flipped through the channels until I found something I could stand, opened the brown envelope and pulled out the file. Artemis Van Oliver. What a stupid name.

TWELVE

THE NEXT MORNING Arnie shocked the crap out of me and trained me on the antique cash register. Who would have thought something so ancient could be so complicated? I found myself glancing around for the red Smart bubble button to help, but it never appeared, so I was forced to take notes. The morning flew by. We had a few customers, just enough for me to practice my place at the checkout counter but not so many as I felt overwhelmed. I manned the register while Arnie helped the shoppers in their quests for the perfect bit of antique crap. I left for lunch and came back to the store to see my boss in a muffled discussion with someone at the counter. The bell above the door announced my intruding presence with its overly cheerful ringing. I couldn't really sneak back out without it looking even more awkward, so I went on in walking quietly past so as not to interrupt what seemed like a very serious discussion.

"Miss MacCann."

It was Arnie's voice. He was peering at me overtop his glasses, like a librarian who catches you talking too loud when you're supposed to be whispering. I'd seen the very same expression directed at me a bunch of times when I was younger and it still unnerved me. The person he was talking to turned his head to look at me. I'd already noticed his height at about six feet and his build, which was probably more to the medium side if he shed the black coveralls and heavy coat. A knitted toboggan covered his head, but there were tufts of dark curly hair sticking out of it at the back of his neck.

I stopped and turned around. "Yes?"

"Would you be so kind as to step over here for a moment?"

I took the few steps to the counter.

The man towered over my five foot four inch frame, so like the intelligent creature I am I stopped before I got too close; a safe distance of about three feet did the trick for me, far enough away I could dodge a punch or a grab if I needed to. The guy turned completely around, putting his back to Arnie. He had a light cocoa complexion, maybe from Hispanic or Middle-Eastern decent. His eyes were a dark chocolate brown with dark brows matching the shade of the curls sticking out of his hat. His nose was more of a Roman shape with a high ridge, very attractive and very proud look-ing. The lower part of his face was covered in a dark well-trimmed beard and moustache although I could still make out the hard jaw line. He looked like he'd fit well on a front page spread of Playgirl if they ever decided to do a winter wilderness theme. I'm usually not the best at judging ages but if I were to make a guess, I would have said he was no older than about thirty.

"This gentleman is Mister Donnelly. Mister Donnelly, this is my new assistant, Miss MacCann."

Mister Donnelly politely stuck out his hand for me to shake, which I did. Now, I normally try to avoid shaking hands for the simple fact that way too many not so nice things have a possibility of happening during those shakes, but since my boss probably wouldn't have taken kindly to me shunning the guy, I gave in. The first thing I noticed was his hand was warm enough to make me wonder how long he'd been inside the shop. He was still bundled up, so I wouldn't have thought he'd been inside long without unzipping something or at least taking off the hat. Arnie kept the store at a comfortably warm temperature in hopes of enticing potential shoppers to come in from the cold. The second thing I took note of was he didn't seem to have any qualms about a nice and firm handshake. Most men will tone down their show of strength whenever they shake a woman's hand. It's one of the few chivalrous acts left, right next to the opening of doors.

"It's nice to meet you, Miss MacCann. I hope Arnie isn't giving you a hard time."

He had a slight Irish accent and a comfortably deep voice, the kind you'd find in some romantic fantasy staged with lots of swords, swinging ropes and damsels in distress. I could picture him swinging down from a rope, his sword in hand, dealing out damage to several of the crew holding me captive. When he'd cleared the path to the pole where I was bound, I could imagine him saying, "Fear not, my lovely wench, for I shall save you." And then my vision went happily off course to the Caribbean Sea and Mister Donnelly suddenly morphed into Johnny Depp. I could have sighed, but didn't. Arnie's voice brought me back. Johnny and the pirates went poof.

"Miss MacCann?"

"No, he's been very kind," I said, taking back my hand and turning to my boss. "Sorry, I didn't mean to interrupt."

Arnie was looking at me overtop his glasses again, but this time it was the look of a cat with his eyes locked onto a mouse. The lines at the corners of his eyes literally smiled, but when I glanced down at his mouth, he wasn't smiling.

"It's nothing to apologize for, Miss MacCann. In fact, you have perfect timing. I need you to do something for me."

"Sure," I said. "What do you need?"

"Mister Donnelly hasn't been in town very long and doesn't know his way around, so I would really appreciate it if you would give him a lift to the airport for me. That way, I don't have to shut up the store to do it myself."

The smile which hadn't made an appearance on his face slid into place. I recognized it as more an expression of patient calculation than just mere politeness, like something I'd be apt to find wandering too close to a swamp's edge. I saw Donnelly wore near the same expression, although his bordered more on amused than calculating. Alligators, both of them. No good thing comes with playing with gators.

"I could hold down the store if you'd prefer to take him yourself."

"You're still new to this job, Miss MacCann. I don't have warm and fuzzy feelings about leaving you in charge of my store or my register."

I couldn't make an honest rebuttal because I wouldn't trust me with the responsibility either. No sane owner should ever leave someone new in charge and expect for everything to go well.

"When's his flight?" I asked.

"In two hours," Arnie replied. "But he'll need a ride to his hotel room to pack. I will, of course, pay you for your time and the use of your vehicle."

"Of course," I said. "When does Mister Donnelly need to leave?"

Arnie's eyes locked on Donnelly. "Now."

Donnelly was studying the floor, silent, as if he wasn't even the subject of this conversation. I let out a sigh, the tension, thick enough it was almost tangible put me into motion.

"I'll just be waiting in my car," I said.

Neither of them said a word. They didn't even look my way as I walked out of the shop. I got in the car and cracked my window; at least I'd be able to hear the reason to dial 911 should their glares turn into something more violent. I didn't know what the hell was going on between the two of them, but since I really didn't know either one, I didn't feel it was my place to interfere. I turned the radio on and listened to the weather report while I waited. They were forecasting snow tonight. Donnelly emerged from the store a few moments later, walked up to my car, opened the passenger side door and got in. He shut the door, buckled up, pulled a pair of sunglasses out of his coat pocket and slid them on.

"Where to?" I asked.

"Ramada on Main," he replied, leaning his head back against the rest.

Figuring his silence to be the result of him losing whatever disagreement he had with Arnie, I kept quiet and started driving. He didn't utter a word while I drove the few blocks to the Ramada where I parked in the lot next to the building. I shut off the engine. He didn't move an inch. I waited. Nothing. The sunglasses were a wrap-around style so you couldn't see his eyes at all. Was he asleep?

"We're here, Mister Donnelly."

He just sat there.

"Mister Donnelly?"

I watched for the rise and fall of his chest to make sure he was still alive. The last thing I needed to make my day was a dead man in my car. His chest rose and fell rhythmically like someone sleeping.

"Mister Donnelly!"

He responded with a light snore and I hit the horn. The Taurus blared out a nice, long, and irritating honk before I stopped pushing against it. Donnelly continued to snore.

I let out a groan, wondering just how much Arnie was paying me for this little favor of his. Then I rubbed the space between my eyes to ward away the headache which was beginning to form there and sat silent for a moment. I hated waking people up. The guy was out like the dead and we'd only driven a couple of blocks. For a moment, I wondered if Arnie might have slipped him a Mickey of some kind, but I decided to give it one more try before I called my boss to ask him about it. I stared at Donnelly, sleeping there in my passenger seat, looking pretty peaceful actually. Who the hell falls asleep in a stranger's vehicle anyway?

I took a deep breath and readied myself, praying I wouldn't get mauled. One does not simply poke the sleeping bear and assume to walk away unscathed. I scooted my back against the door to get some distance in case he woke up swinging and then I extended my hand and gave his shoulder a good nudge. His hand wrapped around my wrist before I could retract and squeezed it tightly. I gave a startled yelp and reflexively drove my left fist straight into his nose. His glasses fell into his lap and his eyes flew open, wide with surprise. He let go of my wrist and covered his nose.

"What the hell did you do that for?" he exclaimed.

"You just tried to break my wrist!"

I wasn't going to give him the satisfaction of seeing me trying to rub some feeling back into my hand or check to see if he'd cracked a bone, but I did undo my seatbelt, ready for fight or flight. He pulled his hand away from his nose and glanced down, it was covered in blood. His handsome Roman nose was already starting to swell. I reached over in front of his legs, hoping he wouldn't try to grab me again, opened my glove box and yanked out a stack of napkins I kept in reserve from fast food places kind enough to give you more than one per visit. I've always saved back the extras since you never know when you'll be in need (like now for instance). I thrust them into his hand and slapped the glove box closed as he began wiping the blood off his face and hands.

"Why didn't you just say something?"

I grit my teeth and handed him a plastic shopping bag I used for the car's trash can. "I did."

"Well why didn't you just say it louder?"

"I did," I growled, "and you obviously didn't hear me."

"Obviously," he said, bending his head forward and pinching his nose with the napkin to stop the flow.

"And I honked the horn," I added. "Who the hell goes to sleep in a stranger's car anyway?"

Donnelly said nothing.

I sat there for a few minutes not saying a word, finally Donnelly raised his head and pulled the passenger side visor down to check out his injury. The napkins had soaked up a lot of blood, but it could only take so much and could do nothing about the red smears drying on his face. I pulled a canister of Handi-wipes (who says I'm not prepared) out from under my seat and gave it to him. He popped the top and yanked a good handful out, using my visor mirror to clean up. He folded the visor back into place and turned to me.

"You know, there are other ways to wake someone."

"I know," I replied hotly, sensing his ways of being woke-up were not something I wanted to hear, "but since I don't have any ice cold water in the car and I left my gun at home this morning, I went with what I had. Now go get your shit so I can take you to the airport and get back to work."

He gave me a boyish grin. "You're not coming in with me?"

"No! Now go before I decide to quit my job and leave you here to hitch a ride from someone else."

He gave a shrug, slid the glasses back on and got out of the car, slamming the door just a little too hard. I rolled my eyes.

"What an idiot," I mumbled. "A good looking idiot, sure, but definitely an idiot." I watched him disappear into the Ramada.

While I waited I checked out my wrist and hand. Nothing was broken, but I did have a nice reddish-purple bruise shaping up like a bracelet around my wrist. I suddenly found myself hoping I'd broken Donnelly's nose or, at least, given him raccoon bruises around his big brown eyes. I had plenty of time to contemplate his demise and after about an hour in the car, I was at my wits end.

"This is way beyond the call of duty," I told myself as I grabbed my purse and headed inside to the hotel's front desk.

I was immediately greeted by one of the staff, a young guy probably barely above the legal working age. He gave me the welcome speech I was sure all the lobby employees were required to recite and asked how he could help me.

"There was a guy that came in here about an hour ago, tall, dark and handsome. He had on a toboggan, coveralls, and sunglasses."

"I'm sorry," the young man said, "I was probably at lunch when he came inside. Is he a guest here?"

I nodded. "Mister Donnelly."

The attendant tapped a few keys on his keyboard and stared at the computer screen in front of him. He finally raised his face to mine and smiled.

"Yes. He is a guest here."

"Good," I replied. "Could you ring his room and tell him to hurry up. He has a flight to catch and I'm his ride."

The smile faded at the edges of the guy's mouth. "I'm sorry. Mister Donnelly has left strict instructions not to be disturbed."

"It's okay. He knows I'm here. Just dial the number to his room and hand me the phone."

The smile on the young man's face faded entirely. "I'm sorry. That's against our policy."

I sighed. "Well, can you at least give me his room number so I can disturb him myself?"

"That's against—"

"Your policy," I finished for him. "Go figure. Look, could you at least make sure he gets a message?"

The smile returned as he realized there was something he could do that wasn't against hotel policy. "Certainly ma'am."

I frowned. Nothing is more wounding to a young woman's pride then being called ma'am. It's meant to be polite, but somehow it never is.

"Something wrong, ma'am?" the guy asked with a nervous and quizzical look on his face.

"No, nothing's wrong," I replied, trying not to wince when he said it again.

"What's your message, ma'am?"

"Tell Mister Donnelly that Arnie's assistant has left to go back to work."

The guy scribbled as I dictated. "Anything else, ma—"

I held up my hand to stop him before he could finish the final ma'am in this conversation. "Now, make sure you get this word for word, okay?"

The guy gave an uncertain nod. He probably hadn't been on the job long enough to be familiar with nut cases such as myself, so I kept my tone very calm, cool, and collected so as not to frighten the bejesus out of him.

"So find your own damn way to the airport, you ungrateful son of a bitch."

The guy glanced up at me with a slacked jaw and wide eyes. I gave him the friendliest smile I could muster up.

"And make sure you spell it out too. S.O.B. just doesn't have as much punch."

THIRTEEN

"WHAT DO you mean you didn't get him to the airport?"

I met Arnie's glare with my own. "I mean exactly that."

"Explain."

I did, adding the last bit about the message I'd left for him at the front desk. It looked like he wanted to laugh, but he didn't, instead he kept up his deadpan expression and peered over his glasses at me.

"How is it an assassin allows someone like Donnelly to get away so easily?"

"Ex-assassin," I replied with a wince as visions of Hawk danced in my head. "Okay, well, sort of ex. Besides, this was supposed to be just an errand and what do you mean someone like Donnelly?"

Arnie smiled. Jerk.

I reminded myself I really needed the job to do things like eat and live before I opened my mouth.

"I think I've done a pretty good job here, Arnie, minus the Donnelly thing."

"Yes, except for Donnelly, you've done okay."

"Okay, so what's with that guy anyway?" I asked.

"There's only one thing you need know concerning Donnelly."

"And what's that?"

"If you see him again, kill him."

MY PHONE RANG at about ten that night just as I had closed my eyes. I growled and picked it up off my bedside table to see who was so bold as to disturb me. It was Dad.

"Sorry if I woke you up," he said.

"I just got into bed. It's okay."

"I looked into John Mathison for you, but I don't think you're going to like what I found."

I sat up and fought off a yawn. "What is it?"

"Two J. Mathisons stick out. One of them is a local guy I couldn't find any background on past two years. The other, well, that's even worse."

"What do you mean worse?" I asked, losing the battle with the yawn.

"The other is one of the many aliases of Artemis Van Oliver."

The last part of my yawn came out like a growling groan.

"I said you wouldn't like it."

"Are you serious? This isn't just some ploy to get me to look into Oliver is it?"

He didn't say anything for a moment and I thought I'd hurt his feelings, so I apologized.

"I told you before, Price, I won't push you into something you don't want to do."

I felt like a heel and hated it. "I know. Just e-mail what you've got on both of them and I'll check into it, and Dad?"

"Yes?"

"Just to ease my mind, you didn't leave those envelopes on my door, did you?"

There was a chuckle on the other end of the line. "Set your mind at ease, Pricey. It wasn't me."

I MANAGED to have as little contact with Arnie as I could the next day. It seemed to be a mutual distancing, as he didn't seem to want to elaborate more about Donnelly and I didn't really want to know anything else right now. Two plus two equals a nice quiet day at work. At quitting time, he gave me a wave and said he'd see me in the morning. I got in my car and headed to the address of the first John Mathison my father told me about, the one with only a two year history.

"Just find this guy and see if he's in danger," I told myself. "That's all you have to do. You're just checking on someone who might need help."

I took the ramp onto the interstate and headed north, flipping on the radio for the weather report and the background noise I needed to keep my troubled mind at bay. The forecast was for snow, but since the front had stalled and not a flake had fallen yesterday, the nice people predicting the weather were promising a big accumulation when it finally did get here. No big deal since it was December and just about everybody likes snow in December, at least until Christmas. Obviously they don't mind if it helps Santa Claus get around in his sleigh. After that, there's more whining and bitching about the white fluffy stuff than you can shake a stick at. Lucky for me, the forecasted snow wasn't supposed to start until after midnight. Hopefully, I'd be back home and in my nice comfy bed by then.

I drove ten miles, took the exit I needed and hit the highway. My destination was one of many small brick homes in a winding subdivision. I slowed the car down to catch the house numbers, found the one I needed and did a slow drive-by for safety's sake and to scout the area. You can never be too careful. In my experience, some of the owners of the nicest homes smack dab in the middle of respectable neighborhoods have been the dens of some of the most notorious crimes, meth makers are a good example. So you couldn't always tell what lurked inside but you could at least stake the place out for a way out of the lion's den if you happened to find yourself trapped.

I spotted a lone red and white Chevy pickup truck in the driveway, nestled beside the large ranch style brick house. The pickup was one of those boxy eighties models which still managed to show up on the roads more times than you'd think. There were boxwoods outlining the front porch of the house, all of them covered in seasonal multi-colored lights. The front window, probably to the family room, glowed from the Christmas tree. Nothing screamed danger, but like I said, you just never know. I went on and did another circuit around the streets, landing me back in front of Mathison's home sweet home and opted to park on the street instead of pulling in the drive in case I needed a quick getaway.

According to the guy's driver's license, he was thirty-five years old, which means, there were thirty-three years unaccounted for. He could have been a born member of a group like the Amish or the Mennonites. It could happen. But more likely he was living under an alias, either one he'd taken for himself or one assigned to him. From there, the assumptions were worse. If he was assigned the persona, then it was most likely by a government or group like the witness protection program we use here in the United States. If he assumed his own identity, then he could really be anything from a spy for another country to some deadbeat dad who faked his death and made a new life for himself in a place where his back child support was no longer a threatening issue.

I tucked the copies Dad had e-mailed me about both Mathisons under the passenger side seat and opened my glove compartment. I pulled the Smith and Wesson 9mm out and shed the pancake holster, opting to slide it in my coat pocket instead of securing the weapon to the small of my back. I got out of the car and walked the few feet to the house. Stepping up on the covered porch, I rang the doorbell and waited. The door opened revealing none other than John Mathison himself. He was dressed only in a pair of faded blue jeans, no shoes, socks, or shirt. Nice smooth skin covered a well-muscled chest and washboard abs. His short dark hair was still wet like he'd just got out of the shower, mussed from a good towel dry. He smelled pleasantly of soap, shampoo, and deodorant; a fresh and clean smell which wasn't the least bit overwhelming. He gave me a slight smile, showing perfectly straight white teeth. I couldn't tell the color of his eyes in the porch lighting, but according to his driver's license, they were blue. I'd have to take the license's word for it.

"Can I help you?" he asked.

"Uh, yeah, my name is Sally Evans and I'm looking for John Mathison. We've been pen pals for years and he told me to look him up whenever I was in town, and well, here I am."

Mathison laughed. "I think you've got the wrong one. I'm nobody's pen pal."

I frowned. "This is the address. Have you lived here long?"

"A couple years," he replied.

"Well that's odd, two John Mathisons living back to back at the same address. Did you know the guy who lived here before you?"

"Nope. Geez it's cold out here."

"It sure is. May I come in?"

Mathison looked uncertain, as if he were weighing his options, either shut the door on Sally Evans and let her figure her own way to her pen pal or let her inside and shut the door to keep my nipples from freezing off. There was even a hint of a third option which was to stay put and demand more information before either of the other two would be acted upon. I waited patiently for the few moments he needed to process it all and make his decision.

"Fine," he replied, sizing me up as he said it, "it's too cold for anybody to be standing outside. Come on in."

"Thank you."

He moved aside and allowed me to enter. The living room was well-furnished but not elaborately so and as I expected the Christmas tree was the centerpiece in the front window. There were several nicely wrapped presents nestled underneath the well-decorated limbs of the evergreen and the scent in the air let me know the tree was real. He shut the door and grabbed a flannel shirt lying over the back of one of those manly recliners you see advertised in furniture stores. He slid his arms into the shirt, motioned for me to take a seat on the overstuffed couch near the door and then plopped down on the recliner. I sat down on the edge. Never get so comfy you can't bolt out whatever exit is available should the need arise.

"So, tell me about this pen pal."

I started to keep up the ruse, feed the guy some cockamamie story about the pen pal that did not exist, and see if he gave me anything useful in exchange to determine if his name was the one someone had been sending me. But it's time consuming and you have to remember all the bits and pieces to the web of lies you weave, which is incredibly irritating, not to mention risky should you ever meet the person again in the future. So, I sat silent for a moment, taking in the very tasteful décor.

"You're not really Sally Evans are you?" he asked.

I looked him straight in those baby blues and shook my head.

"No pen pal?" Mathison asked with a frown.

"Nope."

"Thought so," he replied, sliding his hand between the bulky cushions of the arm of the chair and pulling out a gun.

I reminded myself I was just here to talk and resisted the urge to bring out the 9mm. Mathison aimed the straight at me, clicking the safety off in one fluid motion. The gun itself was one of the Ruger SR9 series, black, sleek and deadly. It could hold enough ammo to blow at least ten holes right through me, and if Mathison happened to be an over-achiever, it would make seventeen holes. That's a lot of bullets for just little old me, best get to talking.

"My name is Price and the real reason I'm here is because you're name, John Mathison, keeps getting dropped at my front door."

He narrowed his eyes. "Uh-huh."

I gave a shrug. "Believe me or not, I don't care. But it's happening and I need to know why. I'm just here to see if you're the right John Mathison."

Mathison kept the gun aimed on me. He was smart, paranoid, or a good combination of both.

"What comes with the name?" he asked.

"An envelope."

He smirked. "You've got a good sense of humor for someone who's getting ready to get shot."

"I know," I said, "but you should hear my jokes when the gun is bigger than yours."

"Who do you work for?"

"An old fart named Arnie who owns an antique shop," I replied. "Now your turn, who are you really?"

He laughed. "John Mathison."

I leaned forward, placing my elbows on my knees and clasping my hands, giving him my most sincere expression.

"Mister Mathison, I am a busy woman and I really don't have time to play games and shoot the shit with you. I know for a fact your current identity is a relatively new one, and well, frankly I couldn't give bigger damn about it. I don't care why you changed your name and I don't care what happened to initiate the change. All I do want to know is why someone might be feeding your name to me."

He paused for a moment and slowly lowered the Ruger to his lap.

"Are you in law enforcement?"

I shook my head. "Are you running?"

"Not anymore."

"Witness protection?"

He didn't answer, but didn't say no. I took it in the affirmative.

"Relax," I said. "I'm not here to break your cover. Any chance the person you're hiding from knows your new identity?"

Mathison shrugged. "I haven't heard anything, but why would someone drop my name to you?"

"Most likely retaliation, nobody feeds me a name without wanting something to come from it. Like, for instance, your death."

He studied me skeptically.

"Look Mister Mathison, I don't like games or riddles and I don't enjoy having people bait me into making a kill. So let's just cut the bullshit alright, you talk and I'll see if there's something I can do to help."

"Are you serious? You really expect me to trust you?"

I reached into my coat pocket and slowly pulled the Smith and Wesson out, placing it on the floor between us before sitting back up and planting both hands on my knees. The Ruger was once again aimed at me.

"I could have shot you at any time if I wanted you dead, John," I said. "Talk to me."

He lowered the gun and slid the safety in place, setting it back in his lap before he began to tell me his story. His wife and daughter were visiting his in-laws and due to come home any time. He'd gotten married and started a family under a new name shortly after being placed under witness protection. For the wife's sake, I hope to God she knew about it. He didn't give me his real name and I didn't ask. It really wasn't information I needed if he was telling me the truth to begin with. At the end of his tale, he looked up at me with hopeful eyes.

"So, what do you think?"

"I think you need to get in touch with your witness protection people and see if you can be relocated."

His eyes widened. "You really think they know where I am?"

I sighed. "I think it's worth taking precautions. You were a mule for a South American drug cartel and a witness to a murder on American soil. The one thing the cartel is good at is killing people who they deem a threat. If they can't get to you personally, they'll hire someone who can. Know what they like better than killing one threat?"

He shook his head.

"Three."

A look of panic filled Mathison's face and he lifted his Ruger, aiming at me for the third time in less than an hour. It's so damned good to have a way with people.

FOURTEEN

"LOOK, it's not me, okay? I told you if I wanted you dead, you'd have bit it before you ever saw me."

Mathison sat frozen, contemplating. I let him. Finally, he eased the barrel down and secured the gun, sliding it back between the arm rest and the cushion of the recliner. I got up to go. I'd done all I could here. He reached down and picked up my 9mm, never taking his eyes off of me.

"Here," he said, handing the gun back, "and thanks."

I slid it back into my coat pocket.

"Call your people. You've got a family to think about."

He nodded in reply and walked me to the door. As I stepped off of the porch, I heard him say, "I sure hope you're being straight with me."

There was no way to make this guy trust me so I ignored what he said and threw my hand up in a wave as I walked back to the car. I got in and closed the door. Mathison was still standing on the porch watching me and I really couldn't blame him, I guess. If the roles had been reversed I'd probably have been suspicious too. I started the engine and was just about to put it in gear when I felt an unsettling twinge deep inside. Call it women's intuition. Call it paranoia. Call it anything you like. It's unnerving as heck and it's meant to be. I pulled out my cell phone and hit Dad's number on my contact list. He answered on the second ring.

"What's up, Pricey? You got snow already?"

"No snow yet. Look, I'm at the house of the two-year-history guy and we just had a nice long talk."

"Witness protection?"

"Uh huh," I replied. "He admitted to being messed in with a drug cartel."

I glanced back towards the house. Mathison had gone in and closed the storm door, but was still staring out at me.

Dad asked, "South America?"

"Yep."

"Shit."

"My sentiments exactly," I said. "I have a feeling there's a leak in the department, but I don't think it was the cartel who passed his name on to me."

Dad sighed. "You know it as well as I the cartel won't leave a hit to chance. Obviously somebody's watching over this guy, maybe whoever it is knows about the leak."

"Possibly," I said, "or maybe the person *is* the leak. I don't have good feelings about leaving this guy to possibilities. Something just doesn't feel right."

I heard Dad blow out a sigh. "You armed?"

"Yeah."

"Pricey, I know you've been out for a while, but this isn't new territory. Go with your gut. If it's telling you to stay for a while and see if anything crawls out from under a rock, do it."

"Okay. Love you."

"Ditto," he replied. "Call if you need me."

"I will."

I ended the call and decided to follow my instinct. I found a scrap of paper and a pen in the deep recesses of my purse, and scribbled down my cell phone number; then got out of the car and went back to Mathison's door where he stood with it open. I handed him the paper.

"Look, I'm not feeling all that great about leaving you to your own devices right now. So, I'm going to hang out for a while just to set my mind at ease. If you see anything out of the ordinary, call this number. Got it?"

He glanced down at the slip I'd handed him and back up at me. "I still don't understand why you're helping me."

I shrugged. I didn't know why either. Maybe it was just the season of good cheer and I was trying to do my part. Maybe it was because, I'd been killing for hire for so long, I just wanted to help someone live for free. Maybe it was because I was on the entrance ramp speeding right back to the highway of my old life. Who the hell knows?

I turned to go, paused, and added over my shoulder, "And for God's sake, get back in the house and keep your gun handy."

I went back to my car, still feeling just as unsettled as before. I put the Taurus in gear, pulled out, and slowly drove down the street. I stopped at a stop sign and took a right, then another right, and another right, kind of like a slow race car driver going the wrong damn way as I circled around. I parked about a block from Mathison's house and shut off my engine. Grabbing a thick blanket stowed on the floorboard of my back seat for emergencies, I covered up and settled in to wait, and wait, and wait.

The first flake of snow floated down and landed on my windshield. It was one of the fluffy kind, like a bunch of small flakes were too scared to make the jump from the clouds on their own so several of them got together held hands and then took the leap. The flake didn't melt, just sat there looking fluffy. It wasn't long before another one came down to join it. A few more trailed after them, settling on the glass and I watched as more of their kind followed. It wouldn't be much longer before my windshield was covered, obstructing my view. I turned the key and let the wipers swish back and forth a couple of times before turning it off again. The glass stayed clear for a second or two before the fluffy flakes turned into kamikaze bits of snow with something to prove. At this rate, there was no way I was going to be able to keep an eye on the house from inside the Taurus without looking conspicuous to anyone who may be watching.

I started the engine and turned on the wipers, making the decision to circle the block again and see if I could find a better position. Maybe there would be an unoccupied house or garage with a view of Mathison's abode. A black SUV came barreling down the street and as it passed I caught a glimpse of a government-issue license plate. I waited, watching it slow and turn into Mathison's driveway. Both front doors opened and two men got out, both of them sporting the typical g-man suit, dress coat, and hair. They walked the short distance to Mathison's front porch and stood in front of the door. I turned my eyes back to the SUV. The windows were tinted but I made out the silhouette of someone in the back seat.

"It takes three agents to move one guy and his family?"

I plucked up my cell from the console and hit my dad's number again, keeping my eyes on the agents at the front door. Dad picked up on the first ring.

"Two calls in one night, Pricey? You're making your old pop feel special."

"Hey Dad, quick question, if somebody needs to move a witness and his family to a new location, who do they send?"

"The Marshalls. Why?"

"Remind me, do they usually dress up like undertakers and travel in packs?"

I heard his breath catch. "Price, give me your location and I'll meet you there."

The front door opened and I could just make out Mathison in the space between the two agents. There was no way I could tell if he'd been smart enough to have his gun with him, but it didn't matter, he opened the door and let them walk inside. The door closed.

"Price?"

"Well, crap. The big dummy just let them inside."

I spotted a vehicle coming up the street and squinted my eyes against the glare of the headlights until it moved past. The small econo-line car pulled to the curbside right in front of the Mathison house and parked. The driver's side door opened and a petite woman got out and immediately went to the backseat door.

"Double crap. Looks like Mathison's family just got home."

I didn't hear my Dad's response to this new development because my full attention went to the third agent in the SUV. I slapped the phone closed and tossed it onto the passenger seat beside me just as the third agent stepped out of the vehicle and reached inside his dress coat. Somehow I doubted he planned to flash his badge. The snow was coming down harder, making it more difficult to see, but I still managed to make out the shape of a handgun when I lowered my window. The woman, completely unaware of what was happening, pulled out a small bundled up child, hiked the bundle on her hip and kicked both doors closed as if nothing out of the ordinary was happening. She didn't even seem to notice the agent coming towards her. I yanked the blanket off of me and threw it on the seat beside me.

My first instinct was to pull the 9mm out of the pocket of my coat, shoot the guy, move on to the house and take out the other two. That would have been the logical thing to do, the old Price MacCann; shoot first, sort out who the undertaker posse really is later, but I wasn't ready to admit I was back to my old ways just yet (maybe tomorrow, but not tonight). I strapped on my seatbelt, shifted my car into drive and hit the gas pedal. The rear wheels spun a little on the slick pavement, causing a little fishtail action which was just the distraction I was looking for. I didn't fight the skid, just rode it. When my tires caught pavement, I floored it and switched my head-lights to bright. The woman whipped around wide-eyed, her mouth in an o shape. She might have looked like a deer caught in my head-lights, but she did have sense enough to move out of the way to the front of her car. The agent, or whoever the hell he really was, took aim and fired.

The bullet took out my side mirror as I veered my car in line with the driveway. The front tires bumped over the concrete curb, bouncing me enough I was thankful I'd strapped on my seatbelt. The next shot went wide as the guy moved to get away from the SUV. He didn't move fast enough and I clipped him with the left side bumper. The force of the hit was enough to throw him back, him going one way and his gun another. I plowed right into the left rear side of the SUV. The airbag in front of me deployed with a loud bang sending white powder all over the cab of the car and out my open window. At the same instant the shoulder strap snapped against me as it locked tight and my face greeted the rough material of the airbag. Adrenaline was pouring through my veins, numbing some of the pain from the impact, but not all. It was like being punched in the face by a gorilla with boxing gloves made of burlap. I popped the release button on the seatbelt with one hand and blindly jerked at my keys in the ignition. The detachable key ring separated, leaving the car key section in the ignition and the other part with the key to my apartment in my hand. A quick jab and downward rip parted the ballooned material of the airbag sending the rest of the powder hissing all around me. Luckily, the door wasn't damaged and I could get out without having to climb out the window.

Several of the neighbor's houses lit up and I knew it would be only moments before someone called the cops. The noise brought one of the agents from inside Mathison's house to the front door with gun in hand. He wasted no time charging out onto the porch, sending bullets at me as I took cover behind my damaged vehicle. The bullet hit one of the side windows of my car, shattering the glass. I glanced over at the woman who was now huddled against her econo-line on the driver's side. She held the child tightly, putting the car to the kid's back and shielding the front of the kiddo with her own body.

"Get the hell out of here!" I screamed at her.

She looked shocked and bewildered, but was coherent enough to yank open the door and climb inside with her kid in tow. The guy on the porch swung his gun in her direction just as the engine came to life on the woman's car. He fired off a couple shots as she peeled out away from the curb and down the street. The passenger side tail light exploded, pieces of red reflective plastic littering the pavement as she went.

I ducked back down when the agent redirected his aim, firing off a few more shots in my direction as he moved forward off the porch closing in on the mess I'd made in the driveway. One of the bullets took out another side window and I vaguely heard him curse me in Spanish. I couldn't help but smile as being called a punta meant nothing to me other than proving the idiot was furious. I glanced to my left where the guy I'd hit with my car lay unconscious. I scanned the snow covered ground and found his gun several feet to my left, partly hidden underneath one of the boxwoods. At least if the guy came to, the gun wouldn't be within his reach; one down and two to go.

I slipped the keys into my coat pocket and pulled the zipper closed with the hope I wouldn't lose it should this night go from gunfire to something more personal like hand-to-hand. The last thing I needed was to have to struggle to get inside my apartment when and if I ever made it back there. I pulled the Smith and Wesson out of the opposite pocket and clicked the safety off as I scanned the ground around me for a needed distraction. Next to me lay a sad and decapitated garden gnome. I guess I must have run over the little bugger with my car as it sped through the front yard. I grabbed the gnome's head, peeked around the side to make sure of the guy's position and gave it a good chuck off to the right into the darkness. The shooter whirled at the sound and discharged the gun a couple times. I eased up to clear my car and fired once, hitting him in the left temple. His gun hand clinched reflexively, causing his index finger to pull the trigger once more before he fell. The bullet hit the ground mere inches away from me. I stayed crouched and in the shadows as I moved away from the Taurus towards the boxwoods where I stopped and peered through the branches to the window of the storm door. Between the limbs of the Christmas tree, I could see Mathison and the last "agent" guy in the living room with guns drawn, screaming at one another. I rolled my eyes.

I didn't have much time to think about their stupidity before sirens pierced the air. I kept my eyes on them and tossed the gun back where I'd swiped it up. Both men fired and both men missed. It was just sad. They were less than twenty feet from one another. Mathison would benefit from some hours on the gun range and the fake agent, well, it would definitely help his aim if turned his weapon the right way up. I don't know why in the world gangbangers hold their gun sideways. You can't hit anything that way. I caught sight of the red and blue strobe lights in the distance just as the last of Mathison's attackers decided to cut his losses and crash straight through the front window. I ducked down and turned my head in the opposite direction to keep from getting a face full of glass shards. The gang banging agent landed right beside me on all fours. I kicked my foot out straight into the back of his elbow, heard the crack of bone, and got to my feet. He let out a scream and clutched his arm just as I thrust my boot straight into the center of his face. His gun hit the ground before he did and I moved quickly, kicking it away as I pocketed the 9mm.

Mathison came out of the house, his plaid shirt open and blowing in the frigid wind, the Rueger held down at his side. I gave him a nod and he nodded back just as police cars screeched to a halt in the street right in front of the house.

FIFTEEN

I FINALLY MADE it back to my apartment at close to four in the morning. The snow was still coming and had been the deadly type driven sideways by cutting wind blasts for quite a while. The kind which stings when it hits you and has a tendency to push all business conducted in its path a little faster, funny how near whiteout conditions can increase the brain power and efficiency of law enforcement. Mathison was conducted with the nice officers (who'd actually taken the call from Witness Protection, courtesy of one of my Dad's contacts) to the police station to reunite with his wife and kid, bound for a safe house and a new identity. The two injured gang members were arrested and then escorted to a hospital, charged with many crimes, one of which was impersonating federal officers. The dead one I'd shot in the head was moved to the morgue, courtesy of a coroner's van, and since not one neighbor admitted to seeing me shoot him it was assumed he was a victim of friendly fire, gangbanger style. I found it odd not one police officer searched me for a weapon, but I guess they just assumed since I was a small woman with a bashed up Taurus, I was not one of the trouble makers. I did not bother to enlighten them.

The cops took my statement, contacted the tow truck driver to move my car once the preliminary investigation was finished, and then designated a nice officer to give me a lift home. All of these things took less than an hour to complete. God bless the snow. The ride home, however, took nearly two hours of snail's pace, nail-biting driving by a rookie cop. I invited him up to wait out the blizzard, but he refused and went slipping and sliding on his way, out into the night and the Antarctic-like weather conditions.

I gave my Dad a call, apprising him of the events at Mathison's house and assuring him I sustained only a few scrapes and bruises when the airbag deployed. He apprised me of the fact he did not appreciate being hung up on, was not at all pleased I'd gone against people possibly from the South American drug cartel without backup of any sort, and then promptly put my Mom on the line. After she ranted for a minute or two, I finally got a word in on my behalf.

"Mom, I know it's been a while, but I'm not rusty. Okay? I'm fine. Everything worked out...Yes, I do realize I should have just shot them and left...Yes, it would have been simpler...No, I really don't know if I'm returning to the business. I was just trying to help someone...Yes, he told me he called his WITSEC contact...I'm sure the Mathisons appreciate it...Yeah, Mom, I do too...

It went on and on like this until Dad took the line and asked me if I had enough food in my apartment to last until the nice folks at the road department could dig us all out again. I told him I was stocked up, told him I love him, and then ended the call. I was exhausted, frozen bone deep and my face hurt, so I moseyed into the bathroom and thawed out in the shower. I stayed awake long enough to catch the early morning news while I made good use of a bag of frozen peas to keep the swelling down on my face where the airbag hit.

I'd completely forgotten about work until the phone woke me up. It was Arnie calling to tell me there was no way in hell the store was opening today and to just stay home, keep warm and ice down my face.

"The tow truck owner is a friend of mine. So is the guy who runs the body shop they use. I'll give him a call and have him take a look at your car."

"You don't have to do that, Arnie. I can make a few calls later today."

"Nope," he replied, "I insist. Just consider it a perk for working for me."

I sighed. "A perk, huh? And just how much will this perk cost me?"

Arnie chuckled. "It's a perk, Miss MacCann, which means it's free. That's why they call it a perk."

I thanked him and hung up, falling back to sleep until mid-afternoon. When I awoke, I stumbled past the window on my way to the bathroom. To say it was a white blanket covering the ground outside just didn't seem enough. It was more like a thick, puffy duvet, one of those really expensive ones made with the down of some unfortunately slow and now naked bird. And what's more, it was still snowing pretty hard. I clicked the television on to see what our friendly neighborhood weather person was saying about our winter wonderland. The first channel I switched to was showing a very excited meteorologist dancing around in front of a map of the tri-state area, flourishing his hands to indicate the movement of the front. He looked like a young kid in a candy shop with a pocket full of money. When he announced the governor's proclamation of a state of emergency, I thought it might throw the little obnoxious man into a seizure. Nobody should be this happy about snow unless you are of the polar bear or penguin persuasion. I checked a couple more stations just to make sure the guy wasn't just tweaking from something like meth, but low and behold, every forecaster on every channel showing the weather sported the same gleam in their eye and the same excited frenzy.

We were going to top out at around twenty inches of snow before all was said and done. And why couldn't they just say that and be done? Why? Because we haven't had a snow like this one in nine years. So everybody get up on the floor and do the penguin dance! Yada. Yada. Yada.

I tossed the remote onto the coffee table and swiped up my phone to give Kelly a call and see how she was doing. I got her voicemail, left a message for her to give me a call back, and went into the kitchen to ease the rumblings in my stomach. More than anything I needed comfort food. Sure, I liked a snow day as well as the next person, but I really wasn't interested in becoming part of an Ice Age. I settled on toast and an omelet with cheese. When I'd finished, I did another cleaning tour around my apartment, called Kelly again and left another voicemail, and then settled on the couch for some quality time with the television.

After about an hour or so, I decided popcorn was in order. On my way to the kitchen, I spotted something on the floor in front of my door, another envelope. I stepped over it and peered out the peep hole in my door. There was no one there. I threw the locks and cracked the door open, careful to leave the chain lock in place. The flimsy metal was a small comfort, but a comfort nonetheless. If someone was really intent on getting in, a chain wouldn't hold them out, but it would delay them a bit until they could either cut it or force the door. However, there was a downside to leaving it in place. It gave you only a narrow field of sight to what lay beyond.

I shut the door and grabbed the first thing my hand could reach for as a sliver of protection should my decision to open the door turn into a huge mistake. The black umbrella was one of those really long jobs like the Penguin used in the Batman movies. Although it wasn't equipped with a knife or a gun built in the end like the famed villain carried, it was formidable weapon in the right hands. I released the chain and slowly opened the door ready for a fight should anyone still be waiting around outside in the hall. No one was there, just an empty hallway with closed doors on either side. I shut the door, set my Penguin umbrella aside, secured the locks back into place and went to the window with the street view. From what I could tell, nobody was stirring outside. There weren't even footprints in the snow. I slid on a pair of boots, grabbed my coat, slid it on, and found the 9mm still in my pocket.

I locked my door on the way out and pocketed the key with the hope there'd be less chance of someone getting in while I was taking a look around, or at least delaying their entrance enough so I could catch them in the act should they be bold enough to give it a try.

I didn't meet up with a single soul until I got to the ground floor by way of the stairwell. When I shoved the door open, I nearly took out Mister Swanson, a seventy-year-old man who plugs along on a cane while carrying his own tank of oxygen. He's probably one of the crankiest old men I know and he's proud of it. I apologized in the process of catching his teetering and decrepit body before he could hit the floor.

"Watch where the hell you're going!" he growled, taking a swipe at me with his cane.

"I'm so sorry," I repeated, steadying him so I could let go and get out of the way.

"Price MacCann, is that you?"

"Yes sir," I mumbled.

"Your father will hear about this, knocking over an old man like me. You could have caused me to break a hip!"

"It's nice seeing you too, Mr. Swanson."

I took a chance he wouldn't fall down and let go. When he didn't tip over, I took off down through the lobby and out the back entrance. One of the building's maintenance guys was attempting to shovel a pathway on what was supposed to be the sidewalk. He turned around when I burst through and grinned from ear to ear.

"Hey Bud, have you seen anybody strange coming through the doors?"

He chuckled and tossed a shovel full of snow off to the side of the path. "Nah, just you. Love the outfit, babe. Classy."

I glanced down at my pajama pants tucked sloppily in my snow boots. I felt my cheeks burn.

"You haven't seen anybody new around here?"

"Nobody's moving, MacCann. It's a state of emergency. Why?"

I glanced to my left and then to my right. The flakes were still coming down pretty hard, but even if they were covering footprints, I should still be able to make out some sort of indentions. The snow in the back of the building appeared completely undisturbed, just a smooth, thick blanket of white.

"You okay?" Bud asked. "You look a little shook up."

I opted against telling him the whole truth simply because I didn't know Bud well enough to go into detail.

"Somebody's leaving love notes under my door. I just got a brand spanking new one just a minute ago."

"Well then your secret admirer lives in the building because I haven't seen anybody outside all day."

"That's comforting," I mumbled. "Thanks."

Back inside, I tromped up the stairs, and exited onto my floor. I unlocked my door and went back in, shedding my coat before I swiped up the envelope. Part of me wanted to tear it in little bitty pieces and toss it in the trash and part of me was curious to know if I'd picked the wrong Mathison. I took a deep breath, tore the seal, and eased it open as if I were working on a bomb instead of a paper envelope. Centered in type were two words. THANK YOU.

SIXTEEN

THE SNOW DIDN'T EASE up until late into the night and it took the city two days to dig out the main roads. Those unfortunates living on side roads were either still snowed in or were finding their own means to dig themselves out. Kelly finally returned my call. Her husband had gone out of town on business the day before the blizzard and was currently stranded in Chicago because all flights out had been canceled.

"It figures," she said hoarsely, "I finally get a break from Corey and Trent breaks with the flu."

"You sound awful," I said, easing the phone away from my ear as she went into another coughing fit. I waited until the hacking subsided and then asked her if she need anything. I didn't know what I could have done in weather like this, but my heart was in the offer.

Kelly declined. "Don't even think about trying to come over. If the blizzard doesn't kill you this flu shit will."

I bid her a speedy recovery and let her know I'd call to check on her later.

Arnie phoned me on the next day to tell me under no circumstances was I to attempt to come in for work until he got an okay from him. I found it odd he'd keep the antique shop closed for so long during the holiday season, but I kept it to myself (his shop, his business). By Friday night, I was suffering from a severe case of cabin fever. My apartment was as squeaky clean as it was ever going to get and I was so sick of watching Christmas shows on television I was ready for Frosty the Snowman to get blasted by a flamethrower, so I opted to pick up a book and start reading. I was barely two chapters into Stephen King's novel Duma Key when someone started knocking on my door. Setting the book on the table, I went over and peered through the peephole. All I could see was a multi-colored knitted toboggan with a pom-pom ball on top of it, stretched over a head with grayish-white hair curling out the undersides. The chubby wearer was bent over a huge, burnt-orange carpet bag, rifling through its contents. I let out a sigh, unlocked the door and opened it.

Aunt Clara looked up from her bag and gave me a huge smile. "Hello dear. I was hoping you were home."

Aunt Clara is short, plump, and extremely well-endowed (a tad bit of the family DNA that was not included in my own genetic chain). Her grandmotherly appearance, with her chubby cheeks and big round eyeglasses, gives most unwary people the impression of esteemed innocence. Slap on a pair of Bermuda shorts and flip-flops with an over-sized Hawaiian shirt and floppy sun hat and she could even be the poster child for hip senior citizens on a cruise line ship. Left bundled up like she was now in colorfully knitted winter apparel and she looked more like Frosty's chubby bride.

I barely got out a hello before she engulfed me in one of her bear hugs which she and my Aunt Lula are famous for; that and long-winded tales of course. After a few seconds, I started frantically tapping her on the shoulder.

"Air!" I gasped.

"What was that, dear?" Clara asked.

"I can't breathe."

"Oh, I'm so sorry," she replied, releasing her boa constrictor grip on me. She held me out at arm's length, looking me over. "Well, just look how much you've grown. I almost can't believe my eyes."

"It's just been a year," I said, still trying to pull some air into my lungs. "You saw me last Thanksgiving."

Clara smiled and patted me vigorously on the arm. "And so I did. And so I did. Wasn't that a wonderful dinner with the family? I had such a nice time."

"I'm sure you did." And before I could stop myself, I added, "You got corked on Irish coffee and did a striptease on the buffet table."

"Now, now, dear, what happens at the buffet table stays at the buffet table."

I stifled a laugh, remembering what actually happened on the buffet table crashed it to the floor of my grandmother's house and sent food and dishes flying all over the dining room.

Aunt Clara bent over to pick up the carpet bag but I beat her to it, swiping it up and closing it with one swift fluid motion as I stood aside and motioned her in my apartment. The thing weighed a ton. I set the bag down by the couch and it thumped heavily to the floor.

"Clara, what the heck do you have in there?" I asked, turning back to her.

"Oh, you know, just the necessities."

"Necessities huh?"

I watched her as she shed the thick coat and all of her knitted accessories, laying them neatly on the back of my couch. My eyes shifted back to the bag. When I looked to her again, there was a twinkle in her eyes, setting my stomach on edge.

"Um, how long are you planning on staying?"

"How long would you like me to stay, dear?"

My stomach fluttered. "The night?"

Clara smiled broadly showing a lot of perfect teeth. "Oh yes and probably then some, dear."

I felt a little sick.

She took my hand and started patting it vigorously. "Now don't you worry yourself. It'll be just like the good old times."

"Good old times, huh? Fess up, Aunt Clara, who's the hit?"

She patted my hand again. "No one you know, sweetheart."

I took a deep breath, trying to form polite, coherent thoughts which would hopefully find their way to and out of my mouth. It took me a moment. All the while Clara kept patting on my hand.

"What's really in the bag, Clara? And don't tell me necessities."

"Some ingredients and a few tools I need, nothing really."

I squatted down and opened the carpet bag, peering at its contents and frowning. A couple of metal pans, a large plastic funnel, three quart-sized Mason canning jars, a folded off-white and thick material which looked a lot like cheese cloth, and one of those big glass pickle jars you see in the cookout section of the grocery store during the summer months. And all of this was just at first glance, I dreaded what I'd see lower in the bag.

"What's in the jar?" I asked, shuddering at the sight of the brown gelatinous muck.

Clara stepped beside me and bent over, examining the bag's contents as if this was the first time she'd look at them. "Which jar?"

I sighed, looking up at her. "The full one, what is it?"

"Oh, well that's Busaa, dear. I made it myself. It's from a Changaa recipe my friend Machupa in Kenya gave me last summer. It should be ready to start working up in the morning."

Changaa, for anyone who doesn't know, is a disgusting alcoholic drink invented in Kenya. It's made from a barrage of ingredients, mostly grains like corn or millet (or sometimes readily available fruits like bananas which are also added in the mix). Sounds delicious, eh? Well, don't hold out your glass just yet. If it's the real authentic deal, then it's mixed with a good portion of feces infested water and a few savory bits of things thrown in for added flavor like used underwear. Just think moonshine on crack because the actual meaning of Changaa is "kill me quick". I was unfortunate enough to have a sip a few years back during a visit to Africa. I spent the next few hours trying to get the taste out of my mouth and I've still to erase it from my memory.

My eyes fell back on the jar of muck. Distillers of Changaa usually use the leftover crap from Busaa as a starter for the "kill me quick" drink; add more sugar and water, put it on to boil and catch the condensation. Whoever thought nastiness could be cooked up so easily? I closed my eyes and took a few deep breaths to calm my upset stomach. There was no way in hell I was going to allow Aunt Clara to put the polishing touches on the brew in my apartment. Aside from the fact I'd probably be the toilet bowl's best friend through the entire process, the smell would permeate my apartment, entire building, and maybe even the whole block. Somehow, I didn't believe my neighbors would appreciate the aroma.

My frown deepened when I moved the cheese cloth aside and spotted a small plastic bottle of Formalin. There was no doubt in my mind I'd seen all I needed to see. I put the cloth back, closed the bag, and stood up to face my mother's sister.

"You are welcome to stay the night, Aunt Clara," I said, propping my hands on my hips like I'd seen my mom do many times when she wanted all of her children to know she meant business, then I gave her the sternest look I could manage, "but you will not be making Changaa in my apartment."

She gave me a cherub smile. "Of course not, dear. I wouldn't dream of making you feel uncomfortable in your own home."

"Good," I replied, carefully lifting the carpet bag and easing it into my living room closet with the hope nothing would get broken and start seeping out. "I'll sleep on the couch and you can have my bed."

"You don't have to do that."

I held up my hand. "No, I insist, you're a guest after all."

I didn't add in the fact that on the couch I could keep a wary eye on the closet door in case she got a wild hair to try something while I was sleeping.

SEVENTEEN

I WAS AROUSED from my slumber by the delicious aroma of bacon frying mixed with the wafting scent of fresh brewed coffee, comforting smells to ease awake a sleepy head. Someone was cooking breakfast. I felt a smile slide across my mouth just before realization kicked in. My eyes popped open and I was off the couch, fighting to free myself from the blanket tangled around me. I nearly toppled over the coffee table in my panic. Aunt Clara had not only slipped by me, but she'd been on her own in the kitchen long enough to heat up smells. I extricated my legs from the blanket in mid-step and caught one of my pinkie toes against the leg of the coffee table. My blurred eyes crossed in agony as the pain shot from my toe, to my foot, to my leg, straight up my spinal cord, and into the son-of-a-bitch sensors in my brain. What resulted was a slew of profanity which spewed from my mouth.

I cracked open my pain-pinched eyes to see Aunt Clara standing at the doorway between the kitchen and the living room (technically, there is no real doorway, it's just were the linoleum ends and the carpet begins). She was in a pair of red, fuzzy reindeer pajamas with her hair rolled tight in curlers and covered by a festive red and green mesh hair net. In all honesty, she looked like a plump elf with a turning fork in her hand. There was a shocked look on her face as if I ran over a puppy with my car. Well, more like I ran over it, backed up, and ran over it again.

"Oh dear! Do you need an ice pack?"

I ignored her for a moment and whimpered, feeling around on my foot for any obvious breaks. When I was satisfied there were no broken bones, I shook my head no for the ice pack and hobbled to the kitchen wincing with every step. Clara shrugged and went back to the stove as I scanned for any evidence of Changaa brewing. The only thing on my stovetop was the skillet filled with frying bacon. I let out a sigh of relief and then nearly choked when I saw what was on my counter.

"Clara, what's on my cutting board?"

"It's just white baneberries, dear. Not a thing you need to trouble yourself over."

I groaned. "You're dicing up poisonous berries on my cutting board with one of my knives?"

Clara smiled sheepishly over her shoulder at me. "I couldn't fit my own into the bag. I hope you don't mind."

"Why would I possibly mind?" I asked, hobbling to the coffee pot.

"Don't worry. I'll clean them well before putting 'em back."

"No need," I replied, bypassing my favorite mug on the counter near the cutting board and pulling another from the cabinet. I wasn't taking any changes on being poisoned accidentally by baneberry splatter. "You can keep them both and the cup too."

Clara gave another shrug and went back to tending the frying pan. I poured my coffee and eased over to the kitchen table to sit down and try to regroup. My toe still throbbed but it was easing down, giving way to a new pounding in my head. I watched Clara bustle around flipping bacon out of the pan, cracking eggs and frying them up. She pulled a cookie sheet filled with freshly baked biscuits out of the oven, all while the baneberries just sat on the cutting board on my countertop awaiting their turn for my aunt's attention. I tried to focus on something else, anything else. What I got was the jumble of nearly incoherent thoughts I usually expect after waking. So I just sipped the coffee and tried not to think at all.

"You know," Clara said as she set a heaping plate in front of me, "I happened to notice you haven't even started decorating for Christmas. There's only a few weeks left. You're running out of time, dear."

"Well, Santa Jonas was in here the other day. Does that count?"

Clara sat down across from me with her own heaping plate. Her eyes brightened. "Jonas? How is he? I haven't seen him in weeks."

"A little preoccupied this time of year," I replied. "You know Jonas, Santa stuff."

"He makes the best Saint Nick," Clara said. She chomped on a piece of bacon, chewed a couple of times, and then asked, "I wonder if he needs a Mrs. Claus for the children. Do you think he'll be visiting the children's home this year?"

I picked at my eggs with my fork. "I don't know. He didn't say anything about it to me."

Clara beamed. "I'll just have to give him a ring and find out then."

"I guess."

I ate while she chatted away between bites informing me of the health and activities of every family member I hadn't been in contact with for a year, which was everyone but Mom and Dad. I finished everything on my plate, got another cup of coffee, and sat back down, allowing her to complete her ramble on my grandmother who was intent on playing Mary in their church Christmas pageant.

"She's over eighty for goodness sake. Now I ask you, who's going to believe she's a virgin, much less one able to bear a child?"

"It's just a play, Aunt Clara. Besides, wasn't Abraham's wife older when she had a kid?"

Clara laughed. "True, but the man playing Joseph in the pageant is over fifty years younger than your grandmother. The dress rehearsal looked like something out of one of those cougar reality shows."

This time I laughed. It was just like my grandmother to cause a rift in the norm and nothing made her more content than to incite controversy. I started to ask Clara what the congregation or the preacher thought about the situation, but my phone started ringing. I got up and answered it. It was Arnie.

"I'm opening up the store today. Are you able to get there by nine or do you need me to come get you?"

I glanced over at Clara. She was stacking dishes in the sink to be washed. She started the water and added dish detergent then went back to tending the bane berries on my counter while the sink filled. I couldn't help but wonder what she could do in my apartment while I was at work. Every imagined scenario ended with either the police or the fire department at my door. Just thinking of leaving my aunt unsupervised was unsettling enough to give me an upset stomach. Arnie's voice interrupted my inner turmoil.

"Miss MacCann?"

"Uhm, Arnie, what would you say to a little extra help today?"

"I'd say they better be able to work a snow shovel."

SINCE ARNIE WAS OBLIGING ENOUGH to allow Aunt Clara to come to work with me, I opted to bundle up and walk the distance to work. I wasn't sure how my aunt would take the news of having to trudge through snow, but I shouldn't have worried. She was thrilled. It's the little things in life, I guess. I quickly washed the dishes, bagged up the berries, cutting board and knife, stuffing the bag deep into the bottom of my trash can while she went off to get dressed. Then I scoured my countertop with the hopes I'd cleaned every nick and cranny where the berries touched.

Clara finally came out of the bathroom sporting a pair of thick black wool slacks and a bright red knitted sweater with a huge reindeer head fixed to the front of it. Attached to the tip of all eight of the reindeer's furry antlers were gold plated jingle bells. I cringed as all eight of them jingled with every movement my aunt made. Clara caught me staring at her sweater and smiled.

"I made it myself. Would you like me to knit you one?"

"Um, no. I'm sure it wouldn't look as good on me."

"Oh, I think you would look lovely. Just let me grab the tape measure out of my bag."

I backed my way down the hall to my room just as she opened the closet door where I'd set her bag. When she bent over to start the search, I ducked into my bedroom and shut the door with the hopes she'd forgotten to pack the tape measure. Unfortunately, when I emerged fully dressed in jeans and a less conspicuous sweater, she was waiting with the tape measure in hand.

"Aunt Clara, can we do this later? I need to get to work and we're going to have to hoof it there."

Clara nodded, looking a little disappointed, and tucked the tape measure back into her bag. It took her a few minutes to bundle up in her coat and all of her knitted wear, but we finally made it out of my building and into the freezing air. Arnie's store wasn't far from my apartment, but walking on sidewalks still covered with snow made it a slower trek even though the city workers had been at it with their shovels and snow blowers. Clara babbled along beside me as we went.

"What took you so long?" Arnie grumbled.

I sighed. "Seriously? Have you tried to walk outside?"

"No, Miss MacCann, I got here this morning by apparition."

I rolled my eyes. "Funny."

"I'm afraid not. I open in an hour."

His expression softened when he spotted Clara waddling in behind me. "Clara! I didn't know you were the one coming in with Miss MacCann. What a pleasure to see you again."

I nearly hurled when he took her hand into his, removed her knitted mitten and kissed it as if he were greeting the freaking queen of England. From there, the day just went downhill.

EIGHTEEN

"MISS MACCANN," Arnie's voice carried down to the basement where I was retrieving a lamp for a customer, "is there any chance I could get you to do a lunch run?"

I grimaced as I pulled one of the gaudiest lamps I'd ever laid eyes on off the metal shelf where it had been rightfully stored in the darkness away from anyone with taste long enough to pick up a covering of dust so thick it muted the color of the paint. I set it down in the one empty space on a folding buffet table Arnie used for prepping inventory ready to move up to the store. Prepping meant dusting, scrubbing, and removing cobwebs or anything else which had adhered to the antique while it sat and waited for its turn upstairs. I pulled out my dust cloth and set to work.

"Miss MacCann," Arnie repeated, this time from the second step of the basement. "Can you make a lunch run for me?"

"Yeah," I replied, "but I need to clean this tasteful antique and get it to the customer upstairs."

I heard Arnie thumping his way down the steps. He came towards me, stopping a good three feet away. I ran the cloth over the tree trunk base of the lamp and around the orange-brown colored owls perched on the stubby branches of the blasted thing.

"That is one hideous lamp," Arnie said.

I whipped my head around to see him with his arms crossed over his chest and a look of distaste on his face.

"You think it's hideous too?"

"Just because I sell it here, Miss MacCann, does not necessarily mean I like it. That particular piece was part of an old friend's estate sale. Lucky for me, no one bought it."

"You're serious?" I asked.

"Not a bit," he replied, "until today. That lovely piece of tacky décor just made this store a hundred dollars."

"A hundred dollars," I said, eyeing the clean but still incredibly horrid lamp, "for this?"

Arnie grinned and shrugged. "Beauty is in the eye of the beholder. I am sure it will make a perfect Christmas gift."

"Yeah, for someone she hates."

Arnie laughed. "How about I finish with this customer and you do the lunch run. I'm starving and so is your Aunt Clara. And I'm sure you're probably hungry too."

He handed me a couple of twenty dollar bills and a slip of paper with both of their orders scribbled on it, deli food.

"Lunch is on me today," he added. "Get whatever you want with the rest and keep the change."

"Thanks," I replied, stuffing the money and list into my front pants pocket as he took the dusting rag from me.

I went upstairs, retrieved my coat from the wall rack in the back room Arnie reserved for an employee lounge (which until I started working here had just been for him), and made my way through the store. Aunt Clara was at the register checking out a line of customers where my boss had set her up all morning. Funny how he had no qualms about putting her in charge of his money, I guess you just have to know someone in this business. I spotted the customer I had been helping gazing at an antique desk near the door and went up to her.

"I have to run an errand," I told her, "but Arnie will be right up with your lamp."

She smiled, showing a lot of teeth, and gave a nod which made her thick jowls jiggle as she made the movement. "Thank you. My uncle is going to love the lamp."

I nodded, went to the door thinking her uncle was more than likely visually impaired, and went out into the cold. When I got to the deli down the street, it was just as packed as the antique store and the line was all the way out the door. The deli is a small locally owned business which has been going strong in the neighborhood since I was a kid. It started out as a little butcher shop tucked between a row of fly-by-night businesses. Now it is the lunchmeat palace of the ville. Named after the butcher who decided to serve sandwiches instead of raw meat, the shop became Smith's (tastefully stitched into the blue and white striped awning over the front entrance) and has been iconic here ever since. The place stays packed, but the food is worth the wait. I took my place at the end of the line behind a short hefty guy in black coveralls and waited for my chance to just get inside the building and warm up.

"Well now," a voice with a heavy Irish accent said behind me, "if isn't Miss MacCann. Long time no see."

I recognized the voice immediately and glanced over my shoulder to see the tall figure behind me. He'd shed the coverall bit and was now in jeans, tan work boots, and a heavy black parka, but the toboggan was still on his head and he still sported the beard and moustache. His wraparound sunglasses hid his eyes, but I'd seen them before and remembered the chocolate color as if it were yesterday. No doubt about it this guy was hot, even with the facial hair, but as they say beauty only goes skin deep. Annoying goes down to the bone.

"Mister Donnelly," I replied curtly as I turned back around, refusing to offer anything more.

"What brings you out on such a freaking cold day?"

I grimaced, wishing I could just ignore the jerk but knowing full well it would be too difficult to pull off with the line in front and behind me without looking like a complete and utter bitch.

"Hunger."

"What a coincidence, me too," he replied.

The sensors to my brain began sounding the alarm as he leaned in close and whispered, "But I guess I'll have to just settle for the hoagie."

I grit my teeth and whirled around, ready to tell him off, and then get the hell out line (Aunt Clara and Arnie would just have to deal with a Big Mac for lunch). Behind Donnelly stood a woman and two young children so I swallowed my profane retort from whence it bubbled and brewed. I was here to get lunch, not teach young children a lesson in cursing. Instead, I glared reproachfully at him, clenched my gloved fists down at my sides to keep from punching the smirk right off his face and turned back around. Thankfully the line moved forward enough for me to open the door, step inside, and close it to leave Donnelly out in the cold.

The unfortunate part of a swinging door is just like it shuts it has the capability of opening again. What's even more unfortunate was the fact the line moved a little faster since two of the customers up ahead at the counter only wanted cups of coffee. When I advanced a couple of steps forward, Donnelly opened the swinging door and came in. I felt him move up close behind me, invading my space and then pushing his body up close to mine. I couldn't move any further up because of the short, hefty guy in front of me.

"Could you scoot back a little?" I asked in a whisper.

I felt his mouth up against my ear, his breath hot against my neck.

"I can't let the kiddies freeze outside, now can I?"

I clenched my teeth and shifted my eyes to the security cameras on either side of the long counter. They were pointed directly at me, so they'd catch anything I physically did to this jerk. I felt him move into me as if I were playing a part in some grind video. I pulled my purse up to block the camera's view of my waist and rammed my obscured elbow right into his stomach. I felt his body give in to the blow just as he let out quiet grunt. The line moved up and so did I.

He stepped up behind me, his breath on my neck again.

"Nice one, slugger," he whispered, "but not very neighborly."

I was going to have to kill this guy. I started to tell him of Arnie's insistence to do the deed when I saw him again but thought better of it. The kids behind us were pretty close and the old saying about little pictures having big ears kept echoing in my head. Their mom might not catch a hint of what was going on, but you can bet your bottom dollar her children would. Kids have a knack for stuff like that. They may not seem to listen or pay attention to a thing their parents say, but get one adult who talks or acts inappropriately and I guarantee they'll hear it, memorize it, and will most definitely attempt to repeat it. The line moved up until the short hefty fellow in the black coveralls was at the counter. If I could just hold on for a bit longer, I could order, pay, and get the hell out of here before I did something I'd regret later.

"Any chance you could give me a lift?" he asked. "You know, for old time's sake."

"I walked here," I whispered. "And I'm not falling for that again."

"What if good ol'Arn said you had to?"

I rolled my eyes and clamped my lips shut. If I just ignored him, he'd go away, right? I felt him brush his lips against my neck, sending shock waves throughout my entire body and making my heart speed up to what felt like a gentle hum. His hand rested against the small of my back, the heat from it alone was enough to send me over the edge. I reached behind my back, touched his hand with my own with just the gentlest caress, grabbed one of his fingers and twisted the shit out of it. He swallowed a yelp and pulled back. The line moved forward, as did I, and the chubby coverall man left with his bagged food in hand.

"What'll it be?" the young guy manning the counter I asked.

I pulled out Arnie's list and handed it to him, adding my own order to the mix. He filled it. I gave him money. He gave me my change and my own bag o' food. When I turned to go, Donnelly was gone.

NINETEEN

"IT WAS VERY KIND of Arnie to give us a lift home," Aunt Clara said as we made it up the last flight of steps to my apartment. "You don't find chivalry like that much anymore."

I pushed open the door to my floor and held it for my aunt to waddle on through. "Yeah, Arnie's a nice guy."

"You know, I think he's always held a lit candle for me. Why, way back in the day when I was just about your age, he would come to our house and spend hours just talking about nothing in particular. But according to your grandmother, he'd never come unless I was there."

I pulled my keys out of my coat pocket and slid the door key in the lock. It was nearly eight o'clock and I felt beat to a pulp. "How come you guys didn't get together? You seemed pretty chummy in the store today?"

Aunt Clara shrugged. "Oh, you know how it is. Sometimes things just don't fall in place. Besides, at that time in my life I was very much in love with another young and flashy stud."

I turned the knob and pushed the door open, allowing Clara to go in first. She gave me a nod of thanks and stepped inside. Who says you have to be male to be chivalrous? I stepped in behind her and shut door. Something white on the bottom of Clara's boot caught my eye.

"Aunt Clara, you've got something caught on your boot."

Clara stopped and lifted up her left foot which had nothing on the bottom.

"No. The other one"

She put her left foot down and picked up the right one, plucking a white envelope off the sole of her boot. "Why it's a letter, dear. Someone must have slipped it under your door."

She handed me the envelope and began shedding her winter wear. I heaved a sigh, tore the corner of the lip and then ran my finger under the length of the envelope, tearing it open.

"So who was the stud which kept you out of Arnie's loving arms?" I asked, pulling out the slip of white paper inside.

Clara plopped down on my couch, wrestling off one of her boots. "Elvis Presley."

I glanced over at my aunt. "You gave up a chance with Arnie for a crush on Elvis?"

She yanked hard on the boot, lost her grip as it slid off her foot, and watched as it went airborne banging the top of my coffee table and then landing with a thud on the floor.

"Whoopsie! Sorry about that," she said as she moved to the other boot. "Well, you can't blame a girl for trying. Back then, Elvis was all the rage."

I turned the slip of paper over to see two words typed dead center, Sarah Nichols. Another boot went flying, following the same trek as its predecessor from my coffee table to the floor.

"Whoopsie again!" Clara exclaimed. "So what did you get, a nice Christmas card from one of the neighbors?"

I pulled my eyes away from the paper, locking them on my aunt. "No, it's nothing like that."

"You look a little pale, dear. Don't tell me someone was callus enough to send a bill under your door. That's just rude."

"Don't worry, it's not a bill. My creditors are kind enough to mail those." I slipped the paper back in the envelope and tossed it on the coffee table, trying to remember if I knew the name. It kind of sounded familiar but since it wasn't a complicated name, I chocked it up to the probability I could have heard it anywhere. I pulled off my coat, gloves, and hat, laying them over the back of the couch on top of Clara's stuff.

"Might I have a look?"

At first I thought it might not be such a great idea. Aunt Clara wasn't known for her discretion when it came to family topics. But then I thought what the hell? If Aunt Clara knew Sarah Nichols, she could definitely save me a lot of work.

"You can peek on one condition, Aunt Clara."

Her eyes sparkled as if I'd just invited her to some sort of secret club. "And what's that?"

"You absolutely cannot breathe a word of it to anyone, especially not Mom or Dad," I paused, "or Arnie or Jonas."

Clara clapped her hands with glee, bouncing her butt on my couch as if she were a chubby four-year-old with an ice cream cone in her sights. "It must be good one!"

"Promise?"

"Oh yes," she said, making a motion to lock her lips and throw away the key. "There will not be a word to your parents, dear."

I held up my hand as Clara swiped the envelope off the table. "Or Jonas or Arnie..."

"Of course, dear," she replied, pulling the paper out. "They won't hear about it from me."

I plopped down on the other side of my couch and propped my socked feet up on the coffee table, waiting for her to respond which I knew she would.

"Why, there's nothing in here but a name," she muttered. "Sarah Nichols, now where have I heard that name before?"

"Sound familiar to you too?"

Clara tilted her head in thought for a moment and smiled.

"Oh, I remember. Sarah Nichols used to be in my bridge club about four, maybe five years ago."

"Awesome," I replied. "Do you know where she lives?"

She gave a nod. "Across town on Willow Street, she's lived in that house all of her life. What's this about?"

"Well, somebody left a note just like this one several days ago with another name on it, so I checked it out. Turns out, the guy was under witness protection and his identity had been compromised. I was able to help him survive a reunion with a South American drug cartel and live to hide another day."

"Oh Price! That's wonderful!"

I wrinkled my brow. "Come again?"

"You helped someone in need. It's such a beautiful thing. I shouldn't be too surprised though, I mean it's in your blood, passed down from generation to generation since way before our ancestors came to America."

"Aunt Clara, I'm not back in the family business. I was just helping someone."

She leaned forward and patted me on the leg. "Oh Price, you don't have to be an assassin to contribute to your family's goals. The only thing they strive for is to help those who cannot help themselves and that can come in all sorts of ways."

"Tell that to Dad. He's trying to get me to help him with the Van Oliver thing."

Clara sat back and sighed. "True, Van Oliver could use the effects of your expertise, but if you don't want to help with it just tell him no. Your dad will understand."

"I know."

"Dearie, the only person making you feel like a failure is you. Losing Michael in the way you did would make anyone rethink their occupation. To take on a job like Van Oliver and not have your heart in it would be a fatal mistake."

"Thanks."

"You're welcome. Now tell me about the delightful person leaving these little notes for you."

"I'd love to, but I have absolutely no idea who it is. I thought it might be Dad or someone else in my family trying to lure me back in, but now I'm starting to doubt it."

"Why's that?"

I thought for a moment. Why didn't I believe it was a family member? "Well, they've always been straight with me before. And besides, the last note I received for the witness protection guy was during the snow storm, so now I'm leaning more towards someone in my building."

"You could set up a camera and find out," Clara suggested.

"I could, but something tells me they'd pick up on it quick and be wise enough to adjust." I shrugged and changed the subject. "So tell me what you know about Sarah."

TWENTY

I MET Sarah Nichols at one o'clock in the afternoon the next day since Arnie kept the shop closed on Sundays. It's not exactly a norm for business owners anymore, but he kept the traditional day of rest regardless of the fact the snow storm shut the store down several days during the week. Clara and I hopped a bus at the stop near my building and rode the cross town distance to the lifelong home of Sarah Nichols. I waited behind Clara when we arrived at the huge colonial house while she pressed the rather elaborate looking doorbell. It rang out a classy rendition of Carol of the Bells. Whoever Sarah Nichols happened to be, one thing was for sure, she was over the top where Christmas was concerned.

"Oh how festive!" Aunt Clara exclaimed.

I shivered as a swift blast of wind rattled by, making my teeth start to chatter. I'd noticed the overcast when I stepped out of my building, but hadn't bothered to look upward since. Dark snow clouds crowded against a gray background producing an ominous sight.

"You didn't by any chance manage to catch the weather report, did you?" I asked her, feeling foolish for having slept until almost noon.

"Well of course I did, dear. I always do. You never know what the weather will do in this neck of the woods."

"And?"

"Well, the nice weatherman on channel five is predicting another snow storm and according to his report, it should start anytime."

"And you didn't think this was information I might need before we went traipsing around across town."

"Neither snow nor rain nor heat nor gloom of night stays these couriers from the swift completion of their appointed rounds."

I frowned. "That's the mail man's creed, Clara."

She shrugged. "Why yes, I guess it is, although I do believe it's quite fitting for us, don't you think? No amount of wind or snow shall stop us from helping someone in need."

I rolled my eyes. "Hit the bell again, please."

After a few moments and several shivers later, I heard the sound of footsteps approaching the door. The deadbolt latch clicked and the door was eased open to reveal a very petite elderly woman with blue tinged hair and horn rimmed glasses.

"Why Clara!" she exclaimed. "I haven't seen you in ages!"

My aunt beamed. "It has been a long time! Do you still play bridge?"

Another blast of wind hit, this one strong enough to dislodge one of the wreaths fixed on one of Sarah's front windows. It flew off the porch and went rolling into the yard. I turned to go retrieve it when one end of the garland she had draped around the rungs on the porch pulled loose and started flapping around furiously. Both women acted as if they didn't notice and were still chatting away.

"I'm sorry to interrupt," I said, "but you just lost your wreath and your garland is taking a good beating."

Sarah looked at me as if I'd just whacked Santa Claus in the nuts with the candy cane of Christmas cheer.

Clara gave me a look of warning I hadn't seen since I was a kid. "It's not polite to interrupt, dear."

I clenched my chattering teeth. Fine then, the little old lady could just toddle on out in the snow and get the wreath herself.

"Please excuse my niece. I'm afraid the cold is getting to her. May we come in?"

"Oh certainly," Sarah replied. "Come on in and warm yourselves up. I'll have James make us some tea."

"That sounds lovely," Clare said.

The elderly lady stepped aside to let us in, closing the door behind us. "Feel free to hang your coats on the rack. I'll just be a minute."

I glanced around the spacious foyer which seemed to be a suffering casualty of Christmas spirit. What wasn't covered or draped in evergreen or snow covered evergreen was drowning in a sea of chubby red Santa Clauses and his magic reindeer. I shed my heavy coat and hung it on one of Rudolph's antlers which was in fact the coat rack she'd pointed to a few feet from the door.

"This is just beautiful," my aunt whispered. "Just look at all these jolly old elves."

I sighed. "Yeah, there seems to be a lot of them."

"We should decorate your apartment like this when we get back," she whispered.

"No."

"Oh, come on. It looks like a winter wonderland in here."

"No," I said, careful to keep my voice low, "it looks like Saint Nick took a huge and festive dump in here."

Clara giggled. "Okay, maybe it is a bit much, but I do think you could use a few Santas around your place to deck the halls."

"One Santa maybe, but not this," I said as I tilted my head to the sideboard crowded with Father Christmas figurines. "This is an army."

Clara shushed me as Sarah stepped back into the foyer to usher us to the living room filled with even more Christmas décor. Clara and I took a seat on an antique sofa which looked as if it had popped straight out of a Charles Dickens novel while Sarah settled herself on the edge of a large winged back chair.

"I'm so sorry, Sarah, I seem to have forgotten my manners. This is my niece, Price."

Sarah gave me a curt nod, undoubtedly still offended I'd interrupted their conversation at the door. I nodded back and gave her a pleased to meet you.

"I've told Price here how wonderful a bridge player you were and I thought it would be nice to pop by and see how you were doing."

I stopped my eyes from doing a good roll as the words liar, liar, pants on fire sang a tune in my head.

"How good of you to think of me, and yes as I'm sure you remember I was quite the player, still am in fact. Do you play bridge, dear?" Sarah asked me.

I glanced at my aunt who had a please play along look in her eye and nodded. "Sure. Do it all the time."

"How wonderful," Sarah exclaimed. "Perhaps we should get together and have a foursome. James would just love to play."

Now, I've never played bridge before and to be quite honest have no desire to do so, but Sarah's statement sent a whirl wind of highly inappropriate pictures flashing through my head (none of which had anything to do with a card game). What's more, a big, burly guy with a black Amish style beard came into the living room holding a huge silver tray in front of him, loaded with a pot, cups and all the fixings for tea. I assumed this indeed must be James.

"Oh, that would be great!" James exclaimed, setting the tray down on an antique coffee table. "I sure do love a good foursome."

Sarah and my aunt clapped their hands in delight as I sat trying with all my might not to burst out laughing. I just couldn't help but think how twisted my mind really was as tea was served all around like nothing was amiss with the proposal. About fifteen minutes into the conversation regarding the game Clara was volunteering me to play, I caught a glimpse of the sky through one of the huge windows across the room. The dark clouds had turned to black as pitch. I tapped Clara on the arm and motioned to the window, hoping the impending storm would help her wrap up the chit-chat and get to why we were here in the first place. I was wrong.

"Drink your tea, dear. We've plenty of time."

I groaned inwardly as to not provoke another reprimand for my rudeness, lifted the cup to my lips, and took a large slurp. My aunt gave me another stern look before turning her attention to the love-me-a-good-foursome man. I lowered my eyes and tried a quiet sip.

"You know, James," Clara said, "Price is single at the moment. And I know for a fact she is looking for a real man to show her a good time."

The tea bypassed its trek to my stomach and went straight into my windpipe. The cup slipped from my hand and hit the carpet, spilling out what was left. I started coughing and just trying to wheeze in a breath. I felt someone popping me on the back and then someone hoisting me to my feet, shoving my arms into the air. The hoister was indeed James and his Amish beard, spooning me from behind while he held my arms up straight.

"High like a tree now Miss Price, just keep them arms up and cough that tea right on up!"

I caught my breath just as I spotted the satisfied look in Clara's eyes and the horrified one in Sarah's. I took the hint and grabbed James's hand with a hoarse thanks to him for not allowing me to choke to death.

"How about we step outside for a moment, James?" I asked with a cough. "I need to get some air and a closer look at those clouds."

James smiled big. "Why, yes ma'am. I'd be delighted."

Out of the corner of my eye, I saw Clara grab a napkin off the tray and begin sopping up my mess off the carpet. "Now don't you worry Sarah, they'll be just fine outside for a moment. We need a little privacy to catch up anyway."

James opened the door for me as I swiped my coat off one of Rudolph's antlers and drew it on, clearing my throat from the inhaled tea as I went. I stepped outside and he followed, shutting the door behind him. The wind whipped against me like a set of flying knives. I zipped up the coat and started to pull the gloves out of my pocket when James threw his arm around me and pulled me into him.

"Whoa there cowboy," I said, putting my hand against his thick chest, "calm your hormones. I'm not here to give you a thrill. I just need to talk."

"Oh come on, just one little kiss. We don't want to let your aunt down, now do we?"

James pulled me in closer and leaned his face into mine. His breath was hot against my cheek and smelled like sausage and peppers. I felt the bushy beard scratch against my skin as he gave me light kiss on the cheek, then he moved his hand under my chin to try and lift my mouth to his. I swallowed the urge to gag and stayed put.

"You get one more chance to be a gentleman, James," I said, praying he'd be as obedient as he seemed inside the house just a couple seconds ago.

It's funny how God doesn't always answer prayers right away. James cupped my ass and I instinctively rammed my knee up hard into his crotch, making him grunt and bow forward just as I shoved the heel of my right hand under his bushy bearded chin with enough force to send him back against the side of the house. And it's also funny how sometimes God just knows a son of a bitch who needs a good ass whipping and keeps his answer to himself just for the sheer entertainment of it.

Plastered against the wall, James slid downward until his butt met the concrete porch. The shocked look in his eyes was evident. It was a look which screamed there was never a woman who'd told him no and succeeded in keeping him off. That was just unheard of.

"Now what would your mummy say if she saw what you were doing?"

"You bitch!" he spat through gritted teeth, both of his hands tucked tightly against his crotch.

"No means no, James, so how about we call this whole thing even and start over, okay?"

He glared at me as I squatted down in front of him.

"Now, I want you to listen to me good, James, and concentrate really hard. Can you do that? And don't try anything stupid because I will finish what I started faster than you can say shave and a haircut which, by the way, you could use right now."

When he just kept on glaring, I added, "I don't want to have to add any more pain to your day, so please just play along."

He gave a slight nod, wincing in pain.

"Good. Now, somebody dropped your mother's name at my front door with no rhyme or reason to go with it and I want to know why. Do you know anyone who'd want to hurt her in any way?"

He shook his head.

"Nobody?"

"No," he groaned. "Everybody loves her."

I sighed. "Do you know anyone else with her name?"

James coughed a couple times and nodded.

"Who?"

"My sister."

"Is she here?"

"No. She lives across town, near Arnie's antique shop."

"Shit," I mumbled, standing back up. "I need her address and phone number now."

He gave it to me without argument and I offered him a hand back to his feet which he waved off with a few colorful expletives about my mother. I shrugged, threw open the front door, and stepped into the foyer.

"Come on Clara, tea time is over, let's go!"

TWENTY-ONE

CLARA and I disembarked at the bus stop just as the sky opened up, pelting something worse than fluffy snowflakes or their tiny evil stinging snow bits. Sleet stung my face as the wind blasted against us, making me wish with all of my heart I'd been smart enough to have brought a ski mask and a pair of protective glasses with me. I glanced over at my aunt who had her head down and was trudging along. She slipped a step and I grabbed her by the arm for support as we carefully made our way back to the apartment.

"Still think it's festive?" I asked as we reached the front stoop of my building.

My aunt smiled, her cheeks rosy from the plummeting temperature and the exhaustive fight to walk only a couple of blocks. "Oh yes, it's like the scene from Rudolph the Red Nosed Reindeer where Santa announces he'll have to cancel Christmas."

I just shook my head with a light laugh and went inside. We made our way up the flights of steps and down the hall leading to my apartment. Opening the door, I scanned the floor for any more mysterious envelopes just in case the mystery writer had grown impatient with my results and decided to send me a reminder note. The carpet was clear and I let my aunt go on in ahead of me. She was already stripping off her winter wear when I shut the door. One of her boots went sailing across the living room, landing with a thump on the kitchen floor.

"Whoops! Sorry about that."

I shrugged. This was indeed becoming a trend. I shed my boots, coat, hat and gloves, and then flipped on the television to hear the weather forecast. We were in for it again and this time the prediction was worse than before, several inches of snow were going to follow the sleet. I groaned.

"Now don't you fret," Clara said as she bustled towards the kitchen. "I'm going to make us some hot cocoa. Everything will look brighter once you warm up."

"Thanks," I replied, dialing Arnie's number into my cell phone. "Cocoa is in the top right cabinet."

Arnie picked up on the first ring.

"Hello?"

"Hi Arnie."

"Miss MacCann, I told you we are not open on Sundays."

I sighed and plopped my frozen behind down on the couch. "I'm not calling about work, Arnie, well not shop work anyway."

"Then to what do I owe this pleasure?"

"I need a favor."

"Continue."

I told him about Sarah Nichols, the one I hadn't met in person and as I expected he pressed me for more information. After I finished relaying all I knew about my mystery writer, I heard him sigh.

"Looks like you're back in the family business after all."

"That's yet to be decided."

"Uh-huh," he muttered. "So what do you need from me?"

What I needed was a scout, somebody who was closer to Sarah's residence and could get to her easier than I could right now, so I gave him the address which was just two houses down from his own. I'd had enough foresight to get Sarah's number from James while my aunt said her goodbyes and asked him to call his sister immediately to make sure she was okay. I wasn't holding my breath for the favor as I'd left him still holding his nuts on the porch.

"Let me call her and get a feel for what's going on," I said. "If you don't hear back from me in five minutes, could you go check on her?"

"There's nothing I'd enjoy more," Arnie replied. "Heat and comfort during a snow storm are highly overrated anyway."

I paused, not sure if he was being facetious or not. "You can tell me no, I'll understand."

"Nonsense, Miss MacCann. If I don't hear from you, I'll go and check the house."

"Thanks Arnie, I'll owe you one."

"Yes you will," he replied and hung up.

I called the number James had given me. After three tries with no answer, not even a voicemail message, I hung up and took the cup of hot cocoa my aunt handed me. I'd just have to wait for Arnie to call me back. Clara sat down on the other end of the couch and propped her pink fuzzy slipper feet up on my coffee table. I took a sip of the cocoa, relishing its yummy taste and the warmth it offered.

"That was a pretty sneaky trick back at the Nichol's house," I told her.

She smiled. "Desperate times call for desperate measures. Sarah will be talking scandalously about you for months I'm afraid, but I didn't really think you'd care what she thought. Besides you don't seem like a bridge player to me so no need to keep up appearances."

I laughed. "No, the idea of a foursome with James sounds too much like a really bad porn flick. What did you talk to Sarah about while I was outside?"

"Bridge mostly, but she did make a comment about her daughter going through a rather nasty divorce."

"How nasty?"

Clara shrugged. "She wouldn't elaborate, but something tells me it may be the reason your mystery writer thinks she needs help."

"I asked Arnie to check on her. Sarah's one of his neighbors."

"Do you think that's wise?"

I sighed and sipped my cocoa. Domestic disputes of any kind were the worst situations to be involved in, just ask any cop around and they'll tell you what a nightmare it is to try and manage those kinds of emotional disasters. Arnie was a family friend but I had absolutely no idea how well he could handle himself in a volatile situation and Clara was right to question the wisdom of me bringing him into it. I picked up my cell and dialed his number. He answered before the first ring ended.

"Arnie?"

"Miss MacCann?"

"Are you okay?"

"Relatively."

I froze. Relatively was the code word my family used when they found themselves in precarious situations. If Arnie was using the code, then something was definitely wrong.

"Arnie, if you mean what I think you mean, tell me goodbye."

There was a pause on the line and then I heard him say, "Dear lady, I bid you adieu."

ALL PUBLIC TRANSPORTATION had been halted until further notice so I would be hiking the distance in the blasted sleet to check on Arnie and Sarah Nichols. I left Clara at the apartment with the strict instruction to call the police if I didn't call her in an hour. Since I'd already held the pleasure of dealing with the authorities over the Mathison incident, I wasn't looking forward to another meeting with them, so I left with the hope all would be simple and quick.

Outside my building, the sleet pounded against anything it could reach. I pulled my ski mask down over my face and donned the safety glasses I fished out of the recesses of my bedroom closet before stepping off the stoop and going against the onslaught of ice and wind.

Grimacing with each carefully placed step, I moved along the walk until I reach a point where it was too slick to navigate. I was forced to trudge through the knee deep snow just to keep from busting my ass.

I made it to the antique shop and paused under the awning over the front entrance for a moment. No vehicles were even attempting to move in this weather and I hadn't passed anyone on foot since stepping outside. It was like the proverbial ghost town, creepy as heck. I forced my feet to keep moving, turning down the street I needed and scanning for Sarah's house number. I didn't spot the 326 on the mailbox until I was almost right on top of it. Glancing up towards the house, I could just barely make out the shape of the standard white, two-story A-frame. I moved off to the side of the icy driveway, around a line of festive looking evergreen trees, and trudged through the crunchy ice-covered snow to the back of the house. Inching between two of the trees, I eased the branches aside to get a better view and gauge the situation. Something grabbed hold of my arm.

TWENTY-TWO

MY HAND WAS in my coat pocket wrapped around the handle of my gun, clicking off the safety and drawing it out before I could even think twice. In a fluid motion, I turned and trained it straight at my assailant's chest. The hand which held my arm immediately released.

"Don't shoot."

Visibility was getting worse by the minute but I didn't have to see the dark beard and mustache to know who it was, I recognized the voice immediately.

"What the hell are you doing here?" I asked.

"I could ask you the same question," Donnelly replied, "but I'd prefer you put the gun away first. It's wet out here and you might accidentally pull the trigger."

Arnie's last words about him came to mind, so I didn't lower the gun.

"Trust me, if I shoot you, it won't be an accident."

Donnelly smiled. "Now that's the Christmas spirit. What if I told you I was here to visit Arnie?"

I smirked. "I'd say you were a fool. Arnie wants you out of town or dead and I don't think he cares which comes first."

"And you, what do you want?"

I paused. I knew two things about Donnelly. One, he was extremely handsome and two, he seemed to be a poster child for the term assface. Unfortunately, the assface always wins.

"I want you to crawl back under whatever rock you crawled out from."

"You wound me, MacCann."

A shot rang out and my heart sped up to near racing. Donnelly glanced down at the front of his thick coveralls and then back up at me as if to make sure I hadn't shot him. I clicked the safety on the gun to keep accidental fire out of the equation should I fall and shoved the weapon back in my pocket. I'd need both hands to maneuver in this slick, snowy mess and trying to keep the gun up and ready was just unrealistic.

"Wait," Donnelly hissed. His hand locked on my arm again.

I twisted out of his grasp just as the second shot sounded from inside the house and took off out of the tree line to the back door.

Running in deep snow looks just as ridiculous as it sounds, mainly because it's nearly impossible to do it. Running on ice (also ridiculous and a tad bit more dangerous) was even worse, a fact I realized all too well when I hit a patch of it and slid all the way to the door. I had to grab on to the handle just to keep from myself upright. I pushed the lever down to find it was unlocked and gave the door a push, hard enough it slammed against whatever was behind it, and pulled out my gun as I cautiously stepped inside.

The kitchen was in shambles, a round wooden table lay toppled on its side and several wooden chairs surrounded it in broken pieces all over the linoleum. I stepped over shards of ceramic and glass, remnants of dishes with food still clinging to them and scattered around on the floor. The stench of fresh blood reached my nose and I stifled my gag reflex as I glanced around for the source of the smell. I sidestepped the mess, careful not to disturb anything in case this turned into a murder scene and kept close to the wall line without coming in contact with it as I made my way to the archway of the next room. A shadow caught my eye and I glanced over my shoulder to see Donnelly coming in behind me.

The living area was tossed over like someone had either been searching for something or succumbing to a really bad tantrum while they searched for something. Couch cushions were pulled off and strewn on the carpet. Books from a shelf nearby lay open and torn scattered around like fallen butterflies all around the room. I glanced at the broken remains of a lamp and scanned the walls and carpet as I moved through, looking for blood, the source of it, and Arnie.

"This isn't good, MacCann," Donnelly said. "I say we get out of here while we can."

I looked back to see him standing next to the couch. I shook my head. "You go. Arnie's in here and probably Sarah or what remains of her. I'm not leaving until I find them."

"Get Arnie and get out. I'll be waiting outside."

He disappeared back into the kitchen and I heard the back door shut a moment later. I grumbled another observation about Donnelly under my breath and moved further into the house. There were two doors on one side of a hallway, one on the opposite side, and another at the very end. The smell of blood was getting stronger, making me a tad nauseous. I wasn't squeamish about blood per se, but no sane human enjoys the scent of someone's life source spilling out where it can be smelled. I took a deep breath through my mouth, praying I wouldn't taste the odor, and held it as I opened the first door to a small bedroom. What little was in the room had been treated with the same care as the kitchen and living area. The covers and sheets were barely hanging on to the corner of a mattress which leaned against a set of boxed springs, teetering on the edge of the bed frame. All the drawers were pulled out of a cedar chest and lay empty, one of them cracked beyond repair by whoever tossed it. A small closet door was opened, nothing inside but a metal rod near the top with a couple of wire coat hangers hanging on. I went around the bed and checked the space beneath the box springs, making sure to look under the bed as well. Nothing.

I left the room, closing the door behind me, and went to the next closed door. The bathroom seemed mostly untouched, only one side of the medicine cabinet lay open, nothing tossed around. I moved on. Just as I was about to turned the knob of the next room, I felt a vibration in my pocket. I pulled out my cell phone and glanced down at the display to see my home number. I flipped it open and answered the call, putting it to my ear.

"Price?"

"Yeah?"

"This is Aunt Clara."

I rolled my eyes. "Yes."

"I thought I should give you a call and let you know that somebody just reported shots fired in the area near Arnie's house. The news anchor said they are trying to get the police out there now."

I groaned. Time was running out.

"Clara, Arnie's cell phone number is on the counter in the kitchen. Call it and see if he answers."

"Okay, dear. I hope you're planning on getting out of there soon."

"I just have two rooms left to check and then I'm out."

I flipped the phone closed, shoved it in my pocket, and opened the next door. I reeled back as the smell of blood and perforated bowl invaded my nose. Swallowing down my need to retch, I peered into the room Sarah must have used as an office. The window next to the desk was shattered, allowing furious blasts of wind and sleet to blow inside. My eyes fell to the casing around the sill. No glass shards; the tell-tale sign of somebody brushing the debris outside in order to pass through. My gaze went from the window to the desktop computer screen on the floor; the black plastic tower accompanied it tangled in black wires and cords. A chair lay toppled on its side with a bare leg and foot draped over it. I stepped forward to see the owner lying lifeless and covered in blood from the neck down. The tattered remains of her fuzzy pink robe ripped in several places and splayed open, revealing the deep cuts in her chest and abdomen. I didn't really know what Sarah looked like, but my guess was this was indeed her. She was beyond any help I could offer now.

I shut the door and went on, opening the last one. Arnie sat on the end of a queen-sized bed in the immaculate bedroom; not one thing tossed and from what I could tell, not one thing touched. He wasn't wearing his glasses, but he was sporting a nice bruise around his swollen left eye and cheek. In his hand and hanging loosely between his knees was a 715.357 Magnum revolver, the source of the gun shots. He held his cell phone in the other hand. He didn't look up when I entered.

"Arnie," I said, stepping towards him, "you okay?"

His eyes slowly lifted up to meet mine. "You're too late, Miss MacCann. We were both too late."

I secured my weapon and shoved it back in my pocket.

"Arnie, we need to get out of here. The cops are on their way."

"Clara called," Arnie mumbled, "said something about the news."

"Yeah, we don't have much time."

I ushered him out of the house, shutting the back door behind me. Donnelly was nowhere in sight. Coward. I shuffled Arnie the short but freezing distance back to his house, once inside, I eased him down on an antique couch which looked a lot like the one Sarah's mother had in her house. I found an ice pack in his kitchen freezer, wrapped it in a dish towel hanging by the sink and returned. Arnie took it with a nod of thanks and put it on his swollen face as I sat down next to him.

"Did you shoot the guy who killed her?"

He nodded. "The first one went wide, but the second was a clean shot to the chest. I didn't see any blood, but the force knocked him out of the window he'd already smashed open before I got in there. When I looked out, he wasn't there."

I grimaced. "Bullet proof vest. The guy was prepared. Did you get a good look at him?"

Arnie shook his head. "Not really. He was covered up pretty well. Average size," he mumbled as his eyes met mine, "nothing really remarkable. Miss MacCann, you need to leave. The cops will be banging down my door as soon as they see our foot prints in the snow."

I stood up and crossed my arms over my chest ready to be defiant just as an earth shattering boom sounded, deep and loud enough to vibrate everything in the wave's path. I grabbed my boss by the back of the neck and shoved him to the floor. The living room window exploded inward, the force of the blast hitting me hard enough to throw me across the room and smack me into the opposite wall.

TWENTY-THREE

I DON'T KNOW how long I was unconscious, that's the upside to being knocked out; time slips away from you. But when I tried to open my eyes everything was blurry, even the hairy face just mere inches from mine. It was talking in a tone so muffled I couldn't make out what it was saying. I pinched my eyes closed and reopened them, still too fuzzy to make out much more than a mouth. It started talking and I read its lips.

"She's coming to. Thank God."

I closed my eyes and faded away to visions of Leprechauns dancing around pots of gold. I could see one of them notice me and approach, talking in a low soothing voice as it came. It kept telling me to just hang on, don't give up, don't go away. It brushed my cheek with a warm hand. I felt the wisp of a breath on my brow as it kissed my forehead. The pot of gold, the dancing leprechauns darkened ever so slowly until they vanished and I was surrounded by the darkness which took me away.

When I opened my eyes again, the face was gone. It was replaced by the flash of red and blue strobes playing along everything it reached, the walls, ceiling, floor, and then the uniformed officer who now knelt down over me.

Shit.

I sat up, my head pounding as if someone was taking a sledge-hammer to my skull, and a wave of dizziness and nausea hit me instantly.

"Wait honey," the cop said, "you don't want to get up right now. Let the medics move you."

No, I didn't want to get up. Everything in and attached to me hurt like hell, but I needed to. I blinked a couple of times and touched the side of my head. I winced, feeling a stinging burn where I touched, and pulled my hand down to see the blood on my finger-tips. My eyes met the cop's.

"Where's Arnie?" I mumbled.

"Your boss is okay," he replied, "a couple of cuts and bruises from the explosion, but that's it. You're lucky to be alive."

I tilted my head, an action I immediately regretted. The room spun around me like a crazed tilt-a-world and my stomach revolted. The cop backed up just in time. I vomited, covering the floor right where he'd been.

I thought I heard him say something like, "Whoa there!" I even thought I felt him grab me, but I can't be for sure because I passed out again.

———

ACCORDING to the news reports televised on our local stations and the nice detective working the case who came to see me at the hospital the next morning, I was lucky to be alive. The explosion completely decimated Sarah's house and the one next to it. Luckily, it only blew out all of Arnie's windows and cracked his foundation. Sarah's remains, per my Dad's inside info, had been torn and strewn all over the sight with the blast and the parts found by the forensics team were charred and damaged beyond recognition. They would be playing the DNA game for a while. The scene itself completely baffled the authorities, considering there were no foot prints left in the snow around the place and they hadn't a clue as to how the murderer fled away.

I sported a couple of deep bruises from my collision with the wall and several cuts which required stitches to close. How I came away without a broken bone I'll never know. My parents were the first ones I saw when I woke up in the hospital. Worry etched in both of their faces. They were well aware of the dangers involved in doing what we do, but I could tell it didn't make it easy for them. The concussion kept me hospitalized for a night of observation, and I was to stay off the roads and away from strenuous activity per doctor's orders for a week. My car was still in the shop so I had no vehicle to drive even if I wanted to be a rebel.

Kelly came to visit me the afternoon I came home from the hospital. After scolding me for not calling her back, she started in on the dangers of texting while driving and why I was an idiot for do so. At first, I didn't have a clue what the hell she was talking about until she excused herself briefly to use my bathroom.

Aunt Clara whispered, "She sounded pretty normal to me when I answered your phone, so I just figured she didn't know anything about you being an assassin. I told her you were texting and driving when you ran into a guardrail with a car. Not your car of course, she knows it's in the shop. I told her you were driving my Buick."

I just nodded my head.

Kelly returned from the bathroom and my aunt left us to our own devices.

"Okay," Kelly said with a grin. "I don't want to hear one word from you about my raccoon eyes after this."

I laughed even though the root to what she was saying wasn't humorous. "Touché," I replied and then added, "Same result, entirely different beast though."

She joined me in the laugh. "I know you worry and I know you think it's stupid for me to stay with Corey." She paused. "And I know you don't believe me when I say I love him, but I do."

"Kelly, he won't change."

"Maybe, maybe not, but I'm not ready to call it quits just yet. Trent needs his father."

I started to tell her Trent needed his mother too, alive and well and not beaten to a pulp, but I didn't. I was, however, thinking seriously about having a conversation with Corey really soon. Kelly changed topics and I let her. We chatted and watched television together for about an hour before she left me to the care of Aunt Clara who was just plain fuzzy peachy in her role as nightingale. She had refused to leave my apartment until I was back on my feet again.

But the best part of the whole post explosion thing was the doctor's orders to make sure I could be awakened at any time once asleep and my aunt took the order damn seriously. Apparently, a concussed person might just snooze themselves right into a coma or, well, death. So, after two days of Aunt Clara waking me up shortly after I'd fallen to sleep (every time I'd fallen to sleep), I was really looking at the coma thing in a whole other light.

The only plus to this entire fiasco was at least I got my bed back. Aunt Clara moved to my couch with the proclamation she would be better able to keep an eye on me should I appear to have a (and this is her term, not mine) comatose expression. Now my problem was who would be keeping an eye on her. I'd already made up my mind if I even smelled one hint of Changaa brewing I would be setting her outside on her ass faster than you can say Ho Ho Ho.

"Now Price, I really need you to be more cooperative with your Aunt Clara. She says you're not resting."

I groaned inwardly as Mom began her lecture, easing the cell phone away from my ear and gave it a few good shakes in the air nobody but me could enjoy.

"She's waking me up every time I fall asleep," I said when I finally stopped shaking the phone and got back on. "How's anyone supposed to rest when someone's constantly waking them up?"

"Keep your voice down," Mom growled. "You know Clara's very sensitive about criticism, especially when she feels so useful." She went silent for a moment and then asked, "Do I need to come over there?"

"Mom, I'm not a kid anymore. I haven't been for a very long time. I can take care of myself just fine."

Mom laughed. "Sure you can. And by the way, I thought you were trying to live the normal life. How does the average ho-hum woman smash her car into a couple of drug cartel hit men and then a few days later get blown up?"

I winced and averted the question altogether. "Uh, yeah, well you don't have to come over. Clara's here. I'll try to be more cooperative. Love you. Bye."

I closed the phone and shuddered at the idea of having Aunt Clara and Mom with me in my little apartment at the same time. This place just wasn't big enough for all three of us (actually I don't believe there was any place on mother earth big enough, but whatever). My bedroom door opened and Clara poked her head in with a big smile on her face.

"You've got a visitor, dear. Are you decent?"

I glanced down at the thick dark blue comforter covering me in my flannel pajamas and then looked back up at her. "I'm about as decent as I'm going to get today."

"Good. Good. I'll send him in."

I sat up. "Clara, wait a minute. Who is it?"

"Oh a very handsome looking gentleman, I'm sure he'll cheer you right up."

My aunt closed the door before I could ask anything more and I flopped back on my pillows with a sigh, thinking my visitor was probably Arnie, Dad, or maybe even Jonas. And then I started thinking about Clara and how, although related, we were so very different. True she was also an assassin, specializing in the art of poison, but there was way more to her than a deadly title. She enjoyed the company of anyone she came upon, being about as bubbly and friendly as one could get without pouring a whole bucket of sugar and spice overtop one's head. Hell, she'd probably let Attila the Hun in my room if he was holding a bouquet of flowers and a get well card. I liberated my 9mm Arnie had seen fit to hide away right after the explosion out from the drawer of my bedside table and drew it under the blanket with me, just in case the differences between Cora and me became life threatening.

I heard the door knob rattle and then Aunt Clara's voice again. "Oh, I'm sure she'll be very glad to see you."

Somehow, I just wasn't so sure. I flipped the safety off of the gun just as the door opened.

"Now look who's come to wish you a speedy recovery," Clara said, motioning as if she were directing traffic. "Come on in now."

I aimed the gun straight at the door. Sure, I'd take out the duvet if I fired, but sometimes sacrifices have to be made when safety is a concern.

"Tell her to put the gun down."

I groaned. Oh, God no. Not now. What have I done to deserve this? Now it knows where I live!

"What gun?" Clara asked. She turned towards me and planted her hands on her hips, glaring reproachfully much like my mother does whenever she'd caught me doing something I wasn't supposed to be doing. "Price MacCann! Do you have a gun under that blanket of yours?"

I gave a sigh, clicked the safety back on, and drew the gun out from its hiding place.

"Oh for goodness sakes!" Clara exclaimed, swiping it up. "This handsome man has come to check on you, not challenge you to a duel. Your mother would have a fit if she saw how you treated this kind gentleman." She turned back to the door as if to tell him it was indeed safe to enter, then stopped and turned back to me. "There's no other weapons under that cover, is there?"

"Nope," I replied.

"No knives?"

I shook my head.

"No grenades?"

I rolled my eyes. "No."

"You didn't make a shiv while I was in the other room, did you?"

"No Clara, I didn't make a shiv. I'm unarmed. Send in the asshole."

"Price! Oh, I am so sorry, Mister Donnelly. She's usually not this rude."

Donnelly came into my doorway and patted my flustered aunt on the shoulder. "No need to apologize. She took a nasty blow to the head. I'm sure the marbles are still rolling around in that skull of hers."

Aunt Clara giggled. "Such a delightful man, well, I'll leave you to your visit. Are you sure I can't get you something to drink?"

"No ma'am," he replied. "I'm fine, but thank you for the offer."

Clara gave a nod and closed the door, taking my gun with her and leaving me alone with the tall bearded man in coveralls.

I glared at him. "How did you find me? And don't tell me Arnie told you because I know that's not true."

Donnelly pointed at a chair near my bed. "May I sit?"

I opened my mouth tell him no, but then thought of Clara who could very well be stationed just outside my door, listening in on the conversation to make sure I was being polite. I gave a shrug which he took as yes. He sat down in the chair and pulled the black toboggan off revealing the short, dark hair beneath, the curls hugged tight against his head. I watched him twist the knitted cap in his hands for a moment as if he was contemplating what to say.

"Actually, it *was* Arnie who told me where you live," he said. "But before you lose your cool, let me explain."

I narrowed my eyes at him.

"Wait now," Donnelly said with a grin, "he owed me."

"Oh really? Why don't I believe you?"

"Come on, MacCann, have I honestly given you a reason not to trust me?"

I glowered at him. "You're kidding, right? You kept me waiting outside of your hotel like a big, ungrateful jerk when I was trying to give you a ride to the airport. You just show up at Sarah's house with some fake excuse about my boss and run off like a big chicken when you see what's inside. That's two very good reasons not to trust you."

Donnelly leaned back and tossed the toboggan back and forth in his hands. "Well, that's a relief."

"What is?"

"Well, I thought you'd be pissed about me grinding into you at the deli."

My frown deepened.

"Did anyone ever tell you that you look beautiful when you're angry?"

"Donnelly, you've got five seconds to come to the point of why you're really here or God so help me I will get up from this bed, get my gun from my aunt, and shoot your Irish ass."

He raised his brow and feigned a hurt expression. "Then what would your Aunt Clara say?"

"She'll get over it. Five. Four."

"You wound my pride, MacCann."

"Three. Two."

Donnelly leaned forward with his elbows on his knees.

"Okay, okay, just stop counting. I really am here to check on you, and by the way, those are very attractive flannel jammies you've got on. Nice pussy cats."

I pushed the comforter off and sat up. "One."

"God, you're a tough nut to crack. Look, I'm here to apologize."

I paused. "For being a rude and cowardly ass?"

He laughed. "Uh, yeah, that and for something else."

I grit my teeth. "What?"

The smile died on his lips as his dark eyes drifted to the floor for a moment and then back up at me. "For being the reason you got hurt, MacCann, I'm sorry."

I started to give a nice retort about leaving somebody in the lurch, but I stopped myself. His expression of remorse looked almost genuine.

"Donnelly, I didn't get hurt because you tucked tail and ran. The explosion happened after I'd gotten Arnie to his house, there would have been nothing you could have done anyway."

"No, I know that," he said, "but you *did* get hurt because I blew up the house."

My eyes widened. "You? I just thought the killer was covering his tracks. You blew up the house? How?"

"C-4 on the gas main, that's why Arnie owes me now. I covered up any sign you guys were there, but I underestimated the strength of the blast. Damn near got you both killed."

My jaw slacked and I just sat there for a moment. Who the hell was this guy? He left before I could either question him further or kill him good and proper.

TWENTY-FOUR

MUCH TO MY aunt's dismay I was finished playing the part of the wounded patient. I've never really like being doted on, even as I kid a hug and Popsicle could cure a ton of hurts for me. So, I got out of bed and went into the living room. Clara was a busy little elf while I'd been tucked away, covering every inch of usable space with Christmas cheer. A tree stood in the corner, completely trimmed with white lights and very tasteful ornaments. She'd draped my end and coffee tables with bits of evergreen, pine cones, and candles of red, green, white, and gold. There were even a couple of gifts tucked under the tree, wrapped in shiny red paper.

"Clara, you didn't have to do this."

My aunt laughed. "Of course I did, but I can't take all the credit. I had Jonas bring the decorations from my house, but they're yours now. I've got way more than I need at home."

I knelt down by the tree to see the gifts were for me. "But I haven't gotten you anything yet."

"Don't worry about it. My present is spending time with my favorite niece during the holiday."

I smiled and wondered if she told that to all her nieces.

"Thank you but I've still got a little over a week to get you something."

"Now you don't have to get me a thing, so don't even worry about it. Oh, I almost forgot, this envelope must have been tucked under the door last night. I didn't open it, but I'm betting it's from your secret messenger."

I took it and sat down on the couch. Tearing it open, I pulled out the sheet of paper and read:

NICE TRY. GET WELL SOON. I'LL BE IN TOUCH.

"What did your mystery writer have to say this time?"

I handed it over and she read it out loud.

"Oh, how lovely!" she exclaimed, waving the paper around excitedly. "It looks as if this person cares about you."

I withheld comment. Whoever this person was, it was becoming apparent they were definitely watching me, a thought which did not settle well.

"You know what I'd love?"

"What's that, dear?"

"I would absolutely *love* a nice cup of your hot cocoa."

Clara smiled from ear to ear. "Coming right up."

I watched her bustle into the kitchen to rustle up my request before I ducked back into my bedroom and called Arnie who picked up on the first ring.

"You are not coming to work today, Miss MacCann, so forget it. And you're car is ready, but forget that too, because you're not supposed to be driving."

"Arnie, we need to talk."

"Miss MacCann, being nearly blown to smithereens has put me a bit behind schedule and now I am elbow deep in Christmas shoppers. Since you and your Aunt Clara are not available to help, I am also extremely short-handed. I'm afraid we'll have to talk later."

"It'll just be a sec, okay?"

He heaved an irritated sigh. "Continue."

"My messenger is giving me the creeps. I think he's keeping tabs on me."

"Then I suggest you call UPS or FedEx and file a complaint."

"Not that type of messenger, Arnie, the cloak and dagger guy who keeps leaving love notes at my door, remember?"

He heaved another sigh. "Hang on for a moment."

I heard the rustling sounds of movement and then a door shut. The background noise of busy shoppers became a distant muffle as he came back on the line.

"Miss MacCann, whether you like it or not you are an assassin."

"You mean was, Arnie."

"No, I mean you *are*. You cannot just drop a skill like that, it's as much a part of you as any other trait you have. So instead of calling me and whining, I suggest you put your skills to good use and find out who this person is for yourself."

As much as I hated to admit it, Arnie was right.

"Fine," I grumbled. "Could you at least tell me who the hell Donnelly really is then?"

He hung up on me.

Clara and I spent the rest of the day watching Christmas movies, most of which I'd already seen this year while we wrote out Christmas cards (or rather, she wrote them out and added my name right along with hers while I put them in the envelopes she addressed and attached the postage stamps). After we'd both decided it was time to call it a night, I took a deep breath and made the announcement I'd been dreading to make.

"Aunt Clara, I'm going shopping tomorrow."

To which she replied, "Not without me, dear."

TWENTY-FIVE

THERE'S something to be said about ingrained skills, they don't just disappear because you'd like them to. I stealthily closed the door to my apartment and locked up, leaving Aunt Clara snoring away like a lumberjack with a chainsaw on my couch. It was like I was a teenager trying to sneak out of the house for a midnight rendezvous, something I'd only seen done in the movies because I'd never been rebellious as a kid. In fact, the only time I'd ever shown a hint of rebellion towards family was when I told them I quit over a year ago. I moved down the hall as quietly as I could, making sure not to tempt fate by assuming my aunt's hearing was slacked, then into the stairwell and down the three flights which took me to the ground floor. I pushed open the door of my building and stepped out into the frigid early morning air. Pulling my scarf up to cover my nose and mouth, I started walking, maneuvering the slick sidewalks as carefully as possible until I came to the service station a couple of blocks away.

Inside the store, the place was as dead as a mausoleum with only a clerk at the counter. She glanced up from the book she was reading, which looked like a steamy romance by the embracing couple on the cover, and gave me a nod of acknowledgement as I moved to the self-serve coffee area. I poured a cup of steaming Joe into one of the Styrofoam cups and secured a plastic lid onto it before approaching the counter to pay.

"Early riser or late night?" she asked, giving me a friendly smile. The diamond piercing in her nose caught the fluorescent overhead light and sparkled when she moved. Everyone loves a good nose diamond.

"Feels like a little of both," I replied, paying for the coffee. "Mind if I wait for my cab in here?"

"Not at all, it's freezing outside."

I thanked her and plopped down on one of the stools next to the front window, sipping from my cup as I waited. A few minutes into the hot brew, I spotted headlights turning into the lot with an on-duty sign lit up on the roof. I gave the clerk a quick thank you and went out, climbing in the back seat of the cab and shutting the door.

"Where to?"

"Ramada on Main," I replied and settled back with my coffee still firmly in my grip.

The hotel wasn't far enough to really justify cab fare, but I was still a little sore from the explosion and felt I owed myself one. The driver had no interest in making small talk, at least not with me, but he did chatter away on his Bluetooth. From his side of the conversation it sounded like he was speaking with a fellow cabbie, so I tuned out the chatter and took in the passing winter wonderland scenery until we made the turn into the lot for the Ramada. The cab stopped at the front entrance and I passed the guy his fare through the window and got out. The hotel lobby was as dead as the service station had been with just one person to be seen manning the front desk. It was an older gentleman who wore the same bored expression of the other graveyard shifter, minus the nasal piercing of course. I tossed my cup into a bin near the door and approached the counter.

"May I help you?" he asked, looking up at me from his seat behind the counter.

"I hope so. I was wondering if you could tell me which room Mister Donnelly was staying in."

"Well, let's see," he replied, tapping on the keyboard. "Ah Donnelly, yes, here we go. Oh, I'm sorry. There's a request to not be disturbed."

I'd figured as much, so I took a deep breath and put on my best confused and slightly annoyed look, which was actually easy to do where Donnelly was concerned.

"That can't be right," I said. "He just called for entertainment about half an hour ago."

"Entertainment, at this hour of the night?"

I gave him a moment to let it sink in. Three. Two. One. I literally saw the light bulb flash on above the old man's head. Add in a twinkling of the eye and a sheepish grin on his face and it was picture perfect.

"Oh, entertainment, I see. Uh, well, he didn't call down to let me know you were coming."

I gave a slight smile of my own. "He did ask for complete discretion."

"Of course," he replied. "Would you like me to call and let him know you're on your way up?"

"You can if you want, but if he's trying to keep it quiet he may not be all that happy about you calling."

"You're probably right. I'll just give you the room number then."

"That'd be great," I said.

I felt a slight tinge of guilt for lying and hoped Donnelly wouldn't file a complaint on the old man later for helping me out. Instead of telling me, the clerk passed me a yellow Post-It with the room number written on it.

"You have a good evening now," he said with a wink.

I gave him a heartfelt thank you and moved towards the elevator. Once inside, I shifted my gaze to the floor, waiting as it moved swiftly upward. I stepped out into the hall when the doors opened, counting down the door numbers until I reached Donnelly's room. I paused for a moment and then knocked softly. The door was opened before I lowered my hand, stopped by the chain lock set in place. Donnelly's face filled the few inches of space, wearing a lazy grin.

"Charlie told me I had entertainment coming up, but I never dreamed it'd be you. Well maybe I dreamt it a little but you weren't wearing so many clothes in my dream."

I grimaced. "Front desk Charlie?"

Donnelly responded by shutting the door and sliding the chain lock off. He reopened it halfway, enough so I could see he was not only shirtless, but barefoot and pantless. The only thing covering what God gave him was a pair of black boxer briefs which were snug fitting enough to ease the work of any imagination. He leaned casually against the door frame and crossed his arms over his well-muscled chest. My eyes couldn't help but drift along the contours of his pectorals and then down the chiseled abs. I stopped at the waistband of his briefs and forced my eyes back up to his face which held a very amused grin.

"Charlie's an old friend of mine and he knows I do not pay for entertainment."

I arched a brow. "So you're a cheapskate? One of those slap-a-ho kind of Johns then?"

Donnelly laughed and opened the door further. "Come on in. I'll slap you around if that's what you're into."

I rolled my eyes. "First, I'm not here for pleasure or pain. And second, you need to put something else on. Your lack of apparel is making my eyes water."

"Okay," he replied, walking off towards the bathroom and leaving me to enter the lion's den all on my own.

I stepped inside and shut the door just as Donnelly returned with only a pair of socks on his feet to add to his apparel. He gave me another sly grin and offered me one of the two chairs at a small table across the room.

"Socks huh?" I asked, pulling off my gloves and scarf, shedding my coat and laying all of it at the end of his bed.

He sat down in the chair opposite the one he'd offered me. "Well just in case you have a foot fetish, I thought it best to cover these puppies up."

I sighed and sat down. This guy was definitely a piece of work. Hot? Yes. Annoying as hell? Absolutely. Mysterious enough to make me come here? You betcha.

"Yeah, you got me. Feet are my weakness. Toes will almost bring on an orgasm."

Donnelly propped his arm on the table, resting his chin on the heel of his hand and feigning a dreamy stare. "I could take them off if you like. Let you rub them to your heart's content."

I managed to not crack a smile. "I'm not here exchange sexual banter with you."

He laughed. "Then why *are* you here?"

"Well, I figure you owe me one for nearly blowing me up and I'm here to collect."

"Hey, I said I was sorry. What more do you want?"

"Answers."

"To what questions?"

"I want to know who you really are and why you're here. And I'd really love to know if you're the jerk who keeps leaving little messages at my door, expecting me to run around like an errand boy all over town and putting me in situations I'd rather not be in. But most of all what I want right now is for you to put your clothes on because your nakedness is very distracting."

He replied with a wink and an air kiss, then got up and snatched a pair of jeans off the dresser a few feet away. I watched him slide them on and then pull a dark colored tee shirt over his muscular torso. A part of me wanted to scream in protest as I sensed my cheeks flushing, not from embarrassment but from some primal need. The scene should be the other way around, I should be watching this guy shed his clothes not cover his gorgeous body with them. I shifted my eyes back to the table top and forced that part of my mind to shut the hell up. The last thing I needed right now was to get involved with someone, let alone someone like Donnelly.

"What do you want to know first?" he asked, sitting back down.

"The messenger, right now it's creeping me out."

"Why would you think I'd know anything about it?"

I was ready for this. "There are two new and strange things in my life right now, you and this phantom person leaving notes at my door. Call me paranoid but I find it more than just a coincidence both of these things are a part of my reality at the same time."

"Why MacCann, I'm touched that you would consider me a part of your reality."

"Don't flatter yourself," I mumbled. "I'm just stating a fact."

Donnelly paused for a moment and then looked me square in the eye. "Well, first off, I am not your phantom. Second, I don't know who in the world with balls enough to be your phantom. And third, I'm a little bit hurt you didn't want to know about me first."

"Oh good grief."

"Come on now, you can't deny there's something between us."

I felt my jaw clench. "No I can't. You're leaning on it."

He laughed. "I wasn't talking about the table."

"Fine then, let's talk about you. Tell me who the hell you really are."

"Donnelly."

I gave him an icy glare.

He shrugged and gave me a grin which went right to his eyes, making my stomach flutter.

"I don't give away information about myself for free, you know? It'll cost you."

"You owe me, remember? So talk or I'm taking my curiosity to my family. And trust me when I say you really don't want to make it on their radar."

"Is that a threat or a promise?"

I got up, grabbed my winter wear and headed to the door. "Somehow I knew this would be a waste of time."

Donnelly was right behind me. I reached the handle as he planted his hand firmly against the door in an attempt to keep it closed. My instinct was to ram an elbow in his gut and follow through with a quick hard jab to his face, but my body refused to do what my brain was ordering it to and all I could manage was to turn around. He was close, way too close. My mind screamed warning after warning as he leaned in closer. I lifted my eyes to meet his just a millisecond before his lips brushed against mine. I felt his hand land lightly on my cheek, his fingers tracing down gently to my chin and lifting it up to deepen the kiss. My heart pounded as my breath caught, refusing air in or out as I felt myself responding in kind. The coat, gloves and scarf slipped out of my grasp but I gave it little notice as I lifted my hand to his chest, feeling the soft material of the tee shirt, the warm sensation of his skin underneath and the intense beating of his own heart coupled with the vibration of a soft moan.

He broke away first and I felt the tickle of his bearded cheek against mine as he whispered in my ear.

"I'm a friend of Michael's, MacCann. That's why I'm here."

TWENTY-SIX

I CLOSED my eyes but it wasn't darkness which greeted me. It was a scene I'd watched over and over in my dreams, a moment which found a way to spill out into the day, leaving me to endure the nightmare again and again. I shuddered as it played another encore in my mind with me begging for Michael to hold on.

"Don't let go!"

"Price, it's useless. Just go!"

"I'm not leaving you!"

An explosion smothered the sound of my proclamation. It blew out in all directions, billowing up choking black and gray smoke nearly obscuring Michael hanging from a beam near the ceiling of the cathedral. He'd caught it on his way down and his body swung gently like a pendulum just above the inferno lying in wait, the flames eating away at everything beneath him.

I shoved my gun back in the shoulder holster, grabbed the beam I'd been squatting on and kicked out to hang from it. The smoke was thick but I could still make out the beam below where the man hung for dear life. I let go of my grip and dropped down, balancing effortlessly. I knelt on one knee, keeping as good a hold on the beam as I could.

"Grab my hand!"

A gunshot blared to the right and I felt more than heard the bullet whiz past my head. I glanced over and saw the shadowy form moving fast along the beam, heading to the balcony.

"There's no time!" Michael yelled. "You save me and you'll lose him!"

There was another gunshot, the bullet going wide, missing both of us by several feet. The shooter was on the run. I grabbed Michael's arm tight, the flesh was slick with either blood or sweat or both, and my hand slid upward. There was no way I'd ever have enough traction with just my hands to be able to pull him to safety. It was a fact I guess we both knew.

"Get him, Price."

He let go and vanished into the inferno.

I opened my eyes before I could scream, my heart thumping so hard in my chest I heard its echo in my ears. I felt the word no escape from my lips in a near whisper and Donnelly eased back, gazing at my face in wonder. Flattening both hands on his chest, I shoved hard pushing him away from me as I swiped my coat up, threw open the door and fled.

"MacCann, wait!"

I didn't turn around, just boarded the elevator and punched the button for the ground floor. The doors eased shut and I collapsed against the far wall just trying to catch my breath. The replay of the memory didn't reduce me to shuddering sobs and leave me filled with the desire to have switched places in the fatality like it normally did, but it still held enough strength to cover me in a thick cloud of guilt, morphing every feeling I'd had about the situation into anger. I was angry at myself for having allowed it to happen in the first place, angry at God for not showing enough mercy to prevent it from happening. And more than all of it, I was angry at my brother,

Michael, for not trusting me enough to let me handle the job he'd asked me to do, for being there, for letting go, and for dying.

The doors slid open and I stomped more than walked through the lobby. The old guy at the front desk glanced up from his news paper as I shot past the counter.

"Well, that was fast. You have a nice evening now."

"Shut up Charlie."

And I went out like I'd come in but just a little more pissed.

I ARRIVED BACK at my apartment shortly before sunrise. Knowing full well I wouldn't be able to sleep, I shed my winter wear and pulled on a pair of pajamas just to feel the comfort of the loose material on my body. Clara was still snoring on the couch, so I put a pot of coffee on and sat down at the kitchen table to wait. It wasn't long before I heard my aunt stir from under the covers and shuffle towards my bathroom. I got up, pulled a couple of mugs from the cabinet and stood by until the contraption stopped dripping. Clara came in just as the coffee was poured. I handed her one, noting her fuzzy red and white candy cane striped footy pajamas, and sat down with my cup at the table.

Clara took a slurp out of her cup and eyed me for a moment. "Did you find out anything while you were out?"

"You sleep with one eye open, don't you?"

"Occasionally."

"And you didn't try to stop me."

"I knew if you were going somewhere in the middle of the night, it had to be important, so why stop you?"

I lifted the cup to my lips and sipped as she raised her brows at me.

"So, are you going tell me what you found?"

I set the cup down and sighed. "I didn't find out anything about the messenger. But I did find out something I wished I hadn't."

My aunt studied my face for a moment and then returned my somber expression with one of her own. I didn't see her hand cover mine, but I felt it.

"You don't have to tell me if you don't want to, but I've learned sometimes talking helps."

"Thanks," I replied.

I started to change the subject, move on to something less depressing, anything but what I really wanted to say. Instead, I lowered my eyes to gaze at the slick surface of the table and took Clara up on her offer.

"Remember the guy who came to visit me the other day?"

"Yes."

"That's who I went to see. He's staying in town at the Ramada."

I didn't have to look up to know she was smiling from ear to ear at the prospect of hearing about a spicy escapade. I ignored it and continued.

"Well, I've had a couple of run-ins with him, all of them leaving me with more questions than answers. And since I thought he may be the messenger guy because of the timing of everything, I confronted him."

"And I take it he's not?"

I shook my head. "No. He's someone else entirely."

"Who?"

I looked my aunt in the eyes. "He's a friend of Michael's. He said it's why he's here, whatever that means."

"And you didn't stay to find out?"

"No. He kissed me. I kissed back. He told me who he was and then I got out of there as fast as I could."

My aunt sat silent for a moment and so did I. She broke the quiet first.

"Price, we all lost your brother that night and we all miss him terribly, but you are not responsible for what happened to him any more than I am."

"I know."

"It was Michael's decision to show up at the cathedral, not yours. And it was his decision to let go of that beam."

"I know."

"Then what you don't know is he would hate to see you beating yourself up for the past year because of decisions he made. And he would really hate it that you didn't even let yourself find out more about his friend before you ran away."

I laughed, thinking about my brother. "No he wouldn't. If Michael knew one of his friends was hitting on me, he'd kick the guy's ass."

Clara smiled. "True. So, what about this friend, are you attracted to him?"

I feigned a shrug. "Attracted, repulsed, it's all the same."

My aunt got up from the table and refilled both of our mugs. "Sounds like the makings of a great romance novel to me."

"Don't get your hopes up," I replied. "He's an incorrigible ass."

Clara set my cup in front of me and then leaned down and kissed the top of my head. "Most of the best ones are, dear."

TWENTY-SEVEN

BY NINE O'CLOCK, Clara and I were walking through the door of Arnie's antique shop. He looked a little surprised to see us, but since customers were already trickling in he didn't object to our being there and were put to work as soon as we'd shed our coats. Clara manned the register while Arnie and I attended the shoppers and kept the shelves filled with overpriced junk. At lunch, Arnie surprised me by making the food run and leaving the store and its patrons to us. Of course he made sure not to stay away for very long, he was showing a bit of trust, not stupidity. All three of us continued on, snagging bites of deli sandwiches and chips between customers. When the store closed and he finally locked the doors, we were all whooped.

Arnie counted the money at the register while Clara and I straitened up the shelved merchandise, sweeping and mopping the floor to make the place ready for the next day. When we'd finished, Arnie motioned me to a stool behind the counter.

"Say, Clara, can you give me minute with Miss MacCann?"

My aunt obliged and disappeared back towards the break room area.

"I'm sorry I snapped at you yesterday."

"It's okay," I said with a shrug. "I know you didn't mean anything by it. Besides, I shouldn't have bothered you."

"No, you had a legitimate concern and I shouldn't have brushed you off." He bent down and pulled a small white jewelry box out from one of the shelves behind the counter and handed it to me.

"For me? Arnie you shouldn't have." I smiled. "What? No proposal?"

"Open the box, Miss MacCann."

I lifted the lid to see two small black pieces of technology at the bottom, one of them circular and no bigger than a dime. The other appeared to be a USB flash drive.

"It's a mini cam, remotes wirelessly to any computerized device you want. Just stick the cam on the outside of your door, I suggest placing it over the peephole, and plug the drive into anything with a USB port. The program will install automatically and you can keep tabs on who comes near your door."

"Thanks Arnie, but I don't have anything for you yet. Clara and I are going shopping after we leave here."

"Miss MacCann, take a good look around you. Do you honestly think I am in need of something else to sell?"

"You'd sell what I'd give you? That hurts, Arnie."

"Just save your money on me and donate it to a worthy cause. Now you two have fun shopping and I'll see you tomorrow."

A few minutes later, Clara and I bid Arnie goodnight and left, catching the bus to the downtown area where the local Wal-mart stood welcoming customers twenty-four seven. My funds were limited and the idea of getting everyone a gift on my list purchased at one location was very appealing. Clara grabbed a cart and headed towards the grocery section and I pulled one out and went the opposite way. We'd meet at the doors later to go home. I perused the crowded isles, picking out gifts for my sisters and my parents, grandparents, and Aunt Clara. I threw in a gift for Jonas and then grabbed a couple of other items I needed for day to day living. I stood in line at checkout for nearly half an hour because the store only had three of its nearly twenty checkout lanes open. When I'd finally paid, I ditched the cart at the front entrance and plopped down with all my bags on a bench to wait for my aunt. After about an hour, Clara waddled out of the store pushing an overflowing cart.

"Good grief, what all did you buy?"

"Oh, everything we need, dear."

I glanced down at one of the bags, reached in and pulled out a plastic see-through container as I made a face.

"Candied fruit?"

"For the fruitcakes, dear, Christmas just wouldn't be the same without them."

I shuddered and put the container back in the bag. "Well, there's no way we'll get to the bus stop will all of this. I'm calling a cab."

"I already have. It should be here any minute now."

"Thanks."

The cab arrived shortly after and took us back to my building where the driver was kind enough to help unload all of our bags and set them just inside the front entrance. I paid the fare and Clara gave the guy a twenty dollar tip and a box of Andes chocolate mints. We packed all we could carry to my door which I unlocked and opened.

"I'll get the rest," I told her, shedding my winter garb and tossing it inside the apartment, "if you can get this stuff inside."

Clara nodded in reply and I jogged down the flights for another load. It took me three trips to get all of it, and by the third run down I felt like I was training for a Rocky movie. I'd saved my stuff to go with the last load just in case Clara was a peeker, taking it to my room to hide the gifts away until I could wrap them. When I returned to the kitchen my aunt shooed me out.

"You go take a hot shower while I put these away."

I didn't argue. I was hot and sweaty and felt the unfortunate victim of one of those Cross Fit classes. I put the box Arnie had given me on my bedroom dresser to be set up when I'd finished my shower, then I grabbed some clean clothes and headed to the bathroom. I stripped down and stepped under the spray, relishing the first relaxing moment I'd had all day. After I scoured every inch of myself, I dried off and slathered on body lotion to fight the dry skin which always comes with winter weather, then I pulled on my comfy clothes and left my hair toweled up until it dried a little more. I paused with the toothbrush in my mouth as the scent of bacon frying wafted under the door. I quickly finished my brushing and headed back into the kitchen.

"I thought it would be a great night for BLTs," Clara said, lifting the crispy slices of bacon out of the pan. "I hope you don't mind."

"Of course I don't mind. It sounds awesome. Here, at least let me help you slice the tomato."

We sat on the couch and watched television while we munched on dinner. When we'd finished, I cleaned up the kitchen and set up the mini cam while Clara took her turn in the shower. That done, I went to my room and wrapped the gifts I'd bought. The ones I'd planned on shipping to my grandparent's house, I packed in a box I'd set aside for that particular purpose and addressed it to go. Like last year, I wouldn't be attending my family's Christmas get-together so they'd just have to be satisfied with their friendly UPS driver bearing presents. The ones for Jonas, Clara, and my parents I tucked under the tree. My aunt reemerged from the bathroom just as I'd settled onto the couch with my lap tap to watch the empty view of my hall via the mini cam. The program was pretty easy to use and would record video data as long as I left the power on to the computer.

"What are you watching?"

"The hallway," I replied. "I'm hoping to catch my messenger in action."

She sat down next to me and leaned in to watch the screen. After about twenty minutes of watching nothing, I heard Clara snoring and turned to see her fast asleep sitting up with her fuzzy pajama feet (this pair taking on a resemblance of Santa's suit, her feet the boots of the suit) propped up on my coffee table. I set the computer on my end table to run the program without me and retrieved the pillow and blankets from the closet. After I'd managed to ease her chubby form around to where she was lying down, I tucked her under the blankets, kissed her forehead and bid her goodnight. She snored in reply. I locked the apartment door, shut off the lights and headed to bed, hoping wholeheartedly I hadn't inherited Aunt Clara's snoring gene.

After tossing and turning for a good half hour, I finally drifted off to sleep. I didn't dream about Michael's death or the part I played in it. What did fill my sleeping mind was Donnelly. I felt his kiss, soft at first like it had really happened, then deeper and more intense (again, like it happened). It was followed by an entirely R rated scene which never took place. Luckily, my alarm sounded before I was faced with the awkward after sex cuddling and small talk. I got out of bed feeling just as sweaty and gross as I had when I'd finished carrying all the Wal-mart bags up three flights of stairs, so another shower was in order. Clara was already in the kitchen, making oatmeal when I walked in.

"Didn't you shower last night?" she asked as I poured a cup of coffee.

There was no way I was going to tell her about my dream.

"One can never be too clean," I said. "It's next to Godliness, you know?"

My aunt shrugged and started doling out oatmeal and toast. She took a seat at the table across from me and sipped her coffee as I took a bite of the hot cereal.

"I found another envelope on the floor in front of the door this morning."

My eyes widened as I nearly choked on the bite. I pushed my chair away from the table and hustled to my computer, accessing the program's recorded files. I waited, watched, fast forwarded, and watched some more.

"You've got to be freaking kidding me!"

"Did you catch him?" Clara asked as she waddled in the living room.

I glared up at her. "No. I didn't catch a damn thing."

TWENTY-EIGHT

I DIDN'T EVEN bother opening the envelope. I was too pissed off. I just shoved it into my coat pocket and headed out of the building with my aunt in tow. She'd already sworn to me she had absolutely nothing to do with it, and to be honest, I believed her. At least, I wanted to believe her. The messenger thing had been going on since before she'd come to visit and quite frankly I really couldn't see my aunt going anywhere in my building without drawing some attention to herself. Even walking out to go to work, she'd bid my passing neighbors and the maintenance guy to have a Merry Christmas, stopping for a few minutes to talk to an elderly couple who'd just recently moved into the building about the weather and the state of affairs in Washington D.C. I finally pried her away with the threat of being late to work. True, I had no real idea how she was "on the job", I'd never actually worked with her, but somehow I just couldn't picture her as the messenger.

"You certainly look sour-faced this morning," Arnie said to me as we bustled inside.

"I'm thinking about moving to a warmer climate," I said. "We had to walk hunched over all the way just to get here."

Arnie gave a slight nod. "I'll have my guy bring your car here today. That way you two won't have to walk home."

I thanked him and reluctantly slid my coat off, keeping my gloves on because my fingers were freezing, and then I took off my hat. I could feel some of my hair rising in response to the static electricity and I resisted the urge to smooth it back into submission with my gloved hands. Arnie let out a chuckle which only confirmed my suspicion that I looked absolutely stunning. I excused myself to the break room where I hung up my belongings and parted with the gloves, then went to the bathroom to assess the hair damage. A few minutes and a growl or two later, I was back at the front counter ready to work. The customers trickled in pretty steadily until lunch time when it slowed to a standstill. Arnie's guy showed up with my car keys and pointed to where he'd parked the Taurus which was a few slots away from the front entrance. I offered the guy twenty bucks as a tip but he refused, saying my boss had taken care of everything including the tip, and then he left. I thanked Arnie profusely and tried to get him to tell me how much I owed him for the repairs. He wouldn't hear of it, telling me once again it was a perk for being his employee.

"Just consider it your Christmas bonus, Miss MacCann."

I started to object since he'd refused to accept a gift from me but he was adamant so I forced myself to let it go. I'd just have to settle for owing him one in the future whether he wanted it or not.

Pizza was delivered a little while later and the three of us actually got to sit down in the break room to eat since the bell at the door would alert us of anyone coming in.

"How'd the mini cam work for you?" Arnie asked.

"I had another envelope under my door this morning and no video of the messenger, just an empty hallway."

"Interesting," he replied, glancing over at my aunt.

I shook my head. "Already been there and I don't think Clara's guilty."

"It isn't me," Clara responded, setting her slice of pepperoni pizza back onto the paper plate without taking a bite. "Price, if I wanted you to do something, I'd just ask. I certainly wouldn't put up a charade like this person's doing."

"I know."

Arnie looked overtop his glasses at me. "So what was in the envelope?"

I gave a shrug and opened my can of Coke. "I don't know, haven't opened yet. I was too ticked off earlier."

"Well, don't you think you should?"

I got up and pulled the envelope out of my coat pocket, then sat back down to rip it open with aggravated vigor. I expected to see "got you" or maybe "nice try" typed in the center of the paper, considering it was obvious this jack nut was keeping an eye on me. Instead, I felt the color drain from my face as I read the two words in the center, Torin Donnelly. I glanced up at Arnie.

"What's Donnelly's first name?"

My aunt grinned from ear to ear. "Donnelly? Isn't that your gentleman admirer? The one you shared a—"

"Drink with?" I interrupted giving her a look I hoped would shut her up. "Yep. That's the one."

She didn't take the hint.

"No dear, I'm talking about that wonderfully romantic kiss."

"You kissed Donnelly?" Arnie asked.

I groaned. "Technically no, Donnelly kissed me."

"Oh she kissed him back," Clara added.

"What part of kill him if you see him again don't you understand, Miss MacCann?"

Something in me snapped. Perhaps it was the result of the frigid weather, the icy air and the mounds of nearly impassable snow. Perhaps it was the fact I been forced to trudge through it all without a vehicle for days. Or perhaps it was just the events of the last couple weeks; being shot at, busting up my car, being blown into a wall, being ordered around by some whacko who knew way more about me than I was comfortable with, or having my dead brother's friend come to town that did it. Hell, it could have even been the fact that my boss had repaired my damaged car and refused to allow me to pay him back. My theory was it was all of those things plus the fact I couldn't get anything real out of Arnie about Donnelly, but whatever the cause of my building rage I'd had enough.

I slapped the paper down on the table, hard enough it caused my hand to sting and my Aunt Clara to nearly jump out of her chair.

"That's it!"

Arnie's eyes widened as I glared hard at him

"I've had enough of the secret crap. So either spill what you know about Donnelly or I quit."

"Price!" Clara exclaimed.

I shook my head at my aunt who looked horrified at the outburst, then turned back to my boss.

"Look, I'm grateful to you for giving me a job, fixing my car, and for the cam but I can't do the secret crap, okay? I want to know why you hate Donnelly enough to want him dead. I want to know why, if there's such animosity between the two of you, he felt the need to blow the damn house up to protect your ass. And I want to know why this guy is really here because it sure as hell isn't to visit my dead brother."

Arnie sighed. "I'd say go talk with your father but I'm betting the suggestion wouldn't fly very far with you, so sit back down and listen up."

I plopped back into my chair.

"Torin is Donnelly's first name. He's a freelancer which as you know is not necessarily a huge deal in this business."

"What's his specialty?" I asked before I could help myself.

Arnie gave me a stern look over his glasses. "Please don't interrupt. His specialty is the same as yours. Now, as I was saying, Donnelly is a freelancer, but he was recruited and trained under the guidance of one of your father's rivals. And before you think about raking me over the coals for the information, allow me to direct you back to your father for the particulars, all I will tell you is Donnelly's guidance came from a member high in government affairs."

I didn't need to question him further about the rival. My Dad hates both the government and their affairs, so I gave Arnie a nod to continue.

"About five years ago, Donnelly broke his connection with his mentor and both the United States and Irish governments. At least that's the rumor although I personally don't believe it. One does not simply get out of the government bed in which you lay, unless of course you trade it in for a grave. Your brother took him on as a partner shortly after and they worked closely together until about six months before Michael died."

I'd never heard my brother ever mention Donnelly, much less bring him around, but then again Michael kept a lot of his life private.

"So what caused the breakup?" I asked.

"The last job your brother worked. Word has it that Donnelly was one of the ones responsible for keeping the leader of a child trafficking ring under wraps which is why I still believe he has government ties."

I felt the color drain from my face. Flashes of Michael falling into the flames replayed in my head, followed by the slow motion feel of me running along the huge beams regardless of the dark and choking black smoke, jumping to a balcony I could barely see as bullets whizzed past me in the target's attempt to get away. He didn't. I'd killed the leader of the ring with one blow to the back of his head and then pushed his body over the railing to burn.

"But that's just rumor," Arnie continued. "All I know for sure is Michael tried to get Donnelly to help him with the job and he refused. Your father and I had to bail them both out of jail because of an altercation shortly before Donnelly skipped town. Funny thing is no charges were filed against either one of them even though the arrest report stated the fist fight had escalated to Donnelly putting a gun to your brother's head. The day I wanted you to take him to the airport was the first time I'd seen him since he was bailed out."

I studied the pizza in front of me and felt sick. I pushed the plate aside and took a deep breath, trying to keep my stomach in line.

"Do you really believe Donnelly was the one responsible for keeping a child molester and his ring hidden?"

Arnie sat still for a moment and then slowly shook his head. "If he were, your father would have killed him himself."

TWENTY-NINE

AFTER WORK I drove Clara back to the apartment in the Taurus. I'd never been so glad to be behind the wheel of my car since I'd bought it and to celebrate the event I made sure to warm the sucker up for a good fifteen minutes before we got in. As a result, the short trek home was so nice and cozy we sat in the parking lot for a few minutes just enjoying the warmth.

"A penny for your thoughts," Clara said.

I leaned my head back against the rest and sighed. "I was just thinking how Michael and I were never really close. We both just always kept to ourselves. I'd even believed we were kindred spirits in that way, like we had some unspoken connection which made our relationship so much better than the one I had with my sisters. But now, I'm not sure. Do you know I honestly couldn't tell you a single thing about his private life after he left home for college? Hell, I don't even remember anything meaningful once he got into high school."

Clara patted my gloved hand. "That certainly is a shame, dear."

"Yeah, it really is. Did you know about his friendship with Donnelly?"

Clara shook her head. "I'd never met him before until he came to visit the other day, but Arnie and your father did. What are you planning to do about the message? The ones you've gotten so far have pointed to someone in trouble. Are you going to help him?"

I closed my eyes for a moment, enjoying the warm air blowing on me, and pondered. I should call Dad, find out anything he knows about Donnelly and get his perspective on everything. Maybe he could add something Arnie couldn't, and then again, maybe I'd just be bringing up memories sure to ruin his Christmas. No, I wouldn't be calling him. I'd handle it on my own. I cracked my eyes open and looked at my aunt.

"I want you to do me a couple of favors, okay?"

Clara nodded, looking a little uncertain.

"First, I want you to promise me you won't breathe a word to anyone in the family about Donnelly, especially my parents. I don't know if Dad realizes he's back in town or not but I do not want to take a chance and rob him of his Christmas spirit, got it?"

Clara smiled. "I think that's very noble of you, dear. A tad bit naïve of course, but noble all the same."

I gave her a sideways glance. "What do you mean?"

"Well, your father and Arnie are very good friends so I'm sure he's been informed."

"Just assume he doesn't know, okay?"

"All right, then what else?"

"I need you to stay at the apartment while I go pay another visit to Donnelly."

Clara gave me a look of concern. "Price, I don't think going alone is such a good idea. Last time you were blown into a wall."

"I wasn't alone. Arnie was with me and so was Donnelly, which was the reason I was blown into the wall in the first place. I want you where it's safe, Aunt Clara. I don't think I could handle you getting hurt."

Clara heaved a sigh and nodded. "Well, I do have some baking to do, but you have to promise me something."

"What's that?"

"You will keep me informed. You won't just leave me to worry myself sick about you."

I nodded. "I promise."

I shut off the engine and we got out of the car, trudging against the cold to the door of my building. Clara shed her winter garb and headed to my kitchen, most likely to start the baking of the dreaded fruitcakes. I went to my bedroom to retrieve my gun, an extra clip of ammo, and a large pocket knife I kept tucked in my underwear drawer. I shed my coat and put on the shoulder holster, then checked my gun which Clara had been nice enough to return after Donnelly's visit. It was loaded with the safety clicked on so I secured it into the holster, pocketed the knife and put my coat back on.

"Please be careful," Clara said as I walked into the kitchen to tell her bye. "And I mean it, keep me informed."

I gave her a hug. "I will and I will. Just don't blow up my kitchen while I'm away."

She hugged back in a bearlike grip. "I love you, Price. Call if you need me."

I left the apartment on that note. My aunt's heart was definitely in the right place, but her specialty was in poison not weaponry or hand to hand combat, and given her age, I doubted she could be of much help aside from calling 911 should trouble arise.

Pushing the door of my building open, I headed out into the cold. The Taurus was still warm from the trip home but I cranked the heat up again anyway just in case whatever predicament Donnelly happened to be a part of required me to brave the freezing air. Part of me wanted to turn on the radio, maybe jam to something like AC/DC while I drove on down the highway to hell, but the rational part of my brain screamed for the solemn quiet and a chance to think things through. Logic won out.

Arnie still believed Donnelly was in the government circle, which could pose a serious problem for me. I'd spent my entire life avoiding the authorities. I sure as hell didn't want to be thrust in the middle of it now. However, the thought of having to gaze upon another corpse created by my failure made me sick to my stomach. What added to my nausea was the uncertainty of what had broken his friendship with my brother. If Donnelly was still a part of a government agency, why would he be covering up something as hideous as a child sex ring? Why would he refuse to help somebody take it down? None of it made any sense but I knew enough about government corruption and their sacrifice of a few for the benefit of many to make any agenda they had on the table work to their advantage. Donnelly could just be an unfortunate pawn in the process or he could very well be one of the sadistic brains behind it all. I could only hope I'd find out the truth and possibly save him from whatever trouble he was in. And if I could manage to do it without getting arrested, maimed, or killed, that would certainly be a plus too.

I slowed the car at the light and made the right turn which put me a few blocks away from the Ramada. Reaching for my cell phone, I flipped it open and then closed it back. Donnelly was probably still under a do not disturb alert and if front desk Charlie answered the phone, there was little chance my call would be patched to the room anyway. I turned into the lot and completed the circuit around the building, keeping my eyes peeled for anything out of the ordinary before I finally chose a spot close to the building's entrance and parked. I shut off the engine and got out.

Zipping up my coat to guard against the cutting wind and to hide the shoulder harness and gun, I entered the hotel lobby. The front entrance wasn't equipped with a metal detector or a guard of any kind so I wasn't worried about carrying. There was only a strategically placed sign posted near the door reminding patrons to please leave their weapons outside the building. It was painted with one of those nice handgun icons encircled in red with a slash right through in the same warning color. I walked on by. As expected, front desk Charlie was right where I'd left him at my last visit. He glanced up from the paper he was reading as I approached the counter and gave me the same smile he'd given me before.

"Long time, no see," he said. "You sure look chipper, looks like business is booming."

"You have no idea. Any problem with going on up?"

Charlie folded the newspaper and set it down on the desk in front of him, giving me his full attention.

"Mister Donnelly has asked not to be disturbed."

I leaned my elbows on the counter. "I'm afraid that train has left the station, Charlie. Do you work for him?"

Charlie chuckled. "Not unless he owns the Ramada."

"A friend? Family member?"

"Why do want to know?"

This time I smiled. "Well, I need to know how delicately I need to break it down for you. Let's try it again, okay? How much do you really like Donnelly?"

Charlie's smile faded, replaced by a look of concern. That concern bred the need to ease his suit jacket open, flashing a gun harness.

"Come on, Charlie, play nice. I'm not here to hurt you or anyone else, let alone Donnelly. Besides, what would your manager say if they found out you'd ignored the pretty sign at the door and brought a weapon into the hotel?"

"I know you're not a call girl," he said, moving his empty hand back where I could see it, "so who are you really?"

"Friend, nemesis, I'm not really sure. But your man Donnelly is in danger."

The old man gave me a sideway look. "Uh-huh. And let me guess, you are Bat Girl here to save the day?"

"Bat Girl is lame. Everyone knows Wonder Woman is the cool one."

Charlie chuckled and I grinned, glad I'd eased the tension.

"Look, Donnelly used to be a friend of my brother's. I don't really know why he's in town, but it doesn't really matter right now. Somebody's been leaking names to me of people who are in dire straits and Donnelly is the third one I've received. I was able to help the first.

The second one I was too late for, she was dead when I arrived. Please don't make this more difficult for me then it needs to be, okay? I just need to meet with Donnelly and find out what's going on." I paused with a sigh. "More than anything, I would love to be able to do this without violence of any kind."

Charlie gave me a nod. "Then you can go up, but there's one thing you should know."

"What's that?"

"He isn't there."

THIRTY

I'D TAKEN the room keycard Charlie had given me and headed on up via the elevator. The old man didn't know where Donnelly went any more than I did, but maybe there would be something up in his room to clue me in on his whereabouts. My goal was to search the room and if I turned up nothing, I'd pay Charlie another visit, see if he knew more about Donnelly than he was letting on. The old Price would have just leaned on him until he spilled all he knew, but I wasn't that person anymore and I sure as hell didn't want to cause an elderly man any undue stress even if it was to help someone else.

I stepped out of the elevator and closed the distance to Donnelly's door, sliding the keycard in. A small green light appeared on the reader with a simultaneous happy beep sound. I pulled the card out and opened the door as I stepped into the room. The bed had been made and the room cleaned, but a pile of Donnelly's clothes lay draped across the back of one of the dinette chairs. I closed the door behind me and unzipped my coat. I didn't take it off and I left my gloves on my hands in case this room became subject to a police search, no sense adding prints or more particulate evidence to place me in the mix. I set to work. The bed was first. I removed the linens and pillows, checking every nick and cranny of the mattress and boxed springs before I moved them off the frame which I also closely inspected. When it turned up nothing but dust the maid service had neglected to clean up, I put everything back as I'd found it and moved on to the night stands, the dresser, the tiny refrigerator, and then the dinette set.

I went through the clothing draped over the chair, piece by piece, checking pockets, seams, any place where someone like Donnelly might hide something important. Nothing. I stepped into the bathroom where the maid service had evidently made their mark, clean towels, new Styrofoam cups, and so forth. On the bathroom counter in a neat line against the mirror stood Donnelly's black zipped-up toiletry kit, a can of shaving cream, a bottle of aftershave, a tube of hair gel, and an open plastic bag of disposable razors. This I found a bit weird since Donnelly sported a beard and mustache, but since he seemed to keep his facial hair neat and trim, I let it go. I unzipped the toiletry kit to see toothbrush and paste, dental floss, a small bottle of mouthwash, deodorant in the fragrance of sport, and a small unopened box of Trojan Magnum XL condoms. I felt my cheeks flush for some odd reason. It wasn't like I hadn't seen a condom before, but Magnum? Shit.

I set the items aside and inspected the toiletry pack itself, looking for obscure pockets, checking the seams and the cloth sides for any out of ordinary bulges. When I'd satisfied my curiosity, I checked the items I'd pulled out, including the condoms which were still sealed in the box, before putting them all back inside the way I'd found them and zipping the kit up. After a complete search of the bathroom and everything in it, I tackled Donnelly's suit case. I was just about to inspect a rolled up pair of briefs when I heard a knock at the door.

Moving to the peep hole, I saw the knocker was Charlie. I opened the door.

"Why didn't you just use the master key?" I asked him.

"It's policy to knock first. Did you find anything?"

I shook my head. "Nothing useful yet, I was just about to look through his suitcase. Care to join me?"

Charlie sat down on the end of the bed. "As far as I'm concerned, I don't even know you're here."

"Got it. What is your relationship with him anyway?"

"Friend, we used to be coworkers."

"Government?"

He nodded.

"What agency?" I asked.

He gave me a wink. "If I tell you, I'd have to kill you."

I pulled out the rolled briefs and the rest of Donnelly's undergarments and clothes, unrolling, inspecting, and then rolling them back up. When the suitcase was empty, I set to looking for secret compartments or anything else which might be hidden in the case.

"What made you trust me?" I asked Charlie, more to pass the tedious time than really desiring an answer.

"Donnelly."

I glanced up at the old man. "What do you mean?"

"Donnelly instructed me to trust you. He said if you came by, needing anything, to give it you."

"Okay," I drew the word out a little bit as I tried to process his answer, "then why the shakedown at the front desk? That doesn't sound like trust to me."

Charlie shrugged. "Old habits die hard in crotchety old men like me. Besides, I don't take orders from Donnelly. What kind of trouble do you think he's in?"

I sighed, repacking the suitcase as I found it. "The fatal kind. I wish I could tell you more, but the truth is I don't know anything else. I know he and my brother were friends for several years before the relationship went to pot. I don't know what happened for sure and to be honest, I don't know how or why they were friends in the first place. My brother had the same aversion to government affairs I have."

Charlie gave me light-hearted grin. "We're not all bad, you know?"

I kept my comment to myself. "Do you know why Donnelly was in town?"

He shook his head. "The only thing he actually confided in me was to trust you, and that was after you'd stomped out of here the other night in a hissy fit."

I blushed. "Uh, yeah. Sorry about that."

"I know him well enough to know he doesn't do the hooker thing and you were upset enough to prove to me he didn't pay for the company."

"Has anyone else been up to see him?"

"Not on my shift, but it doesn't mean anything."

I took a couple steps toward the door as Charlie got to his feet. I turned back to face him. "If you know where he might have gone then now's the time to tell me."

"I wish I knew. Do you have a number in case he comes back?"

I scribbled down my cell phone number using a pen and a pad of note paper from one of the night stand drawers and handed it over to Charlie.

"If he comes back, call me. If anyone comes looking for him, call me. If you see, hear, or smell anything out of the ordinary for this place, call me. Got it?"

Charlie smiled and gave me a mock salute. "Yes ma'am."

"And don't call me ma'am," I growled.

"Donnelly never gave me your name, so what do I call you, Wonder Woman?"

"MacCann," I replied, giving Charlie the old James Bond routine. "Price MacCann."

I could have sworn there was a slight glimmer of something like recognition in his eyes when I told him my name, but he covered it quickly and escorted me out of the room and back down to the lobby, changing the subject entirely away from Donnelly. I should have questioned him further, but if whatever was threatening Donnelly followed the same pattern as before then I really was running out of time to help. I gave Charlie my thanks instead of a hard time and reminded him to call should anything change. I didn't bother to suggest he get Donnelly up to speed on the threat should he see him before I did. If he really was a friend, a suggestion wouldn't be needed.

Back in my Taurus, I started the engine just as my cell phone rang. I glanced down at the display and flipped it open to answer.

"Hey Arnie, what's up?"

"Find him?" he asked.

"Nope, not at the Ramada anyway, if he left town, he did it without his suitcase. You got any ideas where I might find him?"

The phone was silent for a moment but I could hear my boss's gears a-turning, whether he'd come back with a useful suggestion or a snide comment I had no idea.

"Try X-Stay-C out on Buford."

I groaned. "The strip joint?"

"You asked me, remember?"

He hung up and I closed my phone, setting it down into the console next to me. Shedding my gloves and coat, I strapped on my seatbelt and set the car into motion.

"I am so not in the mood for boobs and ass," I grumbled. "Merry Christmas and Happy New Year, Price."

I pressed the power button on the stereo, forewent the radio lottery of anything I wanted to hear actually being broadcasted, and slid an AC/DC disk into the player, cranking the volume up loud enough to match my mood. The opening chords careened into my ears as Highway to Hell began and when I heard Bon Scott's signature voice come in, I let out the breath I didn't even know I'd been holding.

THIRTY-ONE

AS SOON AS I'd made the turn onto Buford, the bright and extremely tacky neon sign greeted me. It was one of those signs you would have expected to see more on the Las Vegas strip than in a small city like this one. Regardless, there it stood towering over top the metal-sided building, X-Stay-C in lights so bright it made me wonder if the city's zoning committee had all been tying one on when they passed the request for this monstrosity. Below the flashing neon name was an electronic billboard with a black background, a computerized image of a woman dancing topless with only a g-string to cover her digital modesty. She moved in provocative ways for her audience, beckoning them to come in like the Sirens of old (if the Sirens were hookers, of course).

I gave a shudder and turned into the lot, shutting my car off and getting out. I wasn't a prude but my sexuality focused more on the aspect of love rather than following pure carnal desire. I'd had a one night stand or two before and it just didn't do a lot for me. Both times the sex had been great, but it just wasn't me. I needed an actual connection with my partner. I wasn't a saint but going to the door felt a whole lot like approaching the gates of Sodom or Gomorrah. I mentally ducked as I entered the building, hoping God didn't decide to rain fire on the joint before I could find Donnelly and get out.

"Hey there, babe."

I glanced at the muscle head guarding the entrance. His hot pink tee shirt was nearly bursting at its seams trying to cover the bulge of his steroid induced musculature. Like a lot of men these days, he'd shaved his head. I had to choke back a laugh. He looked like a hot pink dick.

"Hey there back," I replied. "Have you been on shift long?"

"All night, sweetie, got a break coming up soon if you're interested."

"No, but thanks for the offer. Have you seen any dark-headed bearded guys come through tonight?"

"We've had a couple, why? Looking for your old man?"

This time I did laugh.

Pink Dick's eyes lit up with interest. "No old man, huh? So which way do you swing, baby?"

I ignored the question which was both rude and inappropriate. "How much to get inside?"

He grinned. "Ten dollars, but if you join me for break, then I'll let you in for free."

I gave him a ten dollar bill and a smile which felt like a grimace. "I'll pay my own way thanks."

Muscle head gave a shrug and opened the door for me. Fortunately, the music was so loud I didn't hear his parting remark. Unfortunately, X-Stay-C had decided now was the time to get festive and the song blaring through the speakers was the original recording of Santa Baby with Ertha Kitt singing about hurrying down the chimney tonight. I glanced through the crowd of packed tables to the bar side which encircled the entire stage, every stool was occupied with horny men and women waving dollar bills in the air as Mrs. Claus removed her Santa-like oversized coat to reveal a red thong trimmed in white fur. She, Claus's missus, sported a pair of red sequined pasties complete with tufts of white fur in the center which covered the nipples of her very large (and obviously surgically enhanced) breasts. There was no hint of jealousy in the observation. I just knew enough about gravity to know boobs that large do not stand up and out like that without assistance.

Mrs. Claus shimmed around, putting her back to the audience and then proceeded to get down on all fours, twerking to the slow beat of the song just a foot from where a group of males whistled and hooted. I diverted my attention away from the stage and moved from table to table checking out the patrons who were all watching the routine with hormone filled comfort and joy. Who says Christmas can't be fun?

The lighting in the place wasn't the best for getting any real detail of the people inside with the strobe effect reflecting off the stage in some areas (which was probably what the owner was going for) but I strolled along the front anyway, checking the bar stool people for anyone resembling Donnelly's sex, build, or what I could make out of appearance. I got nothing except for a pat on my ass by a guy who was three sheets to the wind and smelled like his own distillery. I let it go and moved on, circling the huge room until I spotted Santa Claus sitting at a table near the far back corner. I took a seat in an empty chair beside him.

"Price, what are you doing here?"

I gave Santa a sly smile. "I guess I just needed to see if the real Santa was going to twerk on the stage with Mrs. Claus. Oh and please give me a wink and nod if you plan on keeping your sexy boots on when you do."

I knew Jonas blushed without actually seeing it.

"Hey, I just needed to wind down before I headed home."

"It's all right your secret is safe with me."

"Well, I know you're not here for the show, so who are you looking for?"

"A guy named Donnelly; tall, dark hair, beard and moustache, usually wears coveralls and toboggans just to be sexy. Arnie said I might find him here, but in this crowd I really can't see squat."

"Yeah, the Christmas show is pretty popular."

I glanced up with a wince as Mrs. Claus left the stage with a final ass shake only to be quickly replaced by a completely topless lady elf with pointed shoes. In her hand was a red leash and at the end of the leash was a real-life reindeer with its nose painted red. I just shook my head as Rudolph the Red Nosed Reindeer began blasting through the speakers. The elf danced, gyrated, and twerked all around the poor beast.

"This is disgusting, Jonas."

He gave me a wink. "Yes, but it's been a Christmas tradition for years."

"Ho. Ho. Whore. Yeah, I can see the appeal. But since I've already had my dose of annual porn for the year, can you tell me if you've seen this guy so I can get the hell out of here?"

"Seen who?"

I groaned. "Jonas, look at me. Come on now pull your eyes away from the nasty lady on the stage and pay attention. Good. Have you seen the tall, dark, and coveralled guy I just described?"

"Donnelly?"

"Yes."

"Of course, he's standing right behind you."

I whipped around in the chair to see a clean shaven Donnelly indeed standing behind me. The loss of beard and mustache was enough of a change to his appearance I probably wouldn't have been able to pick him out of the packed house even in perfect lighting. He'd forgone the coveralls, replacing them with dark colored jeans, sweater, and leather jacket.

"Hello MacCann," Donnelly said with a grin as he pulled an empty chair from the table next to us and plopped down. "What's a beautiful lady like you doing in a dive like this?"

Jonas leaned forward. "Do you guys want some privacy?"

"No," I replied, "you're fine where you are."

Donnelly scooted the chair closer to me. "Do you come here often?"

I grit my teeth. "Apparently not as often as you because Arnie sent me here."

"I'll have to thank him when I see him."

"I'm not here for hank or pank, Donnelly. If I wanted that, I'd have taken the pink dick at the door up on his proposal."

"So why are you here?"

"Looking for you," I replied. "Remember my messenger?"

Donnelly gave a slow nod.

"Well, Merry Christmas. You just made his list. Your name was on the paper he left at my door last night."

Jonas leaned in closer. "What are you talking about, Price?"

I quickly filled him in as best as I could, sometimes having to raise the volume of my voice to be heard over the blasting music.

"Have you told your Dad about this?" Jonas asked.

"He knows some of it," I replied, "but not the latest about Donnelly. I didn't want to ruin his Christmas by dredging up stuff about Michael."

I glanced over at Donnelly and caught a hint of sadness in his eyes, somehow the lighting played around just at the right moment.

"I thought you were going for a normal life?" Jonas asked.

I rolled my eyes. "I didn't go looking for this. It came to my door. If I had my way, I'd be back at my apartment helping my aunt bake fruit cakes."

I felt Donnelly shudder next to me.

"Exactly," I said.

"Hey, I love Clara's fruitcakes," Jonas said. "I look forward to them every year."

Both of us stared at Jonas as if he had corn growing out of his ears.

"She soaks them in Kentucky bourbon, so don't knock it till you try it."

"Let's get back to Donnelly and his impending doom, okay?"

"Sure," Jonas replied, "but hurry it up if you can, the next act is Frosty the Snowman."

I groaned. Oh, dear Lord let get out of here before they desecrate another holiday icon.

THIRTY-TWO

WHEN I WAS A LITTLE GIRL, my Dad would always make a point to read the 'Twas the Night Before Christmas poem to all four of us kids right before we were tucked into our beds to anxiously await the arrival of Saint Nick, his reindeer, and all of the toys we had wished for during the year. It was one of the most clichéd, yet memorable, traditions for me and I took a bit of the peace and tranquility it offered wherever I went, through whatever challenges life had thrown at me. It also was the one seed of normality from my childhood I hoped would somehow breed more of its kind. I'd never been the sort of girl to wish for the American dream of a loving husband, two point whatever kids, a cat and dog, a house with a garage, and so forth, but I had dreamed of a life where the topic of discussion did not revolve around assassination or any other types of actions considered to be taboo.

But as I sat in the chair beside Donnelly and across from Jonas, trying with all of my might not to look in the direction of X-Stay-C's stage while Frosty bared all of her buttons to show the audience there really was something beneath all the snow, I realized not only had God not granted my prayer to remain outside of tabooed subjects but also he seemed to be telling me that my dream for normality was just a wee bit out of my reach.

"What do you propose I do, MacCann, hide out until your mystery guy sends you an all-clear message?"

"Well, yeah, that's exactly what I propose."

Donnelly shook his head. "It's not happening. There's no way I'm tucking myself away and leaving you to figure out what's going on by yourself."

"Very noble of you," I replied, "but I'm not impressed by your idiotic chivalry."

He leaned his shoulder against mine and I smelled the sweet musky scent of his aftershave. I felt his breath in my ear.

"So if chivalry doesn't do it for you, what would impress you?"

"Well," I breathed, focusing my attention on Jonas to keep my own raging hormones in check (if I pictured this Santa naked, well that should do the trick), "I guess what would impress me most is to not have to look at your battered and bloody corpse this close to Christmas."

Donnelly eased up off of my shoulder. "Got it."

"Good. Jonas how fortified is your place?" I asked as I mentally wiped Santa's naked image from my troubled brain.

"It depends. I don't know what we're dealing with any more than you do. So I can't assure you of anything."

I pondered for a moment. Jonas was right. Without knowing what trouble was chasing Donnelly, hiding him out at Jonas's place might not be such a great idea. I wasn't any more certain of Jonas's skills than I was of Clara's. Arnie was out of the question for the very same reason, plus their dislike of one another only spelled disaster. After a brain wracking moment, I came to the only obvious solution.

"Looks like you're coming home with me then."

Donnelly's mouth stretched out into a shit-eating grin. I did not smile.

"This if for your protection only, so don't get any stupid ideas or I'll sick Aunt Clara on you."

"I think Clara likes me," he replied.

"She likes everybody."

"Well," Jonas said, "now that that's all settled, how about we all sit back and enjoy the show?"

I looked up at the stage to see stripper Frosty waving her top hat in the air while she bounced her black button pasty boobs all around. "How about we don't and say we did."

I grabbed Donnelly's hand and pulled him to his feet. Thankfully, he didn't object and together we left Jonas to enjoy the tacky show all on his own.

"I KNOW, dear, but why didn't you just bring Jonas along with you? It would have saved me the trouble of shipping his fruitcake to him. Oh, and speaking of that, the FedEx guy came here and I sent your packages with him to Mom's house for Christmas dinner."

I thanked her for shipping the presents and then added, "Trust me, a team of wild horses couldn't have pulled Jonas out of his seat."

Donnelly shrugged off his leather coat. "It's a great show, MacCann. I'm actually sorry we left before it was over."

I wrinkled my nose. "It's disgusting."

Aunt Clara's eyes sparkled. "It's legendary."

I glanced past my aunt to the line of fruitcakes sitting on little cardboard platters all along the length of my kitchen counter. The smell of alcohol was pretty strong, so I'd noticed it immediately when I opened my door. But since I knew what she'd been baking, I didn't comment on the fact it smelled a lot like the strip joint I'd just left, minus the scent of horny of course. At the back corner of the counter, sat a closed white cake box, far enough from the other cakes to incite suspicion. I shed my winter garb and moved to the counter intent on opening the box. Aunt Clara cleared her throat and I looked her way with raised brows.

"Not that one dear."

I stood there waiting, almost dreading what I was sure to hear next.

"You've limited my options so I had to improvise."

"And what, pray tell, is in the box?" I asked.

"Oh it's a fruitcake, my special recipe," Clara replied. She turned to Donnelly. "How about I brew a nice pot of coffee to warm you up?"

"Sounds great," Donnelly said, taking a seat at the table.

Clara moved to the sink to fill the decanter with water as I closed in on the white box, lifting the lid to see a fruitcake completely encased in plastic stretch wrap and sitting snuggly on a cardboard platter. I avoided fruitcake as a general rule in life. And because of that, I'd never opened one of my aunt's boxes before whenever the friendly UPS guys delivered them to our front door, so I had no idea if wrapping them in plastic was the norm but something just didn't set right for some reason.

"Why is this one so special?" I asked.

Clara flicked her eyes to Donnelly and then back to me as if to remind me we shouldn't discuss such things in front of company.

I grimaced. "I'm sure he's heard worse."

Clara gave Donnelly an apologetic smile and shrugged. "Like I said, my options were limited so I had to improvise."

"What's in the cake, Clara?"

"Fruit."

"And?"

"Nuts."

I let the lid of the box fall, turned to face my aunt who was busying herself with making the coffee, and crossed my arms.

"And?"

"Well, let me see. There's flour, sugar, butter, bourbon of course..."

I tapped my foot. "Yes, but what's the secret ingredient?"

She gave me a sheepish grin and set the coffee to brew. "Oh nothing too concerning, just a little bean powder, dear."

"Bean powder? I'm guessing it's not from a green bean."

Clara giggled. "Now that would just be silly. Who would put green bean powder in a fruitcake?"

I glanced over my shoulder at Donnelly who appeared to be very amused by our conversation.

"What kind of bean, Clara?"

She sighed, knowing I wouldn't let up. "Castor."

I groaned, plopping down in one of the chairs as I felt the twinge of a headache coming on. "You put ricin in the cake?"

"Only a little."

"You only need a little," I grumbled.

Donnelly laughed. "Your aunt's like that guy on Breaking Bad."

I shot him a look of reproach. "It's not funny."

"Now don't blame me, Price. Ricin is never my first choice, but you've limited my options."

I rubbed my head as I thought about the Changaa I'd forbidden her to brew in my apartment and the baneberries I'd disposed of into the garbage can.

"What have you got against ricin?" Donnelly asked, genuinely interested. "I mean, it's pretty much undetectable, right?"

"True," Clara replied, "but it's extremely unpredictable and you basically have to hope for a misdiagnoses should the partaker seek medical treatment. Besides, it takes longer. I find waiting for organs to fail quite tedious."

"Interesting," he said. "So what's your basic go-to then?"

I glared at Donnelly. "Seriously?"

"What?"

"You're seriously having this conversation right now? Don't you think you've got enough on your plate? I mean, somebody out there is probably getting ready to kill you and here you sit shooting the shit about poisons—"

Clara interrupted me. "But we aren't discussing poisons, dear, ricin is a toxin."

"What?"

"Well, toxins are always naturally produced, while poisons can be natural or synthetic."

"Semantics," I grumbled. "Tell me who the mark is or dispose of the cake. I'm not keen on having poisonous toxins just sitting around on my kitchen counter."

Clara sighed. "It's for your father."

My jaw dropped.

"No dear, I mean the cake is for your father to use, not eat. He requested my help with one of his projects but he didn't tell me who it was for and I've been trying to oblige him ever since I got here but you keep stifling my efforts." She gave me a serious look. "You are very difficult to work around."

"Clara, what part of I'm not working for my family anymore do you not understand?"

"But it's for your father and it is Christmas after all. Doesn't that count for anything?"

I grit my teeth. "Sure it does. It counts for peace and goodwill towards men, not toxins in the freaking fruit cake, and certainly not bloody diarrhea, organ failure, or death. For goodness sake, buy him a tie like I did."

Donnelly grinned. "You bought your Dad a tie for Christmas?"

"He likes ties," I said defensively.

"It's okay," he said, "just chill. If you want to give your father a tie, give him a tie."

"I will."

"Do you want me to throw the cake out?" Clara asked, disappointed.

"No," I replied with a sigh. "With my luck, some homeless guy would decide to rifle through my trash and eat it. Just send it to Dad and let him deal with it."

"How wonderful!" she exclaimed just as the coffee pot beeped, sounding the end of the brewing process and the end to the conversation.

THIRTY-THREE

CLARA BEGAN her death gurgling snore at about two in the morning, which was barely an hour after I'd finally drifted off. Unfortunately, there wasn't a wall or a closed door to muffle it in any way. She'd fell asleep in my living room chair and since Donnelly was lounging on one side of the couch with his feet up on the coffee table and I was on the other side stretched out long ways, the noise startled the living crap out of me. There are just some things which should not be experienced through surround sound.

I opened my eyes to see her head lulled off to the side and her mouth gaped open as she sucked in and blew out air with much the same vigor as a congested chain saw. Groaning, I pulled the afghan off of me and set it aside as I got up. Donnelly was supposed to be on watch while I napped, but it looked like the only thing he was watching was the inside of his eyelids. I nudged him in the leg with my knee but he didn't open his eyes.

"I'm not asleep."

"Looks like it to me."

"I'm just resting my eyes."

"Yeah and Clara's just resting hers," I mumbled as I went to the bathroom.

I finished up my business by splashing cold water on my face, trying to revive myself a bit before returning to the couch. Donnelly was engaged in a good standing stretch with his arms above his head and his back arched. He released it and gave me a sly grin as I plopped down.

"Come here often?"

"Too early for a pickup line, Casanova," I mumbled. "Did you catch anything on the cam?"

He shook his head. "Not really. Your neighbor across the hall came in shortly after you fell off to sleep. She looks quite the peach."

"That's Jasmine Grey."

"Sounds like a stripper name."

I shrugged. "I don't know her well enough to say what she does for sure but the word from one of the maintenance guys is she's a lawyer."

Donnelly chuckled. "The word from maintenance? Well there's a reliable source. Don't you care who your neighbors are?"

"Not really, at least not until I started getting the crazy notes anyway, before I didn't care who they were as long as they kept quiet and away from me."

Donnelly glanced at the television for a moment which was playing some old John Wayne western with the volume barely up. When he looked back at me, I detected a hint of sadness is his eyes.

"I am really sorry about Michael. He was a good a friend of mine."

I wanted to ask him if he was such a good friend then why didn't he help on Michael's last job, but it would just make me sound like a spiteful bitch.

"What happened between you two anyway? Arnie said you guys broke it off?"

"How much do you know?"

I yawned and rubbed my eyes. "I know Dad and Arnie bailed

both of you out of jail for bar brawling. Arnie mentioned you put a gun to my brother's head and said you skipped town after."

He sighed. "Best leave it there."

I sat there for a moment watching John Wayne tilt his cowboy hat at some pretty little lady as she promenaded past him in some one horse town off in the land of television make believe. Dad and Michael were always watching Westerns when I was younger. I guess Donnelly was a fan of them as well.

"What else *is* there?" I asked.

Donnelly paused. "How much do you really know about your brother, MacCann?"

I shrugged. "Not a lot after he became a big boy and moved out on his own, I mean, we'd see each other on holidays and stuff, but to be honest, I didn't even know you existed."

Donnelly paused while Aunt Clara's snoring rose to a mighty crescendo, then muted down a bit to a couple of snorts as she readjusted her sleeping position in the chair.

"Michael wanted to introduce us but I was the one who refused."

"Why? Wait a minute, were you too involved?"

He laughed and shook his head. "No, we both played for team female."

"Then why didn't you want to meet me?"

Donnelly sighed. "I've met your Dad, Mom, the twins and most of your family, except for Clara over there. I've even spent time at your grandparent's house. I think you were away on a job in Cancun at the time. It was on your Independence Day about three years ago."

I'd done several jobs in Cancun. For some reason it was one of the hot spots where the dregs of humanity all seemed to fly after they'd finished wrecking their bit of havoc on American society.

"Your family thinks very highly of you. Price this, Price that. It was as intimidating as it was entertaining. By the way, I've seen you naked."

I felt my face flush. "What?"

He laughed. "Baby pictures, your Mom was passing photo

albums around while the burgers cooked. I guess she forgot to take the ones out of you showing your tiny bum in the bathtub"

"Oh my God, she *didn't?*"

"She did. So, as I'm looking at your baby bum and listening to your family tell childhood stories of you, I think 'Donnelly, this woman is way out of your league. And since you've nothing to offer her worth having, it's best you just stay under wraps.' And so I asked Michael not to breathe a word about me to you."

I felt a grimace coming on. "Oh, I see, because you thought if I met your tall, dark and handsome Irish self, I'd just fall in love and drop everything to pine over you? And you'd have to break my heart by telling me it's not you, it's me?"

Donnelly laughed. "You're brutal. You know that?"

I gave shrug. "I thought you said you'd come back to town for Michael."

"Aye," he replied with a sad sigh. "Your brother and I did have a falling out six months before he died and I did leave town, but I got a call from him the morning of Thanksgiving. He filled me in on what he'd be asking you to do and then told me he would be following to make sure the target didn't pull a fast one and get away. I told him it was a bad idea to put you on it and an even worse idea for him to tail you. The mark had a security detail team protecting him a mile long, but Michael said you'd probably be more than willing to take it on just as an excuse to get out of the family event and you wouldn't fail the kill."

I felt guilt rear its ugly head. Donnelly must have sensed it.

"Family crap is always hard to deal with, MacCann, so don't sweat it. I'm not thrilled to go to family gatherings either. Anyway, your brother asked a favor of me and I obliged."

"What was the favor?"

"Michael wanted me to keep an eye on you if anything happened to him, just to make sure you're okay."

I leveled my gaze at him. "If you guys weren't friends, why would he ask that?"

"He knew I'd keep my word because he knew how I felt about you."

I sat silent for a moment completely unsure of how I felt about the confession. Part of me wanted nothing more than to be held in his arms and feel loved no matter what may come along the way. And part of me knew better. A relationship right now would more than likely end flat, with both of us feeling disappointed and resentful. It was out of the question. I leaned back and rubbed my tired eyes, opting to change the subject.

"So who could possibly want to do you harm?"

He looked a little disappointed at the change in topic, but covered it quickly with a smirk.

"You better get a pad and pen for that."

THIRTY-FOUR

I WAS STANDING guard for the rest of the night, keeping tabs on my computer cam in case anything changed. Since the system failed me once already, I made sure to check my peephole ever so often to double check. I don't know what the messenger did to prevent his/her presence from being on the cam when the last note was delivered, at least nothing concrete anyway although I did have a few theories running through my head, but whatever it was, it didn't seem to be affecting the cam now. I added on perimeter window checks around my entire apartment just to be safe. Donnelly had moved from resting his eyes to sleeping honest about an hour after I'd taken over watch. When the sun began stretching its rays over the horizon, Clara's eyes popped open like a rooster fixing to crow. She smiled at me as she got up folding the blanket she'd used to keep warm during her snore-fest.

I'd already put the coffee on, so the aroma was wafting through the air and giving my place a homey early morning feel like those Folger's commercials. Too bad I couldn't afford Folger's at the moment. So the best part of waking up would be store brand in your cup.

"Good morning," Clara beamed.

"It is morning but I don't know about the good yet, too early to tell."

"Well, just let me freshen up and I'll be right out to cook us some breakfast."

Clara waddled off to the bathroom and shut the door just as Donnelly's cell phone started chirping on the side table next to him. He threw an arm over and plucked it up, swiping the screen with his thumb before he even cracked his eyes open. I watched him heave a sigh and get up as he swiped the phone again and tucked it into his pocket.

"I have to go," he said with a yawn and a stretch.

"We still don't know what we're dealing with yet," I reminded him.

He gave me a sly grin. "You're worried about me, aren't you? No, don't deny it. I see it in your eyes."

"That's sleep deprivation. Look, I just think you should lay low for a while, let me try and find out what's going on."

"Admit it. You think I'm sexy."

"That's beside the point."

He leaned in and brushed his lips lightly on my cheek. It sent tingles rocketing through me as his dark eyes met mine.

"I appreciate your concern, but I'm not one to hide away for very long. Thanks for letting me crash on your couch."

I started to argue, tell him how stupid he was being, but I didn't. Something inside me urged me to let it go and wait. All I did manage was to ask if he was armed.

"Never leave home without it," he replied. "I'll call if things get too hairy."

I peered at my computer screen watching him disappear down my hall. I was still staring at it when Clara emmerged from the bathroom a short time later, ready to tackle breakfast duty.

"Where'd Mister Donnelly go off to?"

I told her, not taking my eyes off the screen.

"Well, that's not very wise. Didn't you try to stop him?"

"Not really."

Clara sidled up next to me to see what held my attention.

"And just why not?"

On the screen was a view of my across-the-hall neighbor's door. It opened and Jasmine Grey came out, dressed in casual jeans, boots, and a black pea coat. I watched her shut the door and begin walking down the hall.

"That's why," I replied, plucking up my shoulder harness and gun, strapping it on quickly, and shrugging on my coat. "Stay here and keep an eye on the cam."

"Where are you going?"

"Fishing," I replied as I went out the door. "I'll give you a call when I catch something."

There had been quite a few thoughts circling my tired brain all through the night, one of those being Donnelly's comment about Jasmine Grey being quite the peach. It was a benign statement which anybody else would have probably disregarded as soon as it was said, but somehow I'd managed to observe a very slight change in his facial expression when he said it and it was enough for my mind to replay the scene a couple of times as I stood sentry over my guests.

I made my way through the front entrance of the building and immediately spotted Jasmine next to her car, opening the door and getting in. Donnelly had vanished out of sight. I waited as she started the engine, letting it idle for a few moments before she backed out and left the lot. I headed to my Taurus to do the same. Early morning traffic any day of the week is a bitch in my area so I wasn't in a hurry for fear of losing her, besides her red Audi stood out like a beacon anyway. I maneuvered in behind her about three cars back and waited on the stoplight. When it changed I followed her through the intersection and down the next two until she made a right turn on State Avenue. The cars ahead of me continued a straight path, so I approached the turn at a slower speed to put some distance between me and Grey's Audi. State Avenue is comprised of mostly businesses, the few homes nestled amongst the office complexes, service stations, and the occasional fast food joints were occupied by an older generation of folks who'd yet to sell out to commercial zoning.

The Audi veered right in the turning lane for Kabodo Drive which is actually just a small inlet to a huge building full of offices, at least that's what it is supposed to be when they finish construction. From what I could tell, they'd managed to erect the bare bones of the place, but things like glass panes in the windows had yet to be installed. The parking lot was paved but unmarked for spaces and there were several work trucks and mechanical apparatuses I couldn't begin to name scattered at various intervals. At the far corner closest to the building, I spotted a black SUV. Jasmine made her turn into the lot and I went straight on, passing Kabodo before turning right at the next lot which just happened to be for a fast food place. I parked in one of the few spots left and got out, making my way out of the lot and over to Kobodo on foot via a pathway which had probably been shoveled out by hungry construction workers. The Audi was parked next to the SUV where Jasmine stood at its driver's side window.

I took a position behind a huge generator strapped to a trailer and watched, noticing the serious expression on Jasmine's face as she spoke to the driver who I couldn't see from my current angle of sight. After a few minutes, Jasmine climbed back into her car and left. The SUV stayed put and so did I, watching and waiting. Finally, the engine started and it backed up, slowly making its way past me. The driver was wearing a dark colored toboggan, a pair of wrap-around sunglasses, and a beard, much like Donnelly had when I'd first met him. His complexion was a much lighter shade and I immediately noticed the difference. The vehicle slowed at the entrance of the lot and I caught sight of the Government Issue license plate, reciting it in my head a few times as it drove off. I quickly went back to my car and headed out after it.

Tailing a black SUV these days in a city full of them is a little more challenging than tailing a red Audi. I moved in behind it about three cars back and followed it onto State Avenue and then onto

Main before I pulled out my phone and dialed a number I hadn't used in well over a year. It rang a couple times before connecting.

"Hello."

"Hey Uncle Vinnie, it's Price."

"Hey Price, how are you doing sweetie?"

"I'm fine. Look, I need a quick favor. I'm tailing an SUV with government plates and I would really love it if you could track it down for me and get a name."

"Wonderful. I guess that means you're back in the business?"

"Well," I replied with a sigh, "technically no. Do you mind running it anyway?"

"Sure. Just give me a minute to get into my study."

I waited until he gave me the okay and then spouted the number off just as I veered onto the interstate ramp, still a few cars behind the SUV. The cars ahead of me were content to stay in the right lane and I cruised in behind them, grateful for the cover. Vinnie's voice came into my ear about a mile later.

"Where are you right now?"

"A mile off ramp twenty-two," I replied. "I've got a three car cushion. Why?"

"Keep it," he said. "The SUV is one of ours."

In this case, one of *ours* meant CIA. Vinnie may have retired and moved on to freelancing but he'd kept all of his old agency contacts, making him a great resource for my former line of work.

"Can you trace the driver?" I asked.

"It's assigned to Agent Black."

"Seriously?"

"I'm serious. Jessup Black is the name. He must be pretty new to the agency. I've never heard of him before. Wait a minute and let me peek into the records."

Another mile and I heard Vinnie heave a sigh. "Why are you tailing this guy, Price?"

I told him.

"You're running on a hunch?"

"Yep."

"I suggest hanging back for a while."

"Why? What have you got?"

"Not a fucking thing. This guy's a blank sheet. Give me a little bit and let me see if can dig up something from one of my contacts."

He hung up before I could get a word in edgewise, which was not at all like my uncle.

THIRTY-FIVE

THE CELL PHONE trilled against my leg and I looked down at the display. It was Arnie. I glanced over at my dashboard clock to see it was after nine o'clock, had a slight moment of panic at the thought of being late for work and then felt like an idiot when I did a quick mental calendar check. It was Sunday. I exhaled in relief and answered the phone.

"Hey, Arnie, what's up?"

"Good morning Miss MacCann. Sorry to call you so early on a day of rest, but I need to ask a favor from you."

"What do you need?"

"Well, under normal circumstances I would refuse to open the store on a Sunday, but I am making an exception today because of a couple of requests I received last night. Feel free to say no of course, but would you be so kind as to come in to work today?"

"Uh, sure," I replied. "Give me a little bit though. I'm tailing someone."

I heard the sound of silence on the line and wondered if my phone had dropped the call until he asked, "Would you please be so kind to tell me what the devil is going on? Is Donnelly with you?"

Traffic was moving pretty steadily, so I propped the phone against my chin and set the cruise control. I filled Arnie in on Donnelly's reaction to seeing Jasmine Grey and then Grey's rendezvous with Agent Black in the parking lot.

"Vinnie's got nothing for me but a name. Why wouldn't the CIA have a file on him?"

"Miss MacCann, I could have sworn your goal was to live a normal life, feel free to correct me if I'm wrong."

"Normal people don't have whacks leaving anonymous notes at their door, Arnie."

"Oh, I'm certain many of them do, but normal people call the police instead of tailing a covert operative. What do you know about Grey?"

"Second hand info, she's a lawyer. What she's doing meeting with an under the table agent, I've no idea."

"My advice is to scale back off the agent. Those federal types get a little edgy when they're being followed."

"You sound like Uncle Vinnie," I said.

"If Vinnie is wary, you should be too."

I heaved a sigh and conceded. "Okay. I'll circle back and be at the store as soon as I can."

"I look forward to your arrival," he replied and then hung up.

Setting the phone between my legs, I changed to the passing lane and moved past the three cars ahead of me and then the SUV, catching Jessup Black in my peripheral vision. He didn't seem to pay me any attention, so I drove on and eased back over into the right lane, leaving him behind. I went up a ways and then exited off the next ramp, circling back towards the antique shop. My phone rang again, this time it was Vinnie.

"Hey Price, you need to break away from the guy as quick as you can."

"Already did," I replied. "What did you find out?"

"He's not CIA."

"Okay, so what is he?"

"Technically NSA, but his file is locked up tighter than Fort Knox used to be so he's probably in the Special Activities Division, although it seems a little weird they'd have anything on him at all."

I agreed. The Special Activities Division or SAD as they are called is a covert branch off of the NSA (National Security Agency). Specializing in anything the United States government needs done but does not want to be associated with, they are your stereotypical secret agents which found a home many decades ago in fictional media (the red-headed step-children of the government). For there to be any record of Jessup Black existence was more than just a little weird.

I thanked Vinnie for getting back with me and hung up, cutting him off for the chance at a good interrogation, which really would have been a waste of time on his part since I really didn't know what the hell was going on anyway. When I finally made it back to the shop, my head was beginning to throb. I called Clara and let her know what I'd found, which wasn't much, and to tell her where I was. I thought for sure she'd want to come join me, but she declined, saying she needed to meet a friend for lunch and she'd see me after work at the apartment. I hung up and went to the diner for a large coffee before walking back across the street to the store which was getting ready to open for business. Arnie allowed me time to put my coat and purse away before setting me to work. I wasn't hungry at lunchtime so I worked the register while Arnie ate in the break room. The store was pretty busy throughout the day with a lot of browsers and quite a few buyers. I guess the snowy weather had delayed a lot of Christmas shoppers who were trying to make up for the loss of time. Who knew people could be so excited about purchasing antique junk for their loved ones?

By quitting time, I was ready to fall down. Arnie locked the front door, flipped the open sign over to announce we were now closed and then went to the register to count the till. I grabbed my coat to leave but he stopped me before I could get to the door.

"Miss MacCann?"

I sighed and turned around. "Yes?"

"Thank you for helping today. I really appreciate it."

I gave him a smile. "No problem. You've helped me out a bunch already."

"Would you be so kind as to allow me to give you a piece of advice?"

"Sure," I replied.

"Don't trust Donnelly. I've been thinking about your situation all day and something keeps bothering me about it."

"How so?"

"Well, what if you misinterpreted the message you received and Donnelly isn't the one in danger?"

"You mean what if he's a danger to someone else?"

Arnie gave a slight nod. "If I were you, I'd keep a watchful eye on your neighbor."

––––––––––

I'D THOUGHT about Arnie's advice on the drive back to my apartment and he did have a point. The message I'd received was just Donnelly's name, so in all honesty, anything could be assumed. I'd just been going on the events from the first two names dropped at my door. Those people needed help, so it made sense Donnelly did too. Give a human brain a nice and sensible pattern to follow and just see how everything falls neatly into place. I got out of the Taurus and slammed the door shut. My mind reeled at the possibilities once the danger to him was taken out of the equation. I crossed the parking lot to the front entrance of my building and yanked open the door as if I held some personal vendetta against it. Inside, all was quiet so I hiked up the steps to my floor and opened the door to the hall, making my way down it with equal vengeance. I paused at the door to my apartment, then turned and walked the few paces across the hall to Jasmine's door. I gave it a couple raps with my knuckles and waited, and waited. I knocked again and the door opened, revealing my neighbor in a short, blue satin robe with a white towel turban wrapped tightly around her head.

I managed a friendly smile. "Hi. I'm Price, your neighbor from across the hall."

Jasmine gave me the proverbial lawyer smile, one of those expressions set aside for attorneys, bank loan officers, and politicians. She extended her hand for a shake and I obliged, paying close attention to her body language as I did so in the off chance the contact might prove dangerous.

"I'm Jasmine Grey. It's nice to finally meet you. Is there something I can help you with?"

"Maybe," I replied. "May I come in?"

Jasmine gave a nod and a flourish of her hand, ushering me inside. She closed the door and motioned me to have a seat on a gray plush couch. I took the offered seat, noting the expensive furnishings of the room. The couch, loveseat, and recliner all appeared custom made. Gorgeous landscape paintings of winter scenes hung tastefully on the walls, most were woodlands blanketed in white but I noted a couple with fox hunt motif, the hunting parting paused forever in mid-pursuit of quarry not painted by the artist. The mahogany coffee table alone was probably worth a month's salary. I guess being a lawyer was quite the profitable career choice. She plopped down on the opposite end, readjusting her robe so all of her secrets would stay secret and gave me another one of her case winning smiles.

"So, to what do I owe this honor?"

I wanted to lead with the possibility of her imminent danger. She might believe me right off and then she might not, so I decided to just speak the language she'd be familiar with as an attorney and proceeded to lie my ass off.

"Well, we've been neighbors for a year and I thought it was high time I came over and introduced myself. Besides, I'm thinking about starting a neighborhood watch kind of thing for our building and I was wondering if you might be interested in joining in."

"I think that's great," Jasmine replied. "We could use a watch here. What can I do?"

"Well, I'm still in the recruiting phase but I'm taking concerns from anyone who is interested in the idea. I plan to have a meeting sometime soon and start from there. Do you have anything you'd like me to bring up?"

She tilted her head in thought for a moment and then nodded.

"Yeah, actually I do. I think we need to address building security."

"How so?"

"Security cameras would be nice and maybe adding on a key pad or maybe a card swipe lock on the outside doors. I've got a friend who owns a local security company. He'd probably be willing to give the building owner a good deal. I can give him a call tomorrow and see."

"That would be great," I said. "Is there any particular problem sparking the idea?"

"Well, I am a lawyer so there's always the chance someone's nose will be out of joint for something I do, just part of the job I guess. But it would be nice to feel more secure at home, you know?"

I nodded. I did know. "Is there something you'd like to share? I'm a really good listener."

Jasmine's lawyer façade faded a little. "Did you ever get the feeling you're being watched?"

"You mean like stalker watched or big-brother watched?"

She gave a slight shrug. "I haven't actually seen anyone following me. But I've just had that weird feeling, you know? I know it makes me sound paranoid."

"Sometimes paranoia is justified. Have you had any weird phone calls or anything?"

"A couple of wrong numbers on my home phone, but nothing on my cell or at the office."

"Have you been in contact with anyone recently that set you on edge?"

The lawyer smile returned. "I'm a defense attorney so naturally all my clients set me on edge."

"What about outside of work?"

"It's probably nothing but—"

I raised my brow, an action beckoning her to continue. She heaved a sigh and gave me look of uncertainty.

"Well, there was this guy I saw about a week ago and then again this morning. I know it's probably just my imagination running wild, but both times I swear I thought he looked at me funny. It was one of those looks where your eyes meet for just a millisecond, but not like the romantic connection kind, more like a look of recognition."

"Can you describe the guy?"

She did. And while she did, my blood began to boil.

THIRTY-SIX

AUNT CLARA RETURNED about an hour after I'd spoken to Jasmine. I glanced up from my laptop to see her come in with a large Go Green shopping bag hung on her arm. She waddled over to the coffee table, set the bag down, and then started shedding her layers of winter apparel.

"Hey there," I said as she plopped down on the opposite side of my couch to tackle the difficult task of pulling her boots off. "What's in the bag?"

The trend of Clara's sailing boots repeated itself, one of them whacking into the door and the other one bouncing along my floor a couple of times before slamming into the wall.

"So sorry, dear, I just can't seem to hold on to the buggers. And dinner is in the bag, although I hope you don't mind leftovers, there was just too much food for two people to eat so I brought quite a bit back with me."

"Sounds great, I just hope it's stuff we can eat in the car."

"Hoagies travel quite well, why? What do you have in mind? Is it a girl's night out? I just love those! Are we going to a strip club? I hear the Hunt and Peck will be doing a Christmas Carol featuring ghosts with really big presents if you know what I mean."

I wrinkled my lip. "Yes on the girl's night out. No and hell no on the other two. One strip show is enough to last me for a lifetime. I don't even want think about what their version of A Christmas Carol is. By the way Jonas is on his way over."

"How delightful, is he coming along on our trip?"

"No, he's staying here to babysit the cam. He should be here any moment now."

Clara gave me a quizzical look and retrieved her boots to put them back on. I set my laptop on the side table and got up to stretch. My butt had fallen asleep and my legs were stiff from sitting for so long.

"Did you turn up any big fish while you were out?"

I shrugged. "Arnie doesn't trust Donnelly and reminded me to do the same. And I've got a sneaking suspicion Arnie's right. When I followed Jasmine Grey out this morning she met up with a government agent, a guy with no public file."

My aunt's eyes widened a bit. "Price, that's not—"

I held up my hand, interrupting her. "I know. I'm not interested in the agent. But I am very interested in my neighbor's connection with him and I've got a sneaky feeling whatever she's doing might have put Donnelly on to her."

"So the message was wrong and Mister Donnelly isn't in trouble?"

"No message, remember? Just a name. So anything can be assumed."

A knock on the door interrupted my aunt's retort about assuming making an ass out of the assumer. I opened it to see Jonas in his Santa garb, holding a couple of nicely wrapped presents in his arms.

"Ho. Ho. Ho."

"What's in the boxes, Santa?" I asked.

"Depends," he said with a chuckle, "have you been good this year?"

I stood aside and motioned him in. "Nope."

"Well, then yours is filled with coal. How about you Clara, have you been behaving yourself?"

My aunt tittered. "Oh, I make it a point never to behave myself. It seems to set a standard people come to expect."

Jonas set the gifts on my coffee table, handing me a cardboard box he pulled from inside of his Santa coat which I laid on the table.

"Ah, you've got coal too then. Well, at least you'll both keep warm for a spell."

He took my aunt's hand and raised it to his lips, giving it a light kiss much like Arnie had before, and then turned to me. I shoved my hands in my pockets, not really appreciating the antiquated greeting. He chuckled and threw his arms around me in a tight hug.

"Now," he said, loosening his hold, "as I understand it, you want me to run surveillance?"

I told Santa Jonas what I'd like for him to do, asking him to stay put in the apartment regardless of whether Grey left hers or not, only to call me if she did. Donnelly knew about the cam and I doubted he would try anything at Jasmine's apartment, but if she were to leave that was a whole other story.

Clara and I hustled out to the Taurus to make a trip to the Ramada. I parked the car midway in the lot, nestled between two other vehicles nearly the same size as my own. They provided some cover against quick glances towards the Taurus but weren't big enough to block my view in any direction. I opened the box Jonas had given me and extricated a pair of night vision binoculars I had asked him to bring when I called. I adjusted them while my aunt began setting up our dinner, pulling out a couple of bottles of water, two wrapped hoagies, and a large unopened bag of chips.

"Won't it be difficult to use those things with the lights in the lot?" Clara asked.

"Not these. They have a filter which screens the brightness, supposed to be state of the art." I put the binoculars up to my eyes to see if they did what they proclaimed to do. "Wow. Jonas wasn't exaggerating. I wished they'd come up these years ago."

I set the binoculars aside and took a hoagie off the dashboard unwrapping it as I watched the front entrance of the building. The sun had set hours ago, thanks to the winter season, but since it was still early in the evening the hotel was still busy. I took a bite of the sandwich filled with a variety of lunchmeat, cheese and veggies, savoring it as I chewed and watched people coming and going. Clara passed me a napkin.

"I love a good stakeout as much as anyone, dear, but do you really think we'll learn anything new from this one? I mean Mister Donnelly knows his name was passed to you, so don't you think he'll be wise to the possibility that you're keeping an eye on him?"

I swallowed. "Yep."

"Then why bother?"

My phone rang and I grabbed it from the console, flipping it open. Jonas. I thanked him kindly for calling and closed the phone, setting back in its place.

"Jasmine Grey has left the building."

"You should have told her to stay put," Clara said. "It's not good for her to go traipsing all over town with the possibility of someone like Donnelly after her. So again I ask, why bother staking out the hotel?"

"Just give it a few minutes," I replied. "Girls night out remember?"

THIRTY-SEVEN

I AM NOT CLAIRVOYANT. I don't have extrasensory perception or any other paranormal ability which might help me manage complicated tasks more efficiently. What I do have is an imagination to aid me through possible scenarios of what I could expect a person to do next. It's not rocket science. Most people with an active brain can do it, but it does require you put yourself in another person's shoes for a while and take a walk around. Granted, the shoes I happened to be strolling in were very stylish, high-priced designer heels, but I found I could manage to conjure up a few possibilities with several facts while waiting for my dearest assumptions to prove real.

Fact one, Jasmine Grey was a lawyer. Fact two, she'd met up with Jessup Black, an undercover government agent. Fact three, the Black and Grey meeting took place at a construction site in the early morning hours before the crew arrived, which could mean whatever they talked about was too private to be accidentally heard in a normal setting. Fact four, the look Donnelly gave Grey had set up my suspicion to begin with, but the conversation I'd had with Jasmine proved she'd seen Donnelly watching her more than once. The description she'd given fit both Donnelly and Black but since she was already acquainted with Agent Black, I could safely assume it was Donnelly she described to me. Fact five, Donnelly used to be in bed with the government, a position Arnie assured me was not easy to leave. My mind reeled at the possibilities of that little tidbit. And all of those "facts" were just the tip of the mountainous iceberg concerning Donnelly, Grey and Black.

Now, what really seemed to make my thoughts swirl was the broken friendship between Donnelly and my brother. Somehow I just didn't believe it all fell apart because Donnelly refused to help Michael take down an insane ring leader who preyed on little kids. My brother's personality had been a lot like Dad's so refusing to help may not get you the friendship of the month award but it wouldn't have caused the whole thing go down in a bar brawl. At least I didn't think so, but if Arnie's suspicions were right and Donnelly wasn't able to make a clean break from his old job, that might have been the cause. Might, maybe, possibly, probably, all of it just a crap ton of speculation. My aunt's voice pulled me out of my whirlwind thoughts.

"Is that Jasmine Grey pulling in?"

"Yep," I replied, taking a bite of my sandwich.

I could see Clara's eyes widen behind her glasses. "You knew she would be coming here didn't you?"

I took a drink from my bottle of water to wash down the bite.

"I knew it was possible."

"Do you think she came to see Mister Donnelly?"

"Nope."

"Who then?"

"Watch and see," I replied.

"Oh you're no fun. I'm old. You could at least give me a hint."

I laughed. "You're seasoned, not old. And I'm not giving you any hints just yet, so eat your dinner."

Grey got out of her red Audi, shut the door and crossed the parking lot to the front entrance. When she went inside, I lifted the binoculars up to my eyes to see her approaching the desk where she stood for a few minutes talking to Charlie who handed her a room key card. She disappeared shortly after into the hall where I knew the elevators were located. I set the binoculars down and continued eating. When I'd put the last bite of sandwich in my mouth I spotted a black sedan pulling into the lot. It parked in a spot next to the hotel entrance as I finished my bottle of water and screwed the cap back on, handing it over to Clara to tuck into her Go Green bag. Jessup Black got out of the car and went inside.

"Bingo," I mumbled, "looks like possibility number one was correct."

"Care to share?"

I glanced over at my aunt who was trying to brush crumbs off the front of her Christmas sweater with a napkin. The garment was knitted out of some sort of dark blue fuzzy yarn which made it look like a light coating of fur rather than an actual sweater. On the front was a plump little elf dressed in green flannel with bells on his pointy shoes and a creepy smile on his face. Clara seemed to be driving the crumbs deeper into the thick fabric instead of sweeping them off.

"That's Jessup Black, the agent I was telling you about."

My aunt tore her eyes away from a stubborn crumb on the elf's nose and gave me a stern look.

"My interest isn't in Black, Aunt Clara."

"If what you're thinking is true, then they're a packaged pair, dear. You're not going to be able to address one without the other, especially if you go in there and catch them doing the wild thing on a Ramada mattress."

"Ugh, thanks for the visual I didn't need."

"Well it's only natural, two young and attractive people enjoying a secret rendezvous, keeping each other warm during a cold winter evening, taking part in the bounty which is the human—"

"Please stop."

"Why? Does it cause your romantic instincts to go all tingly?"

"No. It's annoying and gross."

"A naked human body can be a beautiful thing, dear."

I groaned. "Aunt Clara, I have to go in there and be face to face with those people. I don't want to do it with visions of them naked or doing things I shouldn't see."

Clara chuckled. "Didn't Edith ever talk to you about the joys of sex? She had such wonderful encounters--"

"Stop right there."

My aunt grinned. "But everyone does it."

I grabbed my coat and began pulling it on. "I don't want to hear about my Mom's sex life, or for that matter, anyone else's. I have enough nightmares as it is."

I zipped up the coat and handed her the binoculars, giving her a quick lesson on focusing before I silenced my cell phone and slid it into the front pocket of my jeans.

"What would you like me to do, dear?"

"Just stay put for now. Call me if you see Donnelly, Grey, or Black leave the building, okay?"

"And you'll be doing what?"

"Hopefully, I'll be having a serious conversation with Irish Casanova before he tries to off my neighbor."

My aunt reluctantly agreed as I got out of the Taurus and headed in the building to have a quick chat with front desk Charlie who was seated behind the counter appearing to enjoy the few minutes of downtime before the next hotel guest arrived. I gave him a friendly hello and told him what I needed, making sure to keep my voice to a level only he could hear.

"He's not in his room," Charlie replied. "I saw him leave earlier."

"There are other entrances to this hotel. He could have slipped back inside without you being the wiser."

He studied me silently for a moment and then glanced over at the front doors when they swooshed open allowing more traffic in the lobby. I stood there waiting for his response, the proverbial stubborn mule in the road with no intention of moving. His gaze finally shifted back to me as he let out an aggravated sigh.

"There are too many people here to cause a scene," he mumbled.

"A scene is what I'm trying to prevent, Charlie," I said. "A double homicide is probably not the best way for the Ramada to assure everyone this is a very good place to be."

He chuckled. "Nice play on the company motto."

"Thank you."

"And this can't possibly wait until things calm down a bit and the guests are sleeping?"

"Well," I replied, "that depends on Donnelly. Do you think he'll wait if he can conveniently kill two birds with one stone?"

Charlie grimaced and handed me the room key which I slid into the front pocket of my coat. "I could have sworn I retired from all of this shit."

I ignored him. "And the one for Donnelly, please."

His grimace deepened as he glanced to someone behind me. I looked over my shoulder to see a middle-aged man in a tux with a very attractive and very snockered woman in a red evening gown hanging on his arm. I turned back around facing Charlie, giving him my most winning smile and holding out an empty hand.

"My key card, if you please."

"Enjoy your stay," he mumbled, handing it over.

"Thank you. I'm sure I will."

THIRTY-EIGHT

I FOREWENT the elevator on the hunch it was less likely Donnelly would take it down to the lobby floor if he were really in stealth mode. It's much easier to become a blur in an innocent passerby's memory by stepping past them on a stairwell then it is to stand in an enclosed space while waiting for the doors to open and praying the cables don't break. Of course, if he were really gung-ho, he could always double-o-seven it out of one of the windows.

I came out through the stairwell door on Donnelly's floor with his key card in hand. Since I wasn't one hundred percent certain of what was going on, I would give him the benefit of the doubt and knock first. Who says I'm not polite?

I gave the door a couple of raps and waited. I knocked again, still nothing. I slid the key card in the reader and opened the door. The room was dark so I flicked the light switch next to the door up. One of the bedside lamps clicked on with a comforting glow revealing an immaculate room, maid service clean. I walked to the bathroom and turned on the light. All of Donnelly's stuff was gone. I picked up the phone and hit the button for the front desk. Charlie picked up on the first ring.

"Front desk. How may I help you?"

"You didn't tell me he checked out," I said.

"You didn't ask. You only asked if he was in his room. I said no, remember?"

I sighed. "Yeah, I remember. I just thought you were covering for him. He didn't tell you where he was going, did he?"

"No."

"Thanks."

I hung the phone up, thinking about my next step. The whole reason I was here in the first place was to keep Jasmine Grey alive. I had no interest in involving myself with Jessup Black. I left the room, closing the door behind me, and went back to the stairwell feeling unsettled like I'd walked out on a job or something. I don't know why. It wasn't like my mystery messenger was paying me for services or anything. The jerk was just feeding me names and creeping me out. As for Donnelly, I wasn't sure if it was a win or a loss. My theory had obviously been way off base, but if he had been in danger then at the very least I'd warned him. Maybe he got smart and left town.

I quickened my pace down the steps with a plan in mind. When I got to the lobby, I'd return the keycards to Charlie and go home. With any luck, I could forget this entire thing and try to enjoy the holidays with my aunt, after which, I would bid her adieu and get back to living my life as I had for the past year. The messenger could just go screw himself because anything else he sent me would be promptly tossed into the trash. I was assuming he was male, but who the hell knew? The point was the messages would go unanswered by my refusal to be a puppet any longer and either he'd stop bothering or come out of the woodwork and confront me. I breathed a sigh of relief, suddenly feeling a smidge better about myself as I pushed open the stairwell door and headed toward front desk Charlie.

"Looks like the calm right after the storm," I said, noting the empty lobby as I handed him the cards.

He gave me a half-hearted smile. "Peace be upon us all."

"Charlie, why do you work here?"

"Good company, nice benefits."

"No other reason?" I asked.

"Not that I'd tell you."

I shrugged and walked off, stopping right in front of the door as he let out a light whistle. I looked over my shoulder at him.

"There's nothing left upstairs for me to clean up is there?"

"Nope, nothing to clean and nothing to haul away, you have a good night, Charlie."

He nodded in reply and I went out the door, ready to follow through with operation I'm-done-with-this-crap when I noticed the outside lights for the parking lot were out and paused mid-step on the walk right in front of the entrance. They'd been working when we'd arrived here and since most all business lighting worked on timers of some sort, there was no reason they shouldn't be on and lighting the way. So either something went kapooey all on its own or someone helped the kapooey along, and I was really hoping it was a self-kapooey. I glanced back to make sure no one was behind me, then to the right and left.

Straight ahead, I could see the Taurus and Clara's silhouette in the passenger seat with the binoculars up to her eyes. She wasn't looking in my direction though, but off to the right. I slid a hand into my coat pocket, pulling my phone free as I inched back towards the door and punched in my aunt's number. I saw one silhouetted hand move while the other kept the binoculars in place as she put the phone to her ear.

"Hello dear."

"See anything interesting?" I asked, keeping my voice low.

"Just a man, quite handsome even with the beard on his face, he's repelling down the outside wall."

I sighed. Jessup Black. "What's he doing now?"

"Ah, he just landed very stealthily on the ground and, ah...he's heading your way."

"Who turned off the lights, Clara?"

Her binoculared silhouette turned slowly toward my direction following Black's movement. "I don't rightly know, but it certainly is dark, isn't it? You'd better get ready. He doesn't look all that cheerful."

I closed the phone, slid it in my coat pocket and zipped it up with one hand as I used the other to draw out the folded knife I had stashed in the opposite pocket. It fit well in my grip and wasn't a threat until the studs on the sides of the handle were pressed, releasing the over three inch tanto blade. It had been one of the "necessities" I'd picked up when Clara and I went Christmas shopping. I sidestepped away from the glass entry way, put my back against the wall, and waited for Black.

He rounded the corner at a steady jog, keeping close to the building as he moved. I steadied my breath as I felt my body relax with a sense of familiarity, the cool handle of the knife warming from the heat of my skin. He stopped about ten feet from me next to a bare branched tree, just shy of the direct light from the entrance, his stance was nonthreatening but I heard the sound of metal sliding along leather. I didn't need to see the gun to know he'd drawn.

"Hello there James Bond," I said.

"Care to tell why you're following me?"

"It's not you I'm following," I replied.

Out of the corner of my eye, I saw Grey approach from the opposite side. "Guess she's following me then, some neighborhood watch you've got there."

I stood stalk, waiting. No sense moving when I was still in the light of the entranceway, especially if Charlie was where I'd left him at the front desk. "Yeah, it's a full service watch."

Grey laughed. "I'm sure. So, who are you *really*?"

All three of us turned our sights to the sound of an engine starting up. Aunt Clara's silhouette was now in the driver's seat. The headlights turned on simultaneously with the motor and then grew brighter when my aunt found the switch.

"Price MacCann. Neighbor. Concerned citizen," I replied.

"Besides, you said you were worried someone was watching you, so I decided to check it out. Consider it complimentary for joining up."

Grey moved closer. "Somehow I just don't believe your story."

"Neither do I," Black added.

"Well that's too bad," I said as the Taurus backed up out of the parking spot. "It's a believable story with a very useful moral."

"Moral, huh, and what would the moral of this story happen to be?" Grey asked as she stepped closer.

I kept my gaze on the Taurus instead of Jasmine Grey as Clara shifted into drive and slowly began making her way around the parking lot. Grey was in my periphery of course but all I needed to know was her position relative to my own. I didn't need to watch Black. I knew his gun was aimed at me. He wouldn't come any closer because he didn't need to. He could shoot me from a safe distance.

"The moral of the story is that sometimes paranoia is justified, sometimes it just means you're bat shit crazy, and sometimes it can be a very useful tool. Unfortunately, using it too much will usually make you bat shit crazy. So I always recommend moderation. It tends to keep the straightjackets away."

Jasmine laughed. "I like your spunk."

"Thanks," I replied. "Any chance my spunkiness will encourage your buddy to put the gun away?"

"Not likely," she said, "at least not yet. I want the truth first. I suggest we take this upstairs for a little more privacy."

"Not happening, stranger danger and all."

The Taurus completed the circuit and stopped at the far end of the lot, a straight shot to where I stood. No high IQ would be required to know what was in the cards for my trusty automobile, just the basic understanding of physics mixed with the probability of an irrational lash out from a questionably stable relative riding an exciting adventure high and tapping into her reserve of maternal instinct. In other words, crazy aunt stomps gas pedal and uses Taurus as a deadly weapon to save her endangered niece from a dangerous situation. The engine revved a couple times and I winced, feeling a sudden sympathy for my car and its inevitable fate should I fail to diffuse this situation. Black glanced over his right shoulder and then back at me, his facial expression hidden in the shadows.

"I take it that's your ride," Black said.

"Yep."

"Your mommy?"

"Aunt. She's visiting me for the holidays."

"Oh," Jasmine glanced at my car and then back at me, "I met her yesterday, actually she seemed quite friendly, and she brought over the most delicious fruitcake. You should have thought of that excuse instead of the cockamamie story about the neighborhood watch. I might have believed you, at least until I caught you following me in my rearview mirror."

I paused and shifted my gaze to Grey. "Um...you ate some of my aunt's fruitcake?"

THIRTY-NINE

AGENT BLACK MADE a sound of disgust. I guess, like most of the world's population, he wasn't a fan of fruitcake either.

"Yeah," Jasmine replied, "like I said, delicious. I had some for dinner."

My brain began swirling to the chant of liar, liar, pants on fire. Oh, I believed Grey when she said she liked the cake. It wasn't that. The tune played only for Clara who may have very well fed me a huge whopper of a lie covered in just the right amount of truth to make me swallow it whole; although it was very possible the cake she gave Jasmine wasn't tainted but if it was, then Clara and I were going to have a sit down discussion. Either way, I could definitely play it to my advantage.

"How much of it did you eat?"

Jasmine flashed me a look of uncertainty as she moved into the light of the entranceway. "What do you mean?"

"I mean do you have digestive issues, like the green apple trots or have you had the urge to bow to the porcelain queen? Anything which might make you wonder if you gobbled up something you shouldn't?"

"I, uh, I don't know, I—"

Black took a couple steps forward, enough so I could now see the profile of his face.

"Don't listen to her, Jas. She's just trying to get under your skin and dragging this out."

I shrugged. "Have it your way, but you may want to visit the hospital and have your stomach pumped just to be sure. My aunt doesn't see very well and sometimes, well, let's just say we don't keep the rat poison out in the open anymore."

I spotted the look of panic on Jasmine's face and knew I had her, whether it was true or not, it was a distraction I needed. Grey hit her knees and started tossing her cookies onto the pavement. The engine of the Taurus revved again and Black whipped around, stepping back into the shadow of the tree as he aimed the gun towards my car. I caught sight of Clara's silhouette diving to the right down onto the seat just as the gun let off a muffled whoomph sound, followed by the slight crunch-like noise of a bullet passing through the laminated glass of my windshield. And then, everything seemed to happen at once.

My ears registered the fact Black's gun was equipped with a silencer. Almost instantly, my brain took the recognition and began putting two and two together with lightning speed. Black may indeed hail from the Special Activities Division and be a respected member of the governmental powers that be but this was just what he did, it was not who he was. I allowed my reflexes to have their way, pressing the studs on the sides of the knife and feeling the steel blade click into place.

I closed the distance just as he turned his eyes back to me, shoving the blade deep into his side and up at an angle which would puncture his left lung. I yanked it out at a downward angle, feeling the fabric of the coat and the shirt he wore beneath it tear under the strain of the sharp blade as his flesh and muscle succumbed to the swipe. Black gave a gasping grunt as his left hand went protectively to his side, his body fighting the need to bow forward. He pivoted my way, attempting to swing his gun arm around towards me, pulling the trigger prematurely and making the whoomph sound again. I caught his wrist with my left hand, stopping the momentum of his gun arm, simultaneously moving my body forward with my right side leading as I flipped my knife blade end to the ground and rammed the butt of it up under his chin. The force knocked his head back enough to throw him completely off balance.

I shoved him into the trunk of the tree hard enough to hear the air expel out of his good lung in one hard gasp. I pulled the wrist I held tight up and against the bark while twisting the knife around again in my hand and stabbing just below and dead center of the ulna and radius bones with everything I had, pinning his wrist to the tree. Black let out a guttural wheezing sound, his lung trying to pull in the air he needed to scream as the gun fell to the ground with a thud. I gave the weapon a sweep with my foot, making it skid off the walk and onto the paved lot under the front end of a parked car.

Over to the side, I saw Jasmine indisposed, still retching in front of the entrance as the door swished open to let front desk Charlie outside with his weapon drawn. He wasn't aiming at me. The gun was trained on Jessup. My gaze fell back on the agent.

"When someone tells you they are not following you," I said, moving to my left out of Jessup's punch or kick range, "be thankful, take it as a sign of good fucking cheer and move the hell on with your night, asshole."

He coughed hard a couple of times and glared at me, his words coming out low and raspy. "Who the fuck are you, FBI?"

Charlie sidled up next to me. "She isn't, but I am. Agent Black, you are under arrest."

I glanced over at him. "I thought you were retired?"

"Cameo appearance," he said.

"What does Donnelly have to do with this?" I asked.

"Not a damn thing," Charlie replied. "I told you he left."

The headlights of the Taurus dimmed to nothing as the engine shut off and Clara opened the door. She got out, looking a bit frazzled but none the worse for wear as she made her way across the lot. A huge grin spread across her face.

"Oh Price! You sure do know how to make girls' night out memorable. Your grandmother would be as pleased as punch if she was here and as mad as hell she missed it, best keep it to ourselves then. Oh hello, Charlie. How's it hanging?"

I rolled my eyes. "Seriously? You two know each other?"

"Of course we know each other," Clara replied, "got married in Vegas about thirty years ago in a little chapel just off the main strip."

Charlie laughed. "Yep. Best damn two weeks of my whole life. How are you doing these days, sweetheart?"

I glanced from Charlie to Clara and back to Charlie again. "You're kidding right? I never knew you ever married."

"Well it was just two weeks, dear. We had it annulled on account of our jobs at the time. Charlie's a g-man you see and I don't think being married to a poisoner would have been a boost to his career."

"Oh God," Jasmine muttered, wiping her mouth with the back of her hand. "What did you put in the cake?"

My aunt gazed down at Grey. "Nothing but love, dear girl, and a tad bit of Christmas cheer."

I raised my brow at her. "You didn't give Jasmine the ricin cake?"

"Now why would I do that?" Clara asked. "I told you who I made the cake for and I only made the one."

CLARA and I were back at my apartment, both of us way too wired to turn in for the night. Santa Jonas went home after letting me know about the big fat nothing happening on the cam. Clara brewed up some of her hot cocoa and we plopped down on the couch to enjoy it while we relaxed.

"Does anyone in the family know you were married?"

Clara laughed. "No. We kept it to ourselves and since it was all on friendly terms, we stayed in touch. Charlie met his current wife about a year later, lovely woman from Oregon."

"Do you ever wish you married again?"

Clara shook her head. "No, I'm afraid that's just not in the cards for me, so no sense wishing over it. Besides, I'm too much of a free spirit to allow a man to order me about. What about you?"

I sighed. "I don't know. I see Mom and Dad and my grandparents and I think how special their relationships are, then I turn to the public records in the newspaper and see the divorce actions are the longest column on the page. It kind of fizzles out the dream, you know? Besides, I guess I'm sort of a free spirit too, whatever that means."

Clara giggled. "I think it's the theme song of all bachelors and bachelorettes."

I laughed with her and then paused, thinking about my dubious neighbor.

"You know it really is too bad they didn't have anything on Jasmine Grey. I would have loved to see her locked away."

"Oh, I don't know, dear. I found watching her on all fours violently upchucking to be quite satisfying."

I had to agree, even if it was all due to her overactive imagination. The police had released Jasmine without charge, even offered to drive her to the hospital if she felt she needed to be seen by a doctor. She'd refused of course and nothing was mentioned about the possibility of her being poisoned by Clara's fruitcake. I guess they just assumed Jasmine was one of those people who couldn't stand the sight of blood and there had been quite a bit of it on the tree where I'd pinned Black's arm with the knife and on the ground from the wound I'd given him in the side. Somebody would be doing a lot of power washing the next day.

As for me, Charlie gave them a very nice cover story, all of it pointing to self defense. And since Black was stupid enough to have put a bullet through the windshield of my car, nearly killing my aunt, it only strengthened Charlie's tale (although my retaliation was viewed as a little extreme, especially when it took two medics to pull the knife out of Black's wrist). Agent Black didn't protest, because he couldn't. He passed out cold as soon as the knife was pulled and I highly doubted he would be telling any tale of a woman getting the better of him. Jasmine Grey didn't argue about the role I played in the whole ordeal either and was assumed to be the innocent caught in the crossfire, much like my aunt who appeared as nonthreatening as they came. I as sure as hell didn't argue because Charlie had saved me from quite a bit of trouble, countless probing questions, and possibly a nice prison sentence.

"Do you think your neighbor will come back to her apartment?" Clara asked.

"Maybe, but something tells me if she does come back, it will be to pack up and move."

"And you still think Mr. Donnelly is after her? Even after Charlie said he didn't?"

I thought about it for a moment.

"Yep."

"Huh. What are you going to do about that?"

I shrugged. "Absolutely nothing."

FORTY

MONDAY MORNING FOUND me dragging my tired ass out of bed, to the coffee pot where I could attempt to wake myself up from the inside out, and then to the shower where the goal was to rouse myself from the outside in. My aunt had fallen asleep on the couch in a post hot cocoa coma and was happily snoring away in dreamland. I scribbled a note about me going to work and if she wanted to join me there later to feel free. I didn't know whether it was a product of exhaustion or if I was just becoming content, but the whole idea of Clara joining me at Arnie's store actually felt like a positive thing. I checked the security cam before I headed out, rewinding and fast forwarding what was recorded overnight. My hall remained empty and Jasmine Grey hadn't returned to her apartment. On my way out, I glanced down to make sure the mystery messenger hadn't left another message; nothing on the floor, nothing on the door. I knew better than to think I'd seen the last of the notes, but as soon as the next one arrived, I would be wadding it up and tossing it in the trash can with a lit match. My immediate goal in life right now was to have a nice and quiet Christmas, hopefully in the company of my aunt. I hadn't asked her if she would be attending the annual Christmas shindig at my grandparent's house yet, mainly because I knew she'd try to talk me into going with her. I was just now coming to grips with Michael's death and the part I played in it. I was not ready to confront the whole fam-damily yet. I didn't want their pity and I sure as hell didn't want to be the brunt of their anger or disappointment should they hold any resentment against me.

I locked up and headed to work on foot since the windshield of the Taurus was nicely decorated with a brand new bullet hole on the driver's side complete with the spider webbing pattern which surrounded it. I would definitely be making a call to my insurance company today. Hopefully, they could find some sort of bullet clause in my policy which would pay for a new windshield although I wasn't holding my breath.

The air was frigidly cold, just as I'd expect this time of year and from the looks of the sky, it appeared we may have more snow on the way. I must have been feeling some bit of wintery spirit because I found myself actually looking forward to the chance of it, that is until I came upon a huge mountain of the dirty gray and black stuff some moron pushed onto the walk which blocked any chance of moving over it (unless I wanted to slide down the other side on butt). I grumbled as I was forced to tread through knee deep snow to circle back to the walk. Okay, so maybe looking forward to more accumulation was a bit farfetched.

Back on the walk, I caught the sound of humming and was surprised to find it was me, to the tune of God Rest Ye Merry Gentlemen no less! I couldn't remember the last time I'd hummed a Christmas carol.

I opened the door to the shop, starting the little bell above the entrance to dinging which I usually found a tad annoying, but this morning it almost sounded festive.

"Good morning, Miss MacCann. I trust you rested up and are ready for another fun filled day."

"Good morning to you," I replied with a smile.

Arnie paused and gave me a wary look.

"What?"

"You seem chipper this morning."

"Is that a bad thing?" I asked, heading towards the break room to shed my winter wear and hang up my purse.

"No, but you're never chipper in the morning. And it's a Monday morning, no less. You usually smell of fire and brimstone on Mondays. Where's Clara?"

"She's at the apartment, sleeping off her hot cocoa."

I walked off, put up my stuff away and came back into the front room to see my boss standing at the register looking puzzled.

"Clara's fine," I reassured him. "She was just sleeping so well I didn't have the heart to wake her."

"Where's Donnelly?"

"No idea," I replied, leaning my elbows on the counter. "He checked out of hotel Ramada and disappeared."

"Ah, now I'm in a good mood."

Arnie flipped the front door sign to open and together we managed the few customers who trickled in to shop. It was definitely quieter than it had been yesterday. I was assured this would probably change during the lunch hour. Most of my time was spent in the basement, cleaning and preparing antiques for their debut upstairs in the front room or packaging up a few items which had already been purchased and needed to be shipped. I'd gone up and down the steps so many times that my thighs were burning. Lunchtime came and Arnie was correct with his prediction of a fun filled day. The lunch hour of hell (which was when a lot of shoppers came around on their way to eat or on their way back to work) stretched to two hours of hell and I found my good mood waning with each stupid question. I know. The customer is always right, yada, yada...bullshit. At one point, I felt like I was running a neighborhood yard sale, dealing with hagglers too cheap to pay the asking price.

"Excuse me, but how much is this statuette, *really*?"

I sat the lamp I was carrying down on the floor next to my feet and lifted the little statue of an avenging angel holding a sword down at its side with one hand and what looked like a Bible in the other. I turned it upside down and showed the middle aged and paunchy bald man the price tag.

"I know what the tag says, but surely you don't mean twenty dollars."

I placed the statue back on its resting place. "Well, the tag says twenty dollars and tags never lie."

The man chuckled, his jowls jiggling with the action.

"You misunderstand me. You see I am willing to give ten dollars cash."

I smiled. "Thanks, that's very generous of you, but if you want the angel that will be twenty dollars."

His sickly sweet smile faded a bit. "No, I mean I am willing to give you ten dollars, in cash, right now."

"Good. Do you want to put the other ten owed on your credit card then?"

The smile completely disappeared and was replaced with a rather nasty looking grimace.

"May I have a word with your manager, please?"

My smile grew more genuine. "Oh, I can do better than that, see the guy in the horned rims manning the checkout counter? That's the owner. Have as many words as you like."

The paunchy brute stomped over to the counter as I picked up my lamp to place it on display in the front window. I didn't bother to see how the scene between them played out, I just continued on with my work. After the store cleared out from the rush, Arnie called me over to the counter.

"Miss MacCann, I received my first customer complaint regarding your service."

"Short guy, looked like a bald wheeble-wobble?"

"Indeed. He says you were very rude to him."

"I wasn't impolite at all. He was haggling for half price on the angel statue. I didn't budge. He asked to speak to the manager and I sent him to you. I was very professional."

"He said you tried to take ten dollars off of him."

"Nope. He offered me ten cash. I thanked him and then told him the statue was twenty. So did he buy the thing or not?"

"He did."

"You gave in, didn't you?"

"I settled on fifteen. It's Christmas time after all and the angel was for his pastor."

"Okay," I replied with a shrug. "So, am I in trouble?"

Arnie studied me overtop his horn-rimmed glasses. "Why would you be in trouble? You were professional and when you couldn't satisfy the customer you sent him to me. I think you handled it well. I just wanted to let you know about what was said."

He glanced down at his wrist watch and then back up at me.

"I thought you said Clara was coming in today."

"I left her a note to follow me over if she wanted. She may still be snoring on the couch. I can call the apartment and see if she's coming in."

"No, I can do that. Would you mind running to the deli?"

I told him I didn't and took the money he handed me, grabbing my coat and heading out to get a couple sandwiches. When I returned, Arnie alerted me of the fact he had to leave a message on my answering machine. I called Clara on her cell phone and got her voicemail. I left a message for her to call me back, but by closing time I still hadn't heard from her. Arnie looked as concerned as I felt and offered to drive me home.

"That's okay. I'll walk if you're all right with me leaving now."

"Absolutely, call me when you find out something."

I grabbed my stuff and headed home.

FORTY-ONE

I OPENED the door to my apartment expecting to see my aunt doing something industrious like cooking, be it a festive menu or a poisonous one. I was praying for festive, but was disappointed to find neither option in the mix. Clara was usually pretty active so I knew she wouldn't have slept the day away and I was right. She wasn't in the apartment at all. I checked my answering machine which had only one message from Arnie earlier in the day. I looked in the closet and saw her carpet bag was still inside. My first thought was she'd gone off shopping or visiting, although it was strange she didn't leave a note, but then again she was a grown woman and could do as she pleased. I called Arnie and let him know what I discovered, which was nothing. He assured me she was probably just fine and would probably be back soon. I was supposed to give him a ring whenever she made an appearance.

I took off my coat, scarf, hat, and gloves, shedding the rest of my apparel like a second skin as I went off to the bathroom to shower away the grime of the day. After I dressed in my comfy ensemble of Hello Kitty pajama pants and Is Monday Over Yet? tee shirt, I went to the kitchen to rustle up supper and that's when I spotted Clara's cell phone by the coffee pot. Picking it up, I roused it from sleep mode and swiped my finger across the slick glass-like front to get to the home screen. An alert for two missed calls prompted me to check her voicemail. The first message was from me. The second one was from my Dad. Not wanting to go all crazy and invade her privacy completely, I hung up right after Dad made his introduction and set it aside. I really wasn't in the mood to cook so I pulled a bag of salad mix, a green onion, tomato, shredded cheese and ranch dressing out of the fridge. After I'd chopped, tossed and dressed the veggies, I poured a glass of coke to wash it all down and then went to the couch to enjoy.

I took a couple of bites before grabbing the remote and flipping the channel to the local news report where our friendly neighborhood weather man was predicting the time of the snowfall for tonight with enough added zeal to make a kid with ADHD look calm, cool and collected. I'd called my insurance company earlier and they assured me they would have someone over to look at my busted up windshield today, but I'd been so worried about my aunt I forgot to check it on my way in. I let out a grumble as I pulled the boots and coat back on, then went to the kitchen and rummaged through the drawers to find what I needed: a flash light, a couple of plastic trash bags, a towel, and a roll of duct tape just in case the glass was as damaged as I'd left it this morning.

I said a couple of choice words (which would have prompted my mother to grab the nearest bar of soap if she'd been around) when the dark frigid air cut into me. Glancing skyward, I noted the shadowy thick covering of the clouds, no moon or stars out tonight. I shivered and clicked on the flashlight, following its luminous beam to the Taurus. Indeed, it was just as broken as I'd left it. I set the bags and tape on the hood, using the towel to wipe off as much of the moisture as I could and then set to work covering the windshield with the plastic bags and securing them with duct tape. The finished product certainly wasn't pretty but at least it would keep the interior of the car from getting wet. I swiped up the roll of tape, towel, and flashlight and ran back to the building, nearly taking out Mister Swanson as I pushed open the door.

He teetered a bit, steadying himself with his cane, and glared at me. "Price MacCann is that you?"

I groaned. I'd almost caused the old man to fall by bumping into him once this month already and here he was again on the verge of breaking a hip because of me.

"I am so sorry, Mister Swanson. I don't know what's got into me these days. Are you okay?"

He glared at me with cloudy eyes. "I do. You run too much. You got no respect for old folks like me."

"Again, I am very sorry," I said with a sigh, "please accept my apology for being so clumsy. I would never purposely try to run you over."

Swanson gave a slight nod. "Next time, just watch where you're going. You might want to try and be like that aunt of yours. Woo buddy, is she a looker."

He gave a throaty chuckle which made me want to step back a few paces out of his reach as he continued.

"Polite too, why if I was a decade younger I'd be—"

I coughed. "Mister Swanson, I hate to interrupt but when was the last time you saw my aunt?"

He gave me a stern glare. "See? No manners."

I took a deep breath and swallowed the urge to push him down on his cranky old ass.

"Look sir, my aunt seems to be missing in action right now and I really need to find her and make sure she's okay before the snow gets here. Did you see her today?"

"Missing huh? That's no good. A beautiful woman like that could freeze to her death out there tonight."

"Exactly, so when did you see last?"

He was silent for a moment as if all of those elderly gears inside his head were slowly turning, probably trying to recollect the time rather than the event. Clara was nothing if not memorable. I waited patiently. About a minute later, the light bulb clicked on and he gave me a broad toothless smile.

"Saw her late this morning, right here in the lobby. She was about as pretty as a peach, talking about Christmas coming soon."

"Did you see her leave the building?"

He gave a nod. "Yes. She wished me a Merry Christmas on her way out."

"She didn't by any chance tell you where she was going, did she?"

"No, she didn't, but she did say her niece was going to love her Christmas present. I suggest you get her something special in return."

"Yes sir," I replied as I turned to go. "Thank you for your help. You have a Merry Christmas now."

"And you as well, Miss Price MacCann."

I paused at the way he said my name. He didn't growl it or anything it just seemed weird to be addressed full on like that. I glanced over my shoulder and saw him staring out the front window. It made me a little sad. As far as I knew, Mister Swanson lived alone.

"Mister Swanson?"

He turned around with his big bushy eyebrows raised.

"If you're not doing anything on Christmas day, would you like to join us for dinner?"

His toothless grin returned. "That'd be fine. You'll put a good word in for me with your aunt, won't you?"

I laughed. "Of course, I'll be sure to tell how very dashing you are."

Making my way back up to my floor, I entered my apartment and locked the door behind me. I plopped back on the couch and finished my dinner, watching the news.

"A man was found dead in his room at Saint Marcellus Hospital early this morning, but it was the way he died that has everyone

baffled. The hospital director was unavailable for comment, but the orderly who found the man says he was shot point blank in the fore- head sometime overnight."

The screen blinked out the anchorwoman and the face of a clean cut orderly with short, dark hair and piercing blue eyes filled her place. The camera panned back a little and showed him in foam green scrubs standing in front of one of the many trees lining the hospital's entrance. I found it odd the hospital would allow an orderly to speak to a television reporter about something like this, but I'd seen weirder things.

"Yeah, I guess you could say this guy was having the mother of all bad days. He came into the ER with a pretty deep slash on his side and a stab wound that went right through one of his wrists."

I swallowed the bite I was chewing before I choked on it. I didn't need to see a picture to know who the victim was, not many people around here go to the ER with wounds like I gave Agent Jessup Black. I sat frozen as the orderly continued his tale of finding the agent dead.

"The guy never had a chance."

I looked down at the quarter of the salad I had left and pushed my plate away, no longer hungry as the screen went back to the news anchor.

"No noise was heard, leaving the authorities to believe a silencer of some type might have been used. Local police are going through the security tapes and investigating the crime at this time. Now on to much happier events, in Selena's Craft Shop on Main Street you can expect to see a lot of festive things including the man himself, Santa Claus."

I glanced up to see Santa Jonas standing beside a television reporter, grinning like the jolly old elf he portrayed and asking the reporter if he'd been a good boy this year. As I watched the brief interview, sipping my Coke to keep my salad down, I pondered over the fact somebody cleaned up after me. It could have been the agency

Black worked for, cutting its ties to a man who'd attracted too much attention, or it could be someone else with an axe to grind (maybe Jasmine Grey for all I knew). That's when the image of Donnelly's face flashed into my head, followed by the memory of the house explosion which nearly took both me and Arnie to the great beyond. Maybe Black was the one with ties to my brother's last job. Maybe. Maybe. Maybe.

I shook it off and changed the channel when Jonas's ho-ho-ho interview ended. There was nothing I could do about any of it anyway so it looked like Bing Crosby would be the center of my attention. After another hour of sitting and waiting with Mr. Crosby, watching his merry song and dance, I grew more concerned about my aunt and finally called my Dad. He answered the phone after the first ring.

"Hey Pricey, are you calling to tell me you're going to take the Van Oliver job?"

"No, I'm calling to see if you've heard from Aunt Clara. I haven't heard a word from her all day and her stuff is still here. I'm really getting worried."

There was a brief pause, followed by a sigh. "She didn't leave a note?"

"No. If she'd left one, I wouldn't have called."

"She was supposed to leave you a note."

I blew out a breath of relief. "Good. She's with you guys then."

"Well, she was but we found a back door in the Van Oliver job."

Tension replaced my brief feeling of relief. "What do you mean back door?"

"Funny thing about people like Van Oliver, they always seem to want to put on a show no matter how much they claim to break from society."

I rubbed my temple where a stabbing pain was beginning to pierce my skull as Dad continued.

"He's hosting some sort of local Christmas soiree and I doubt it's to celebrate the birth of Jesus. Anyway, he hired your Uncle Sandor's wife to cater it, looks to me like his security is slipping."

"Or he's on to us."

"Possibly, but I'm trying to look on the bright side here."

I heaved a sigh, knowing full well there would be no way round it if I wanted to keep my Aunt Clara out of danger. I gave Dad my final answer about the Van Oliver job.

FORTY-TWO

"I'M NOT BACK," I told him, "and I'll probably never be back."

"I understand," Dad said.

"So don't even ask."

"You have my word," he replied.

He gave me what information he'd obtained about the venue, told me he loved me and hung up. I was gathering the things I'd need for the job when the phone rang. It was Kelly.

"Hi Kel, what's up?"

"Not too much. Corey went out of town on business again. What's going on with you?"

I pulled my duffle bag out of the closet and opened the drawer where I kept my 9mm.

"Oh, not a lot," I lied, "I'm just packing for an overnight stay, kind of ho-hum really. There's a Christmas get together my Dad wants me to attend and you know how much I love those."

"It'll be good for you," Kelly said. "You need to get out more and socialize. Is this a family thing?"

I pulled the gun out and set it aside, along with a box of ammo and the knife I'd used on Agent Black.

"Kind of," I replied, releasing the blade and inspecting my cleaning job. "My aunt will be there. Does that count?"

"Sure, aunts count. I'm glad you're seeing your family more. It'll help you get things back to normal."

I sighed, staring at the knife in my hand. "Touché."

"What's that?"

"Nothing," I replied, folding the blade back into the handle.

Kelly was silent for a moment and then said, "I need a favor. All of my babysitters are tied up with the holidays coming and I really need to do the Santa shopping for Trent. So, I was wondering if you'd be willing to sit with him for a few hours next week while I shop."

I paused. In the entire year I'd known Kelly, she'd never asked me for a single favor, yet she was always offering to do things for me. I couldn't say no but the truth was I never babysat, not my little sisters, not my cousins, not even neighbor kids. Images of what it might be like to watch over Trent for a few hours flashed to mind and left me feeling like I had a better chance of surviving a few hours with Van Oliver.

"It's okay to say no, Price. Really, I'll understand. He can be a handful sometimes."

That was a huge understatement. Kelly I liked. her notorious three-year-old? Not so much.

"It's okay," I said. "I'll do it."

"Great. Thanks. I'll get back with you on the details."

After I hung up with Kelly, I called Arnie to apprise him of what was going on with Aunt Clara, and in turn, me. He offered to come along, which I declined; one loved one in the mix of things was enough. He didn't argue and I didn't prolong the conversation. I hung up feeling much like I always had before a job with the slight buzz of adrenaline kicking around inside of me. The sensation was a lot like what you'd get if you were poised to jump out of an airplane. The outcome would be completely different of course. There would be no winner, not really anyway, losing my brother from my last organized job was proof of that. Before his death, I'd looked upon my work as a game not unlike chess, plotting my moves as if I were the queen, protecting royal interests and taking out the opposing side piece by piece until the marked king stood before me. I thought I knew the seriousness of it, spending so many nights either rehashing it while I tossed and turned or suffering through the nightmares such things bring. But in reality, I didn't know as much as I'd thought. It wasn't a game, someone would die and it was nothing to take on lightly.

I exited my building and headed across the parking to where an old eighties model Toyota truck sat idling; the driver gone from the cab as soon as I picked up the call alerting me of its arrival. The door gave a long and metallic creak on rusting hinges as I pulled it open. It didn't matter. I wasn't attempting stealth right now anyway. I set the duffle on the passenger side seat and climbed in, noting the wear of the interior in a beaming glare of an exposed overhead bulb. The hinges sounded their creaking disapproval as I shut the door, an action which gave an empty metallic echo of old and overly used metal hitting another of its kind. I reached up and took out the bulb of the overhead, setting it in the empty ashtray. The dash light illuminated the gage display and I could see right off a couple of these were useless, their arrowed arms pointing wherever they'd been hovering when they stopped working. One of these was for the fuel but it didn't worry me. I knew the tank was full, just like I knew this monster was equipped with four wheel drive if I needed it, and if the predictions were correct about the snow, I would.

Pulling the worn and potentially dry-rotted seatbelt across my torso, I slid the end into the buckle and made it snap just like all of the state paid actors and actresses recited on the television commercials. "Buckle up before you drive." "Click it or ticket." "No belt. No brains." "Click. Clack. Front and back." And my personal favorite, "Trust your captain but keep your seat belt securely fastened." Too bad I was the captain of this dilapidated rolling piece of machinery with my safe-keeping strapped in by a belt several decades old.

The snow started as soon as I hit the interstate. Obviously, a little start out flurry was not in Mother Nature's agenda because one minute we were flake free and the next minute there were so many I had to slow to a crawl just to keep from plowing off the road or into a nearby vehicle. One idiot in a huge pickup must have decided four-wheel drive gave him the power to speed on at the state's mandated limit of seventy miles per hour. I watched as he passed my beat up ride as if I'd been standing still and roared on up an incline where he did a rather impressive donut which ended with an even more impressing swerve into the emergency lane where it stopped. I passed on by in my slow-and-steady-wins-the-race pace. It took me over an hour to traverse the usual fifteen minute drive, but I finally spotted my exit and slowed my speed even more, gearing down the engine to just one slot above neutral to clear the sharp curve. I turned right and crept on past several stop lights as I made my way to the hotel hosting Van Oliver's party tomorrow night.

I bypassed the lot and took a right in a nearby shopping center lot, squeezing the mound of rattling metal into a space with cars on either side. Dad had not only supplied my more than tasteful ride to this shindig and reserved a room under one of my old aliases, but he'd also been thoughtful enough to supply a few other needful things. I pulled the windshield cover out of the duffle Dad supplied and laughed as I unfolded it and secured it on the glass. I grabbed a purse I'd brought, my own duffle and the one Dad had left for me as I got of the cab, slamming the creaking door shut and studying the front image of the sun shield with R2D2 and C3PO from Star Wars glaring out all who dare get within sight of the truck. May The Farce Be With You, it said.

I walked to the front of the hotel and the doorman opened the door for me, giving me a nod of acknowledgement and asking if I needed help with my bags. I couldn't help wondering if he was really one of Van Oliver's yahoos and so I politely declined and moved up to check in at the front desk.

"You have a good stay, Miss Avery," the attendant said, handing me my key card.

"Thank you," I replied, reminding myself to answer to the call of Miss Avery, Christina, or Christina Avery should the name be called.

I stepped into the empty elevator and then out into the hall where my room was located right across from the stairwell exit. Sliding the key card into the reader, I waited for the green light, turned the knob when it shown and went inside. As rooms go, it was what I would have expected out of a hotel catering to the wealthy, but I wasn't here for the amenities. I set my bag and purse aside on the dinette table, then tackled my Dad's bag. Inside were a couple things I'd asked for and a few things I didn't; a brand new and conveniently disposable cell phone, five hundred dollars in small bills, a can of pepper mace, several pairs of Latex gloves, and last, but certainly not least, my Aunt Clara's fruitcake box tied up with a very festive red ribbon bow.

What I did not bring with me was my own cell phone, Clara's cell phone, the file on Van Oliver, or anything in my purse indentifying me as Price MacCann. My goal was to get in, wait for my opportunity to complete the job, and then slip out during the big Christmas hootenanny without being noticed. I grabbed a bottle of water out of the tiny refrigerator and sat down on the bed. On the side table next to me was the remote, so I clicked on the television and settled in for the night. Around two in the morning, the cell phone chirped and I answered it.

"Hi Dad, whatcha doing?"

He laughed. "Everything's set. He just boarded up and should be there to check in at nine in the morning."

"Room number?"

"There're two, five twenty-nine and five thirty, I'll send you the layout of the building." He paused for a moment and then added, "I love you, Pricey."

"I know, Dad. I love you too."

We both hung up.

FORTY-THREE

THE PHONE CHIRPED AGAIN, this time sounding the alarm I'd set for nine o'clock. If Van Oliver's plane was on schedule, then he should be checking in right on time. I flipped the television over to the local station I usually catch in the mornings and waited for the hyped up weather guy to do his thing. He didn't disappoint. In fact, he was so happy he'd predicted the exact snowfall amount he damn near wet himself with glee. It's funny how someone can just do their job right and they expect the Hallelujah chorus to be singing in the background. If they're wrong, they just shake their heads and explain how the jet stream moved just shy of wherever, upsetting their prediction and they just go on again as if they'd never been wrong. I left the weather guy to yammering on while I stripped off my slept-in clothes and hopped in the shower. Believe it or not, he was still patting himself on the back when I returned to the room to pull on clean attire.

I put on a pair of loose fitting jeans and opened a side pocket on my duffle, pulling out a spandex strap I'd packed for the purpose of securing the weapon to my midsection. I fed the material through the bottom strap of my bra and cinched it tight, sliding the knife in the sheath which had been stitched into the strap. I pulled a black loose fit sweater over it, the bottom hem coming just to the waistband of the jeans making it easier to pull the knife free when needed.

The last thing I pulled from the bag my Dad had given me was an express postage paid shipping box complete with a small roll of packing tape. I packed up my coat, clothes, duffle, and toiletries, securing the box with tape and scribbled a bogus address into the space made for it. The box would disappear into postal oblivion, nestled amongst dead letters and others of its kind. I put the cash, 9 mm, ammo, and the can of mace into my purse along with the keys for the Toyota. The cell phone went into the left front pocket of my jeans and my key card for the room in my right. I tucked Aunt Clara's special recipe fruitcake inside Dad's black bag being careful not to bend the box and then hung my purse on my left shoulder. I shrugged the fruitcake bag on overtop the purse strap and swiped up the box to be shipped out. I left the T.V. on just for the hell of it and scooted out of the room. It was now almost ten.

I took the elevator down to the lobby floor and went straight towards the front desk where a plump and rather stuffy looking woman stood.

"May I help you?" she asked, her double chin waddling turkey-like as she spoke.

"Uh, yeah," I replied, trying not to smile as her bulbous eyes glared at me with everything but hospitality. "I need to have this package shipped."

She took the box, looked to see it was already labeled and set it aside on the counter. "The courier should be here any time. Is there anything else I can do for you?"

I told her no and turned to go in search of the cafeteria for a cup of coffee when two huge gorilla-like men come through the front entrance dressed in what appeared to be Armani suits. Both were clean cut with hair buzzed down in military fashion, their skin sporting out-of-season tans, and muscular builds which shouted steroid use. They parted just inside the entrance and took positions on either side of the door, folding their hands in front of them like honor guards.

I glanced back at the desk attendant.

"Who are those guys?" I asked, knowing full well they some of Van Oliver's hounds.

She rolled her bulbous eyes in a highly annoyed fashion. "Part of his royal highness' entourage."

I put my back to the well-dressed gorillas and leaned forward, lowering my voice. "What do you mean?"

"Well," she whispered, "lucky for us, we get to host his majesty's Christmas party tonight."

I traced my finger along the slick wood of the counter in front of me. "Cool. I was looking for something to do tonight. When does it start?"

She gave a chuckle which caused her chin to waddle again.

"The event is by invitation only, but don't worry you'll have complete access to the restaurant, shops, pool area, gym, and many other amenities; only the ballroom and adjacent courtyard will be in use."

"It's like twenty degrees outside. Who in the world will be using a courtyard?"

Another chuckle, another waddle. "You'd be surprised."

Somehow, I didn't think I would.

FORTY-FOUR

THE MAÎTRE D ushered me to a table which was just a few feet from the entrance and off to the side. I chose the seat against the low mahogany-like divider, its thick lacework weaving around in an intricate and graceful pattern just beckoning the imagination to conjure up the sleek form of long snakes winding and twisting around loosely enough to see through the spaces left between them. With the wall at my back, I couldn't have been more pleased. It was a perfect people-watching position with no chance of someone sneaking up behind me. I set my purse next to me on the short leather-benched seat on the wall side and put the bag with Clara's fruitcake down beside it.

From where I was seated, I could see the two muscle-heads at the front entrance with ease, Thing One and Thing Two. The maître d left and was quickly replaced by a server who set a glass of ice water down in front of me as her way of a greeting, then followed the action by placing a rather large and laminated menu next to it. She didn't look a day over twenty. Her auburn hair was swept up in a loose bun on the back of her head and the glasses she wore were just one angle degree shy of being horn-rimmed. The uniform she wore was definitely the restaurant standard, black slacks and formal vest with a form-fitting white button-down oxford shirt complete with a black bow tie.

"Thank you for dining with us," she said. "Can I get you some coffee?"

"Sure," I replied, noticing the black name tag with gold lettering pinned to her vest. "Coffee sounds great, strong and black, please."

"Of course, I'll bring you a carafe."

"Thank you, Amy."

She gave me genuine smile, seemingly pleased I called her by name, and went off to procure said carafe. I opened the menu, studying my options and sipping the ice water as I stole glances every once in a while at Thing One and Two. Amy returned in a few minutes with her tray balanced on one hand as she gracefully set the white porcelain cup and saucer before me, turning the cup upright and then slowly pouring the steaming brew into it. She set the carafe on the table within my reach.

"Are you ready to order or would you like a few more minutes to decide?"

My stomach was trying desperately to urge my answer in the affirmative but I needed to stretch out my time here for as long as possible.

"I'd like a few more minutes if that's okay."

"Sure, I'll check back with you in a little while."

I thanked her and she went away, leaving me to sip my coffee and people watch while I perused the menu. Thing One and Thing Two stayed where they were through my first cup and on into the beginnings of the next one. My stomach uttered gurgling sounds of protest, feed it or there would be hell to pay and it had an entire plethora of weird noises to choose from, so I nodded at Amy on her next pass by my table and ordered my breakfast. Shortly after she left, Thing Two was switched out by a replacement I'll call Thing Three. He was pretty much the carbon copy of One and Two. I watched Thing Two walk off towards the alcove where the elevators were located, more than likely making a trip up to room five twenty-nine.

My plate came a little while into my third cup of Joe and I took my time eating. Don't worry about me Thing One and Three. I'm just a hungry woman trying with all my might not to scarf down my grub right in front of you.

When I had only a slice of bacon and a wedge of toast left on my plate, Amy returned.

"Since it's so close to lunch, would you like me to bring you a dessert menu?"

I paused, my stomach now happily digesting what I'd given it. A dessert might push my comfortably full stomach over the edge into unbuttoning your jeans territory, but it would also buy me more time to watch and learn. I gave her a nod and then asked if I could use the restaurant's ladies room to powder my nose (and relieve myself of several cups of coffee).

"Certainly," Amy replied. "I'll take you there myself. Would you like me to leave your plate so you can finish it?"

I smiled and told her no, plucking up my purse and slinging it on my shoulder, leaving the bag with cake where it sat. If anyone was stupid enough to steal it they were in for one nasty surprise. I returned to the table to find the goons right where I'd left them.

A half an hour later, I pushed the last tempting remains of the apple pie away from me, the only thing left was one small bit of crust and a thin puddle of melted vanilla ice cream too shallow to scoop up and slurp with my spoon or too ill-mannered to just pick up the plate and lick it clean.

Amy brought the check in one of those tasteful leather binders and left to serve another table. I winced as I opened it. This little brunch just cost my Dad twenty bucks, plus the nice tip for Amy. I unzipped my purse and pulled two twenties out, putting one inside the binder with the check and one on the table under the salt shaker and then I left to check out other sections of the hotel.

FORTY-FIVE

"IF YOU ASK MY OPINION, I think this entire thing is a big pile of cow bunk. To imagine someone like him would even think of hosting a party in honor of the birth of Christ, well, it's just sacrilege!"

"Will you keep your voice down? Do you want to get fired?"

"Not this close to Christmas I don't, but you can bet if that piece of work had decided to throw this thing on New Year's Eve then I'd be walking out shouting the whole way."

"Well, don't start shouting now. I've got a kicker of headache."

"Sinus or tension?"

"Husband, so I guess you can say tension. Can you grab some silverware from the bin over there? I'll be right back. I need to get some Advil out of my purse."

"Well if there isn't anything else we need to add, then I'm giving Jimmy a call and have him porter his ass on down here and take this cart to your highness's guards."

"Sure, you do that."

According to the information Dad had sent me, there were no security cameras in this section of the hotel, but I'd made sure to keep my eyes peeled for anything out of the ordinary. Most places of business post naked cameras up, it's cheaper and it usually deters questionable activity much like a cop car sitting in full view of traffic. Others will use the mirror domed covers, mostly for aesthetic purposes because anyone in the country over the age of six knows what they really are, but occasionally you'll find places who are gung-ho enough to use hidden cameras hidden tucked in false fire alarms, smoke detectors, vents and so on. I knew for a fact this particular chain did not.

I peeked through the window in the swing door and spotted the room service cart unattended and not more than two feet away. The top section was filled with covered plates; nothing like the silver domed covers you see depicting lavish room service but more like the plastic plate covers you'd see rolling down a hospital corridor. The bottom section just held one cake box and a Saran wrapped tray of cookies, leaving enough space for Aunt Clara's fruitcake. I pulled the box out of Dad's bag and carefully took off the ribbon bow, tucking it back into the bag and retrieving the cloth inside, wiping away my fingerprints.

As I eased the door open, I could see one of the uniformed women across the kitchen, her back to me as she went about her business of wrapping silver wear in cloth napkins. I quickly and quietly pushed the door open, took the few steps to the cart and slid my box next to the one already there, taking the cloth with me.

There was no guarantee the cake would be touched, but I'd happily take anything to even the odds a bit. I slid back out through the door before either woman returned and took a position in a darkened alcove near the service elevator to make sure my box made the trip. If not, I would have to retrieve the cake before anyone else decided they deserved a slice of more potent then Ipecac with Ex-lax mixed in holiday cheer.

That's the thing I absolutely hated about working with poisons. You had to make certain it was the intended mark who received the tainted portion, which to me was way too risky. But I had an entire entourage of body guards to take out of commission before I attended to Van Oliver, so the cake would have to do.

It wasn't long before Jimmy the porter came down the corridor towards the kitchen in a long lankly stride. At least, I assumed it was Jimmy since he was sporting a snappy porter uniform. Tall and lanky, he ambled at a leisurely pace past me without so much as a glance my way as I stood quietly in the shadows. I heard the sound of his hand meeting the swing door and then the noise of wheels rolling, bumping over a threshold, and then swishing along the carpet.

I didn't have to move an inch to see the cart as it passed. The tainted cake still held its position right beside the other white cake box and the cookie tray. I let out a sigh of relief as the cart moved on to the service elevator, then put my purse into the bag so I was only dealing with one shoulder strap and made my way back to the lobby as quickly as possible before anyone else came down the hall.

Thing One and Thing Three were still posted at the front entrance just as I'd left them, luckily they both seemed occupied with a couple of teenage girls who were captivated with muscles and possibilities. I scooted past without a glance from either of them and made my way into one of the many shops in the makeshift hotel plaza off to the right of the restaurant.

I wasn't in for a spree. I was biding my time. The party was set for seven in the evening and I hoped I would be out of here with none the wiser shortly after. Strolling through one shop after another, I stole occasional glances at the lobby and kept my eyes peeled for more of Van Oliver's security staff. I'd managed to whittle away three hours, putting the time at nearly three o'clock as I meandered into the last little store in the building, which happened to be a bookstore. The entryway was an open mall-style like the other shops and all of the aisles were set with shelves positioned so the lobby was always visible. Another hour passed before I settled on the first book in Laurell K. Hamilton's vampire hunter series, I paid the cashier and went out to a sitting area in a remote corner of the lobby with a full view of the hotel's comings and goings.

I expected the goons at the door to become suspicious of my loitering, but they didn't seem to notice me. At four o'clock my phone chirped and I flipped it open to see a message from Dad to alert me of the fact Aunt Clara and the catering company had arrived at the hotel and Uncle Sandor would make sure the security cameras on the fifth floor would be temporarily out of commission. I cleared the message and resumed reading.

Several chapters into Anita Blake's adventures with the paranormal, a reporter and her camera guy came in the front entrance. I glanced at the wall clock to see it was nearing six and listened in on the conversation which was starting to grow just a tad heated. Apparently, the reporter was sent by a local news station to cover the party and all of its rumored guests, one of which was supposed to be a state senator. There was a clichéd proclamation from the woman regarding freedom of the press, but the hotel manager stepped up to the plate to inform them they would have to set up their post off hotel property. They were followed by several more members of the media who were also escorted back outside to hold their little media vigil in the cold.

This was definitely going to be an interesting evening.

FORTY-SIX

THE HOTEL LOBBY began filling up a half an hour later with tuxes stuffed with men who appeared as if they had a devil of a time getting their trousers to fit appropriately with the corncobs shoved up their well-to-do asses. Most of these corn-cobbers seemed to resemble faces plastered on Vote For Me signs stuck in the yards of citizens who didn't mind scaring the crows away with the headshot of a "promising" politician. There were women as well, in formal dresses just an inch shy of bridesmaid/prom queen quality, most all of them colored in something so seasonally festive they resembled tree ornaments which had fallen from their branches and gone awry. The ballroom had yet to be opened, so the lobby continued to fill raising the noise level to a low and steady hum of conversational chatter.

I spotted Thing One pull his cell phone off the side of his belt and put it to his ear. The expression he made was priceless and I knew right away the cake had done its job. He stepped over to his partner and whispered in his ear, producing the same grave look on Thing Three's face. I closed my book, tucked it into my bag, and got up, wading through suits and evening dresses until I stepped onto the elevator. I punched the button for the floor to my room and the door slowly closed, beginning its assent upward. When they opened, I stepped out, bypassing my room altogether and headed to the stairwell. It was empty as I knew it would be. Outside of a fire or complete loss of power, hotels usually don't have a lot of traffic on the stairs unless something's wrong with the elevators or there's some sort of fitness convention taking place on site.

Sliding my hand inside the bag and then further into my purse, I felt around for two pairs of latex gloves. I slid on one pair and then put on the second overtop the first as I mounted the steps. I put my hand in again and extracted the can of mace, readying it for use with one hand without one falter in my stride. I moved quickly up the first flight and then slowed my pace to a more cautious speed for the next one just in case Van Oliver had posted a guard just inside the stair well door.

No one was there. I tested the bar and pressed on it gently to make certain it wasn't locked. It gave way without a sound. I pushed it open a few inches and peeked through the gap to see three or four of Van Oliver's guards further down the corridor in front of the elevator. None of them looked particularly spry. They'd all shed their suit coats; their button-down shirts rumpled and soaked with sweat. When the doors opened, I watched them board the elevator; one of them seemed a bit more unsteady, requiring two of the others to help him on. They disappeared as the doors slid back together. Four down, I had no idea how many more to go.

I stepped in, keeping my hand on the stairwell door to make sure it eased shut with barely the sound of a click and then started down the hall. There were a couple of cameras mounted on the upper part of the wall to keep this floor more secure than the others below it, just another amenity provided by the hotel with an extremely high price tag. Unfortunately for Van Oliver, they were useless now compliments of Uncle Sandor and his crew. But I knew guys like "your highness" had other ways of keeping tabs on the goings-on in and around him, so I didn't pooh-pooh the possibility of a hidden camera or two of his own nestled somewhere nearby (like for instance, on the cameras themselves, which wouldn't be unheard of although I could see no added "features" on any of them as I passed).

Van Oliver had paid for two rooms, five twenty-nine and five thirty, but I wasn't certain which room was his and which room housed his men until I spotted the tiny black disk no bigger than a dime on the corner of a framed country landscape painting hanging directly across from room five twenty-nine. I almost missed it, tucked into the shadowy bare branches of the tree line. My eyes shifted to the opposite side of the hall where there was nothing but wallpaper. I knocked softly on five-thirty's door and stepped out of the viewing range of the peep hole for five twenty-nine in case Van Oliver heard the knock and put his eye up to investigate. And then I waited with bated breath. One Mississippi...two Mississippi...three Mississippi...

My back hugged the wall as I imagined what the guys inside would do...four Mississippi, get to the door...five Mississippi, look into the peephole...six Mississippi, what the fuck, no one's there...seven Mississippi, this better not be a prank...eight Mississippi, turn the knob...nine Mississippi, kicking some ass if it is...ten Mississippi, open the door.

I moved in quick, aiming sure and thumbing down the button on the can of mace which sprayed a stream of pepper spray gel in the upper part of Thing Two's pale face. He let out a grunt, pawing frantically at his eyes with one hand (which only rubbed the shit deeper in) and trying to free the pistol on his belt with the other. He'd taken a step back in his surprise, too distracted to get out of the swing line of the door, and I shoved my shoulder hard against it slamming it right into him and sending him reeling back as he pulled his pistol free from the holster on his belt. I shut the door behind me with just enough force so it would close and not slam, caught the back of his left foot with the heel of my own and swept it out from under him. He landed hard on his back and I heard the grunting sound of his breath being knocked out of him. His elbow smacked against the edge of one of the beds and the pistol jarred out of his hand, thudding to the carpeted floor next to him. I plucked it up and clicked the safety off. He froze.

"Hi there," I said in a calm and soothing voice. "I don't know if you looked in the mirror lately but you look like complete and utter shit."

He started coughing, his cheeks blown out like a chipmunk's stuffed with the rewards of foraging, his face reddening from the effort to expel the pepper spray from his lungs as he tried to turn over. I didn't want him to choke to death so I allowed the motion, watching as he struggled. Finally, he managed to sit up and gag up a puddle of nasty between his outstretched legs and onto the dark colored carpet. It was mostly bile and whitish foam, tinged with bright red blood from burst capillaries in the esophagus either the resulting force of his current bout of hacking or excessive vomiting brought on by the festive fruitcake.

Against the sliding glass door across the room, I spotted the makeshift buffet table covered in a white cloth and sporting the remnants of dessert. Both white cake boxes were open at the top and on the end, revealing the white cardboard platters within. The hotel kitchen's box still held a round, two-layer chocolate cake with what looked like one sliced wedge missing. The box I'd added to the room service cart held only a platter littered with crumbs. From what I could tell, the cookie plate was completely untouched; the Saran wrap still stretched tightly across it. I shifted my eyes back to Thing Two who was now taking deep breaths to try and regain some control over his need to start retching again.

"You should see a doctor," I said, setting my purse down on the bed. "You're looking a little green around the edges."

"Fuck you," he mumbled, pulling at the bedspread with unsteady hands.

"I wouldn't do that if I were you. It'll just rub it in deeper."

He ignored me and began furiously wiping at his eyes which were now streaming two trails of tears regardless of his effort.

"Son of a bitch!"

"I told you so," I replied, "best listen up and if you cooperate, I might be able to get you something to put out the fire in your eyes. Hell, I'll even give you a little hint as to why you and your cronies are spewing at both ends. Afterwards, you can make a little trip to emergency room where they keep the stomach pumps, maybe spend a few days in a hospital bed, and there's a happily ever after for you and your buddies."

"And if I don't?"

I gave a shrug, knowing full well he couldn't see me. "Well, if you don't, then I'll put an end to your last really bad day and I'll move on with the rest of mine. Personally, I'd choose option one."

FORTY-SEVEN

THE DAMN WEATHERMAN was dancing around in front of his green screen, moving his hands around as he pointed to the image of the tri-state map with last night's snow fall totals scattered all over it.

"Minimal," he said. "This front has stalled just west of us which is why, as you can see, we've only received barely of pinch of what we're in for. And in the words of Bachman-Turner Overdrive, "You ain't seen nothing yet!""

I watched him swoop his left hand down in a motion which followed the forecasted animation of the radar and the huge purplish-white blob which had been positioned over the northwest section of the map slid down and over to the right of the goon's wide screen television. It stopped right over top of the station's viewing area, causing me to grimace. If I didn't want to be stranded another night in the hotel, I needed to finish my job as quickly and efficiently as I could, grab Clara and high-tail it home. I gave Thing Two the cordless room phone and settled the muzzle of the gun snuggly against the side of his head to keep him honest as I waited for Van Oliver to answer.

"Hey Boss," Thing Two said, his voice raspy from obvious discomfort, "can you step over here for a minute? Yeah, I sent them

on to the hospital...nah, I'll live...must have been something I ate...
uh-huh...okay."

Thing Two gave a slight nod and started to hand the phone back
to me just as a very stupid idea took over his pea-sized brain, causing
him to rear back and try to hit me with it. I dodged the blind swing
effortlessly, pulling the gun away from his head and flipping it
muzzle up while sliding the safety on, then I angled back and
slammed the butt of the weapon to the side of his head. His red and
swollen tear-streaked eyes tried to widen in surprise at the blow, but
couldn't manage it. His body slumped to the right on the floor,
knocked out cold, but alive none-the-less. I set the gun on the night-
stand and yanked the bedspread overtop of his body, moving towards
the room door and pulling the bathroom door closed as I went.
Taking a position next to the entryway, I put my back into the corner,
reached under my sweater and slid the knife free of the spandex
sheath. I clicked the blade in place and held it down at my side. A
minute or two passed before someone knocked at the door.

One Mississippi...two Mississippi...three Mississippi...

I heard the latch on the handle click and the door eased opened
silently as a tuxedoed man entered the room. I stayed where I was,
the door providing good cover.

"Roberts? Good God, this place reeks, what the hell did you
all eat?"

Four Mississippi...five Mississippi...

"Roberts, are you in the john?"

I heard a couple of raps on the bathroom door and then, "Look, I
have to finish getting ready, what did you want?"

I gave the entryway door a gentle push and followed its motion as
it began to slowly swing to a close. The man turned his head slightly
in response to the movement, giving me a clear view of his profile. He
hadn't noticed me yet, but it was risk I was willing to take to make
sure of his identity. It was Van Oliver alright, dressed out in his
formal penguin wear and ready to rub his nasty, psychopathic elbows
with other elbows cut from the same corrupt, but more rich and

powerful cloth. The ends of his bow tie still hung limply against the front of his shirt and he'd yet to pull on the tuxedo coat, but it was apparent he was nearly ready to join the hoopla downstairs. Too bad he would never arrive.

Six Mississippi...

He ignored the entryway door and turned his attention back to the bathroom, knocking harder this time.

"Roberts, answer me or I'm opening the door. And I am not in the mood to see your junk right now."

Seven Mississippi...

Van Oliver's left hand went to the door handle and I stepped out right behind him, glad he was just barely taller than me. I wouldn't even have to stand on my tip-toes to do the job. He raised his right hand up, now tightened into a fist to give the door a good pounding.

Eight Mississippi...

I allowed him one pound, reached out with my left hand and grabbed a handful of his dark colored hair just above the crown of his head and yanked down, bending his neck back. He gave a grunt of surprise and his left hand clutched the door handle while his right, still clenched in a fist whipped up and back reflexively, never even grazing me. I felt his muscles tense in the core of his body, trying to turn. I kept the grip I had on his hair and shoved my elbow deep in the pressure point in his upper back. The action stretched his head further back and the force of my well-planted elbow slammed his chest into the bathroom door.

Nine Mississippi...

His left hand still gripped the door handle while the right hand relaxed its fist, swinging downward and taking the arm with it in an arch to try and get some purchase on me. I raised the knife and moved in at an angle over his right shoulder, touching the deadly edge to the skin on the left side of his neck as I pressed inward, simultaneously locking my wrist, elbow, and shoulder. I could feel the warm sensation of blood flowing over my gloved hand as the flesh gave under the blade and I felt, more than heard, Van Oliver's stran-gled cry.

With my wrist and elbow still locked in position, I yanked my shoulder back hard, tightening the grip on the knife's handle as the blade slid cleanly through the left carotid artery, the front of the trachea, the right carotid artery and then out the other side of his neck. He let out a wet sounding gasp as his body seized in a contrac-ture causing his left hand to yank down on the bathroom door handle. When the latch released, I shoved him forward into the opening door with my forearm and elbow, loosening the grip on his wavy locks and setting his dark hair free.

Ten Mississippi...

No longer holding to the handle or having the support of a solid door to stop his advance, he went down like a falling tree, hitting the bathroom tile face first with bright red blood spurting from his severed arteries. The thump of his body meeting the floor was the last sound he made and the spurting slowed to a flow which slowly began spreading on the floor from the no longer visible wound beneath him like some sort of weird crimson shadow. I watched for a moment, waiting to see if his torso would lift as he tried to breath. It didn't. The puddle's expansion began to slow as I closed the knife and pulled off the outer layer of gloves folding them over the bloody weapon. I turned my eyes back to the covered lump of Roberts and saw the bedspread rise and fall in the slow, rhythmic motion of unconscious breathing. Plucking up my purse, I slid the bloody gloves down into the bottom recesses of the bag and then stepped out of the room, closing the door and leaving Roberts to his own fate.

FORTY-EIGHT

IN THE EMPTY STAIRWELL, I pulled off the second pair of gloves and put them in my purse before I sent Dad a text to let him know the job was done. Halfway to the ground floor, the phone vibrated in my hand. I paused in descent, flipped it open and tapped the message to read his response.

That's good news. I'll inform your aunts.

I texted him back.

Have Clara meet me at the truck in the lot next door.

He responded back immediately.

Will do.

I heaved a sigh of relief, thankful my aunt would be safe. I shut the phone and stuffed it into my purse as I continued on down. When I pushed open the stairwell door, the sounds of the Christmas party greeted me. The volume of Rockin' Around The Christmas Tree rose and fell probably as the doors to the ballroom opened and closed. I moved past the wing where the celebration seemed to be in full swing and walked into the lobby still busy with party-goers meandering about chit-chatting. I pulled the key card out of my jeans pocket and headed to the front desk where the older woman I'd met earlier still held down the fort.

She wasn't smiling and looked exhausted, her waddling chin more deflated than this morning. I watched cautiously for any bit of recognition in her bulbous eyes as I paid the bill in cash. There was nothing evident but fatigue. I signed the check out sheet with Christina Avery's name and passed it back to her. She bid me a perfunctory Merry Christmas and I recited the same, turning to leave. Thing One and Thing Three were still manning the front entrance as I strolled right on by them into the frigid night air where a white limo was parked; the doorman occupied with helping a woman in a black sequined evening gown and long black fur coat from the back seat. Her ebony hair was swept up in an elegant bun revealing white diamonds which sparkled in her ears and just below the front of her neck. She smiled politely at the doorman, gracefully stepping to the side as the car door was shut. My eyes flicked towards the driver in a dark colored suit, donning his chauffeur's hat. He pivoted just enough for me to see his face. Donnelly. What the hell?

His dark chocolate eyes met mine and held them for just an instant before he turned away, stepped to the back of the limo and opened the door for his other passenger. I slowed my pace just enough for a glimpse at who emerged. A tall, slender tuxedoed form folded out of the car. He had short reddish-blond hair in a mussed up gel style like he'd gone to bed with a wet head, did ten rounds of tossing and turning with a disagreeable pillow, and got back up before it could dry properly. I walked towards the front of the car as he turned, noticing his pasty white complexion and the sharp features of his face. Recognition slammed into me and I nearly tripped over my own feet.

Corey. I'd only met him once and once was enough. His reputation preceded him as did the fallout from many of his violent actions. He took a couple of long-legged strides around the back of the car, hooking his lanky arm around the elegantly dressed woman and pulling her close. Out of the corner of my eye, I saw her kiss him on the cheek. He hadn't seen me and I didn't want him to. I lowered my eyes and kept walking, past the limo and out from under the awning into the snow-dusted parking lot. I wanted to turn right back around, catch up with the ginger son-of-a-bitch and slug the living daylights out of him. But now was not the time. Instead, I gritted my teeth and traversed the distance to the lot where I'd parked.

Without a coat, I was shivering when I reached the truck. Pulling the keys out of my purse, I unlocked the door, got in, set my purse on the seat and reached across to unlock the passenger side. Clara was opening the door and climbing in just as I put the key in the ignition. The interior of the cab was dark without the overhead lighting but I could see her plump form squeezed into the bright white server's button down shirt. Her door slammed shut as I started the engine and shifted into drive, not even bothering to buckle up and not waiting for her to do so. I was out of the lot and on the street before she said anything.

"Is everything okay?"

"Yep," I replied.

"Any trouble?"

I shifted into the turning lane and eased the truck to a stop at the light.

"Nope."

"Van Oliver?"

"Dead, just like Dad told you."

The light switched to green and I made my turn, catching the wailing of sirens in the distance, undoubtedly heading for the hotel.

"I'm fine, really," I lied. "I'll be better when we're home."

I wasn't sure about what I'd seen and I was even more uncertain about discussing it with my aunt so I didn't say anything more. Clara sat silent for the rest of the drive. I ditched the truck in the back alley of a convenience store a few blocks from my apartment and left the keys inside for Dad's guy to pick the truck up later. Halfway home, the wind started coming in gusts and it began to snow so heavily that by the time we reached my building, I could barely see a foot beyond me. I fumbled my apartment door open with near-frozen fingers and just stood there shivering for a few seconds.

"You're standing on an envelope, dear."

I glanced down to see she wasn't joking, lifted my right leg, and grasped the corner of it between my thumb and index finger. Peeling it from the sole of my wet shoe, I held it at arm's length, much like one would carry a dead mouse by the tail if the occasion called for such a thing, and stared at it. Now wet, I could see right through the paper to the black type of the name inside. Ten steps to the kitchen, I stopped and pressed down on the foot pedal, lifting the trash can lid and dropping the envelope inside. The lid slammed shut as I turned and faced my aunt, just daring her to object. She didn't.

"I'll make us some cocoa, dear."

ABOUT THE AUTHOR

Mary Ellen Quire is the author of Sheldon's Diary and Dark Deliverance. She has also written two time travel novels, Link Detonator and Detonator Times Up, penned under the name Mary E. Rose. Her compilation of short stories entitled Fairview was released in 2016.

Born and raised in Kentucky, she has been dabbling in the writing world since high school where a creative writing class honed in on an interest shed had since she was a child. Balancing life with four daughters and work, she found time to write in the wee hours of the morning when her interest in writing became a passion. She resides in the quiet town of Crestwood with various animal squatters.